Elise and Andraya Wall, together known as Virginia Mae Brown, are identical twins who share the same passion: a love of telling stories. Together they combine their ideas to create original stories they hope will enthrall and inspire readers. They live in Virginia with their three crazy dogs and two cantankerous but lovable horses.

Virginia Mae Brown

THE MAN FROM ALCATRAZ

AUSTIN MACAULEY PUBLISHERS™

LONDON * CAMBRIDGE * NEW YORK * SHARJAH

Copyright © Virginia Mae Brown 2022

All rights reserved. No part of this publication may be reproduced, distributed, or transmitted in any form or by any means, including photocopying, recording, or other electronic or mechanical methods, without the prior written permission of the publisher, except in the case of brief quotations embodied in critical reviews and certain other non-commercial uses permitted by copyright law. For permission requests, write to the publisher.

Any person who commits any unauthorized act in relation to this publication may be liable to criminal prosecution and civil claims for damages.

This is a work of fiction. Names, characters, businesses, places, events, locales, and incidents are either the products of the author's imagination or used in a fictitious manner. Any resemblance to actual persons, living or dead, or actual events is purely coincidental.

Ordering Information
Quantity sales: Special discounts are available on quantity purchases by corporations, associations, and others. For details, contact the publisher at the address below.

Publisher's Cataloging-in-Publication data
Brown, Virginia Mae
The Man from Alcatraz

ISBN 9781649795366 (Paperback)
ISBN 9781649795373 (Hardback)
ISBN 9781649795380 (ePub e-book)

Library of Congress Control Number: 2022919666

www.austinmacauley.com/us

First Published 2022
Austin Macauley Publishers LLC
40 Wall Street, 33rd Floor, Suite 3302
New York, NY 10005
USA

mail-usa@austinmacauley.com
+1 (646) 5125767

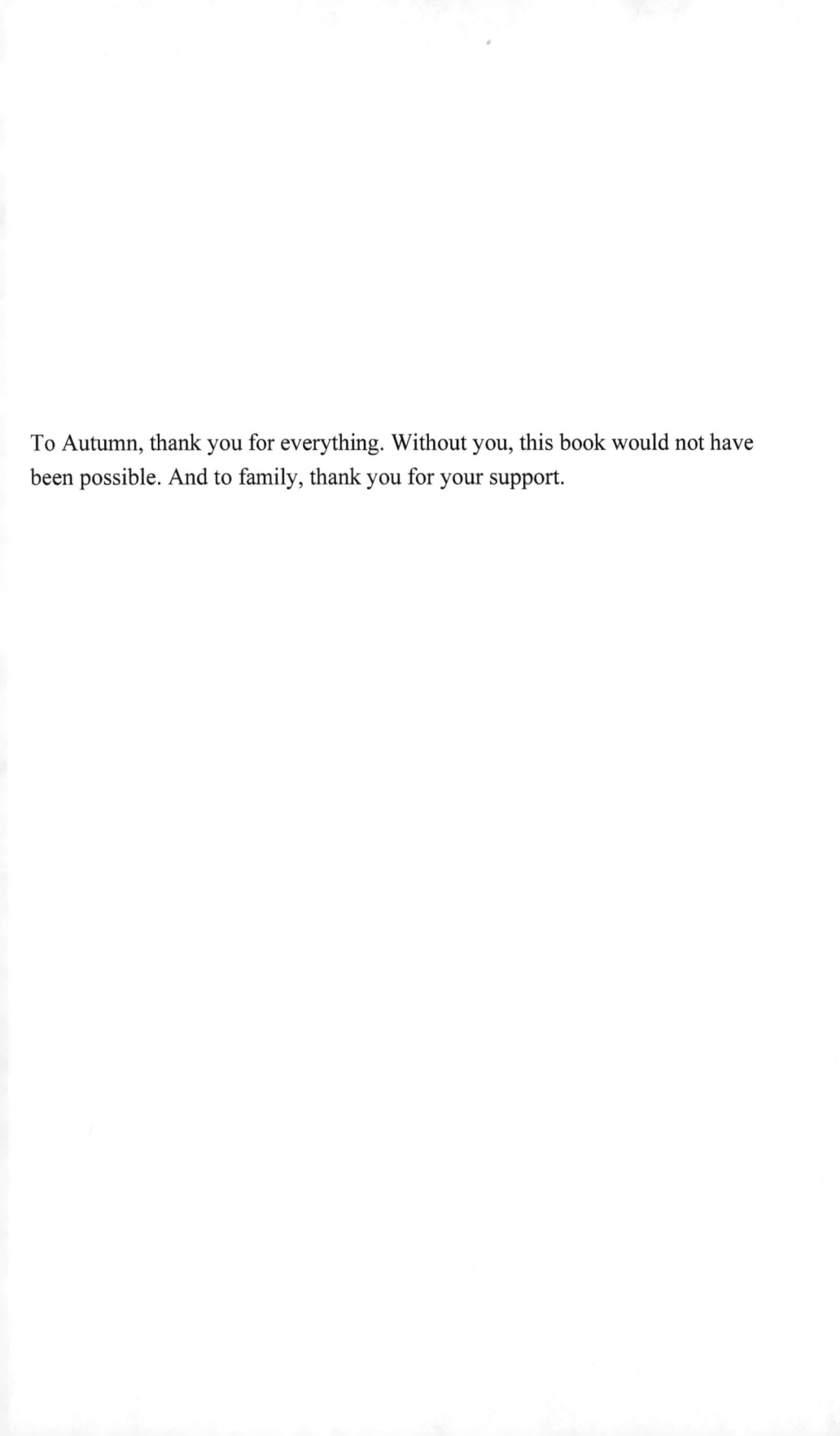

To Autumn, thank you for everything. Without you, this book would not have been possible. And to family, thank you for your support.

Prologue

May 7th, 1949
San Francisco, California

Alexander "Rex" Armati watched his friend Vincent weave the needle in and out of the fabric of the stolen raincoats, his fingers deft and experienced. All was going according to plan, he thought with a smug smile. Soon, they would be free from this hellhole called Alcatraz. They would make it to the mainland and go their separate ways, seek new lives, and remain anonymous from the law.

For months, Rex and his pals had planned this escape. They had stolen supplies, widened the ventilation ducts in their cells to holes big enough to crawl through, and set up a little shop in the utility corridor. There, they worked to make a raft big enough to hold all four of them—Rex, Vincent, Hadley, and Anderson—out of raincoats. They were almost ready.

To disguise their absence, Hadley and Anderson had fashioned dummy heads out of a homemade mixture of concrete dust, toothpaste, soap, and toilet paper. Hair from the barber shop served to add a realistic appearance to these dummies, and once nestled on the pillows on their beds, blankets tucked to the paper chins, the guise could fool even the most careful eye.

Rex was the leader of this escape committee. He dictated and planned, helped out a little on the raft, too. Vincent, Hadley, and Anderson were okay with having him as their leader. This whole thing had been his idea to begin with, anyhow, and Rex felt he had a right to boss them around. After all, he was the son of a man respected throughout New York City as the boss of all bosses. Salvatore Armati was Father to those who were loyal to him, but no more.

Rex was proud of his Sicilian blood. But he was no longer welcome in his Family. He had broken the code of honor by going to the police and providing them with information. Why he had done it was due to broken traditions; all honor had been lost, and that was not the Sicilian way. He had had no choice but to do it—the new Father of the Armati Family was corrupt and deserved Rex's betrayal.

Because of his actions, his Family had fallen, and Rex had wound up here, in this God-forsaken place. He suspected his imprisonment in this particular hell had something to do with his twin brother Stefano.

But Rex didn't give a damn. He didn't crave revenge. He didn't want to start a war. He just wanted a fresh start.

After the Second World War, he had become addicted to morphine, but since his sentence to Alcatraz, he had become clean. Although the wounds he sustained while fighting many-a-battle still ached and throbbed, he refused to numb the pain by resorting to his old ways. Once he'd escaped Alcatraz, he would be baptized by the ocean a new man, and he vowed to never touch a drop of that poison for as long as he lived. Realizing full-well he would be tempted, he decided the best way to completely kick the habit was by finding a place so secluded and peaceful, morphine became an afterthought.

But first, he and friends must succeed in escaping. It wasn't wise to plan ahead and map out one's future when the present was all that mattered. Rex fully understood this. Those were words of wisdom from his father.

"Tomorrow we make our escape," Rex told his squad in his thick New York brogue. "Be ready, men. Our attempt will be at midnight. If you fall behind, then you will be left. Do I make myself clear?"

"'Course, you're the boss," Anderson said respectfully.

"These waters are dangerous. I hope you're all good swimmers, because if our raft fails, that's precisely what we'll be doing."

"And shark infested," Hadley added with a violent shutter. "Remember the sharks."

"Is that raft almost ready?" Rex asked Vincent.

"Yes. By tomorrow, it will be finished."

"That's good."

Rex heaved a sigh. How far he had fallen! He had been Dad's second in the Family, but no more. Now, he was just a man without a purpose. His Family had abandoned him after he'd betrayed them all. Mama was the only one left who understood. Rex loved her dearly, but never again would he ever feel her comforting arms around him. Once he was out of this place, he would forge a new identity, and that meant ceasing all contact with his mother. Perhaps he would send her an occasional letter under an alter ego.

It was time.

Rex's heart hammered wildly in his chest as he crawled out the hole beneath the sink in his cell and into the small corridor leading to the utility room. Anderson and Vincent joined him, but Hadley was nowhere to be found. Rex allowed one minute to pass by, but when Hadley still hadn't joined them, he decided it was for the best to leave him behind. Time was a luxury they could not afford, and Hadley knew that. Rex was sorry to abandon him, but he had no other choice.

The three men gathered the raft and the homemade paddles they'd made and started off, moving quickly. Adrenaline surged hot and welcoming through Rex's veins as he took point and led his team. They climbed up the ventilation shaft to the roof and quickly slid down the kitchen vent pipe. Many obstacles lay in their way, but they cleared them without delay and soon arrived at the shoreline without being spotted by the searchlights. The raft was promptly inflated and placed in the choppy waters; Rex hopped in, took the ore Anderson tossed him, and prepared to paddle with all his might. Vincent was the last one in and pushed them off from the shore. All three men began to paddle, making for the distant mainland.

The going was tough, the waters churning violently. As they reached the halfway point, a current swept them towards the Golden Gate Bridge and they quickly lost sight of the mainland. Working desperately, the men paddled hard. Their strength began to ebb away.

"We'll never make it," Anderson cried. "We're getting swept out into the open sea! We'll be eaten alive by sharks!"

"Ah, shut up, Anderson!" Rex snapped. He was beginning to regret taking the pessimistic fool along. "Keep paddlin', men!"

Vincent began to waver, but he continued to paddle. He was a good soldier, and never complained. Rex would be sorry to part ways with him if—no, *when*—they reached the shore.

"Shark!" Anderson suddenly screamed.

"Shit!" Rex cursed when he saw the fin. He paddled harder.

Anderson stopped paddling, his eyes wild with fear. He took one look at Vincent, made a decision, and grabbed the man by the lapels of his shirt. Before

Rex could stop him, Anderson tossed Vincent into the ocean; the shark immediately took the bait and abandoned its circling of their raft in favor of having Vincent for a meal.

There was no time to berate Anderson concerning the vile act he had just committed. It was either live or die, and Rex was very much opposed to the latter. He was only thirty-one. He had a life to live.

The shore was within their reach, but the raft was useless now. It had carried them this far, but now, Rex realized they would have to abandon it and swim the rest of the way. He informed Anderson of what he was about to do, then dove into the water. Honing the skills his father had taught him, he swam with all his might towards the beach, which was near enough to see in the pitch black of night. Whether Anderson followed or not, Rex didn't know. All he truly knew was a deep desire to *survive*. The will to live fueled him. When his feet struck a sandy, welcoming bottom, he wanted to rejoice. Once on shore however, he collapsed, cold and exhausted. But there was no time to stop now, not when freedom was within his grasp. He got to his feet, looked around for Anderson, and realized with a sinking feeling that he was the only survivor. He didn't pause to dwell on this long, as he was freezing and if he didn't get into warm clothes soon, getting caught would be the least of his problems.

So he started off.

Freedom was his.

Chapter One

Rex inhaled the cool morning air and gazed up at a sky swollen with clouds through half-lidded eyes. Sweat perspired on his skin and dampened his clothes. His racing heart throbbed in his ears and the world felt distant. Like the mainland had been from Alcatraz.

His successful escape seemed years ago when in fact, it had only been a few weeks. In that span of time, he had traveled many miles by hitching rides with kind people, and walking. He had a destination in mind: Wyoming. It was secluded and peaceful, a place where he could lie low for a while and begin a new life. His mother, Maria, had always dreamed of visiting the wild country she had read stories about when she was but a little girl. She had fantasized about marrying a rustic man who rode horses and herded cattle. Such a fantasy! In the end, she had married Salvatore Armati, a brutish man from Sicily with big ambitions.

Up ahead there was a sign. It read: *Welcome to Crowley County. Population: 721.*

Rex paused a moment to examine it; the words swam and blurred together, becoming a big pool of white. He carried on, taking his fedora off to fan his sweaty face. Damn, but he felt like hell. He assumed his condition had something to do with his lack of nourishment and sleep. A kind elderly man he had hitched a ride with had given him twenty dollars to get by. Already Rex had spent twelve of it on food. He was sorely in need of a good night's rest, but first, he must make it to the town that lay fifteen miles ahead. Such a distance intimidated his weakened body. He muttered a quiet curse and willed himself to keep going.

Two miles later, he collapsed in sheer exhaustion to his knees and decided he wasn't longed for this world. God ought to deliver him from his suffering, but he supposed he had sinned too much in his life to receive His mercy. No, if he died, he would be going to hell where he would rot for eternity harboring a vast cavern of regrets.

"Lord," he muttered, "I feel like hell."

He saw something coming towards him, and squinted. It was an automobile, he decided, hope restored. But what were the chances of the driver stopping to rescue a pale, sickly man? He allowed hope to slip through his grasp. He wasn't seeing sense. He felt as though he was being consumed by the fever which wracked his body like a violent storm. He was delusional.

The automobile came to a stop and the door opened. Some big, hairy gold creature leapt out and galloped up to him. It stuck its big pink nose in his face and attempted to lick his cheek.

"Grazer, heel!" a masculine voice called. The dog cantered away.

"Oh, David, look! He's nearly dead," a feminine voice said.

"I can see that, honey."

"Are we going to help him, David?" Another female voice.

"Of course we are, Amanda."

Rex groaned when a cool, soft hand splayed across his cheek.

"Oh, you poor thing," the woman named Amanda crooned. "David, he's burning up!"

"Let's get him to his feet. Margaret, take his other arm."

Grazer—the dog—touched his nose to Rex's hand as the fella named David and the dame named Margaret helped him to his feet. His knees nearly buckled but he managed to remain standing as David and Margaret guided him to the automobile and helped him into the back seat. Amanda slid in next to him and cradled his head on her lap. The dog, it's stale breath on his face, lay on the floor beneath him.

As David put the automobile in drive, Rex lost consciousness and was consumed by darkness. Next he awoke, he was lying in some bed in a strange room. A window was open, and the white curtains lifted gently upwards as a cool breeze floated in. The room was empty save for an armchair and a bookshelf. Rex wondered where he was, how he had gotten here, and who was responsible. As he slowly eased himself into a sitting position, he noticed something big and golden lying at the foot of the bed and realized it was the dog, Grazer. Grazer looked up and blinked big brown eyes at him as if to say, oh, look, you're finally awake!

"Yeah, pal, I'm awake," Rex murmured dazedly.

Grazer stood and stretched. As he made to jump off the bed, he trampled rudely over Rex's feet and Rex winced as he felt the sharp claws dig in to his skin through the quilt covering him. His head still throbbed, but he felt better. Much better.

Grazer trotted off out the cracked door. Rex could hear those unmerciful claws clicking on the hardwood floor. Moments later, a woman with dark brown hair pulled into a tidy bun entered with a tray of soup balanced in her arms.

"Good afternoon, mister," she greeted kindly. "Are you feeling better? I brought you something."

"Uh, yes, ma'am, thank you," Rex answered gratefully, and although he wasn't hungry, he would attempt to eat anyway.

"You gave us quite a scare. My husband David took you for dead. My name is Margaret Chandler by the way."

He hesitated, thinking it would be best if he didn't use his surname. He wracked his brain quickly for another and decided he'd borrow that of his best friend, Al. "Rex Moretti, ma'am. It's a pleasure to meet you. I appreciate you tendin' to me."

"You're not from around here. New York?" Margaret guessed, settling the tray in his lap and handing him a spoon. "My mama came from New York."

"Yes, ma'am. Staten Island, to be exact."

"I'll leave you to your meal. If you should need anything, just holler. I'll be in the kitchen."

Rex ate his soup in silence. He felt fortunate and lucky the Chandlers had happened upon him when they did. Had they not, he would be a dead corpse on the side of the road.

The soup was good, and he polished it off. Exhaustion overcame him as he put the tray on the nightstand, and he decided to rest. Yet sleep eluded him, as he felt strange lying in a strange bed in a strange house probably on some ranch or farm in the middle of God-knows-where. He felt like he was imposing, and the very feeling unsettled him. As soon as he felt up to it, he would be on his way and leave these folks in peace.

As he was drifting off, the sound of a screen door slamming in the distance made him jerk awake. Muttering a quiet curse, Rex rubbed his temples and realized the headache was still going strong. He could still hear his pulse in his ears.

"Amanda Grace, what did I tell you about slamming doors?" he heard Margaret scold. "We've a very ill guest and he's trying to rest."

"Sorry, Peggy," Amanda replied in a tone of voice that implied she wasn't really sorry she'd slammed the screen door. "May I see him?" she asked.

"No, you may not."

"I'm not a child, Peggy. I'm a woman."

"That doesn't give you special privileges to barge in on a poor sick man." She dropped her voice, but Rex still caught the words uttered from her mouth. "You must remember he's a stranger. We don't know him."

"That makes him all the more exciting," Amanda insisted.

Rex smiled. He imagined a little girl in a ponytail when Amanda spoke. She reminded him of his seventeen-year-old cousin Rose. Rose, who talked a mile a minute. Rose, who made everyone laugh. Rose, who, despite her naivety, was wise beyond her years. He sure did miss her.

"All right," Margaret relented on a sigh, "you may see him. But briefly, mind you. You are not to engage him in conversation. I'm sure he is finished with his soup so your only purpose for going into his room is to fetch the tray. Do you understand?"

Amanda muttered that she did.

"Run along, then."

Rex eased himself into a sitting position and maneuvered his feet from harm's way when Grazer suddenly burst in and took a flying leap onto the bed. He was about to use foul language to curse the dog out when Amanda entered. He quickly refrained from swearing in front of her, and as she came to stand before him, what he saw was a woman—not a little girl. She wore her blonde hair long and loose, and a white bow was fastened in place at the back. The shin-length dark blue dress loosely hugged curves and a womanly bust, yet Rex only saw a youth before him.

He was startled when she boldly settled herself on the edge of the mattress and folded feminine hands in her lap.

"Hello, there," she said with a wide, girlish smile. "I'm Amanda. I'm David's little sister."

"Rex," Rex introduced brusquely.

"You sound funny. Where are you from?"

"New York."

"Are you from the mob?"

Rex tried not to look alarmed. If she knew who he was, then her family might boot him out or perhaps even hand him over to the authorities. He was too weak to fight, and too honorable to hurt them. Amanda looked gullible enough to believe anything he told her.

So he lied.

"Sorry to disappoint, kid, but I'm just an honest, hardworkin' man. I've no connections to those bastards—I mean, fools—whatsoever."

She did indeed look disappointed, but she soon brightened. "David likes honest, hardworking men," she told him. "Perhaps he'll hire you. We're short of hands here on the ranch."

At this, he felt hope stir within him. He didn't care what the job was; he was in sore need of one, and any-old position would do, be it to wrangle cattle or herd sheep or whatever it was one did on a ranch. He flashed Amanda a smile and her response was to blush crimson. He had that effect on the dames.

"I'll accept if he'll have me," he said.

"I'll tell him you're interested."

"Thank you."

* * *

David Chandler was a man in his early thirties. He was tall, his shoulders broad, his arms hard with muscle. He was a man who didn't take kindly to those who slacked and failed to follow orders. He was also very open-minded and wasn't opposed to hiring those whose skin color sometimes prevented them from obtaining decent jobs.

Rex quickly found out *whom* he was to be taking orders from—and he was not happy, to say the least.

When David hired him, Rex had fully expected to answer to him and only him, but that wasn't to be so. He would be answering to the foreman, a tall, slightly heavyset man named Solomon Elwood. Despite that Solomon was a friendly fellow with kind dark eyes and a heart of gold, he was black.

Right away Rex knew there would be problems concerning this arrangement. It wasn't that he was opposed to allowing the negro people their freedom; it was the very thought of taking orders from one that had Rex regretting his decision to accept the position offered him. Life simply didn't work that way. There was a pecking order, and Rex considered himself above Solomon's people.

Not David, apparently. David saw Solomon and himself as equals, and told Rex he ought to see things that way too, otherwise he might as well pack his nonexistent belongings and get out. Rex needed this job, so he had no choice but to set his differences aside and begrudgingly accept the fact that he would be taking orders from a black man.

Work for Rex began as soon as he was well enough to stand without staggering. He was given one of the empty cabins about a mile or two from the homestead down a secluded dirt road. The hands called these cluster of cabins "Bachelors' Row," because that was precisely what the inhabits of the cabins were: bachelors. Solomon lived further on up the road with his wife Ellen Sue and his seven-year-old son Billy.

The Chandler ranch sat on almost nine hundred acres of lush, green land. Two hundred acres of it was woods swollen with game which were hunted for food in the winter months when heavy snowfall prevented trips into town for groceries. Next to the homestead was a large garden, and beyond that was a fruit orchard. Pastures held cattle and horses. A large, red barn served to stable the horses used for riding purposes. A smaller one housed milking cows. There was a chicken coop, too, where fresh eggs were collected each morning by either Margaret or Ellen Sue.

Amanda gave Rex a tour of the ranch. Grazer, always at her side, tagged along. As they walked, she chattered on about her teaching job at Crowley Elementary School and her desires in life, which included finding a husband and having five children with him. Rex listened. Privately, he thought she talked too much.

"There's an old homestead in the woods somewhere," she told him when she was finished telling him about her husband, whom she hadn't met yet. "It belonged to my great grandpa, Elmer. There's a pond up near Bluebird Valley I like to walk to when it's dreadfully hot. I sometimes go swimming there. Have you ever gone swimming, Rex?"

Rex wanted to say, *You have no idea*, but he merely smiled and simply told her he had, loads of times when he was a little boy. But no more.

"Why?" she pressed, looking at him strangely.

"I have no desire to swim. It's child's play."

"You're a very serious man, Rex. You ought to lighten up."

He shrugged.

She changed the subject. "Do you ride?"

"Ride?" he echoed, confused.

"Horses, I mean."

"No," he confessed, realizing that might be a problem if he was going to put his heart and soul into this job.

"I can teach you," she offered eagerly.

"I might just take you up on that offer, ma'am."

"Amanda. My students call me ma'am, and sometimes, it's refreshing to hear folks address me by my given name."

"Very well, then. Amanda."

She beamed him with a smile.

They headed to the main barn. Amanda showed him to his mount, a black mare named Esther. Esther reached her nose for his hand as if searching for something to eat. She nickered softly when Amanda produced a sugar cube from the pocket of her jeans and offered it to her.

"My horse is Gregory. He's the appaloosa next to Esther." She gestured to the black gelding who appeared as though a dusting of snow blanketed his back. "Your first lesson will be on how to take care of your mount…"

She spent an hour showing him how to properly groom Esther. Lesson two was saddling and bridling; lesson three was mounting, which he did once he had led the gentle, quiet mare into the corral beside the barn. Once in the saddle, he looked to Amanda for guidance. From her post perched on the top rail of the fence, she told him to gently nudge Esther in her sides and make a clicking sound with his tongue. He did as instructed, and Esther began to walk forward, ambling along at a comfortable pace.

"Once you've learned the basics, David will take you out and have you successfully herding cattle in no time," Amanda said confidently.

"Sounds dangerous," Rex called over his shoulder.

"It is when you're a greenhorn."

"Swell," he muttered sarcastically. "That makes me feel very … at ease."

"Don't be nervous. Esther will sense your emotions and respond to them accordingly."

"Define accordingly," Rex requested calmly.

"If you're nervous, she will be, too."

Rex patted his mount on the neck. For her sake, and for the sake of his life, he would attempt to remain relaxed and focused.

David, Solomon, and the rest of the hands were out moving the cattle to a higher pasture before the storm Solomon predicted hit full-force. Indeed, there were great black clouds in the distance, moving slowly in from the east. Solomon forecasted heavy rainfall, therefore the creek in the pasture the cattle were currently grazing in was liable to flood, putting newborn calves' lives in danger.

David thought it would be best if Rex sat out on moving the cattle, because he felt Rex wasn't ready to take on such a dangerous task. Instead, he had Rex repairing a leak on the farmhouse roof. Rex didn't mind. He was good at fixing things, and was happy for an excuse not to endanger his life. He was good at riding, too, but not *that* good. He had nearly broken his neck this morning when Esther had decided a cat walking across the fence line was in fact a demon with horns fixing to kill her; she had thrown him when she took off in a desperate attempt to flee the threat. Margret had had to patch him up, as he had sustained a four-inch gash to go with the long, deep scar on his right cheek sustained from his war days fighting Nazis.

Now, he whistled Bing Crosby tunes as he fixed that pesky leak Margret had been complaining about. He was enjoying life on the Chandler ranch. It was peaceful, and the hard work ranch life tossed at him kept his thoughts from straying to his mother and Rose, both of whom he missed with a fierce ache. He longed to write to them, and he would, but not for a long while. He would wait until he was but a hazy memory to the law, his Family, and his twin brother. The law would possibly forget him in no time, as they likely presumed him dead, drowned in the ocean after his attempted escape failed. Let them presume that. Let everyone presume that, including his twin brother who had taken over as Father after their dear old papa had been killed by the Father of the Moretti Family after an age-long feud.

Rex heard the screen door slam. Moments later, Amanda came out to peer up at him, one hand shielding her eyes from the bright rays of the sun. She watched him for a moment. He paused to acknowledge her.

"Don't fall," she advised him with genuine concern. "You might break your neck for certain this time."

Rex saluted her causally. "Thanks for the warnin', kid, but I understand full-well the consequences should I indeed take a fall from this here roof. Why don't you pray for my soul? If I fall and die, then perhaps God will forgive my sins more willingly."

"Very funny."

He grinned and went back to his work.

After a while, she went off to the barn with Grazer and left him in peace. Once again, he paused to watch her. She reminded him so much of Rose, it hurt to look at her. The only difference between them was appearances; while Rose had shiny black hair she preferred to wear bobbed, Amanda's was blonde and reached down to the middle of her back in thick, golden waves. And while Rose's eyes were brown, Amanda's was a blue in between light and dark, like the sky just before dusk. Rex knew an ache in his heart and bent to his work once more, concentrating on getting that leak repaired before the storm hit.

Later, as the sky became dark and forbidding, he went to his cabin to do a little work there. If he was going to live here a while, he wanted to feel at home. The cabin was dusty, the floors in need of scrubbing. There was a kitchen, a small living area, a bathroom (he was told by Solomon such an amenity was a luxury on a big ranch such as this one), and a bedroom. The living area was sparsely yet properly furnished; he felt the only thing missing was a bookshelf full of books. He would soon change that, however—once he received his wages. He would also buy a new wardrobe. As of now, he was wearing clothing David had lent to him. He hated to borrow.

As thunder sounded overhead, Rex stood in the middle of his new kitchen and decided what he really needed was a wife. And perhaps a son or two, and even a daughter. Now that he dwelled on his feelings, he realized he was lonely. But there was plenty of time to go searching for a wife. In the meantime, the dust was making him sneeze. He set to work.

Chapter Two

It didn't take long for Rex to settle in and get used to his new routine. He started to enjoy ranch life, something that was ironic, considering he'd been a city dweller most of his life. It was very refreshing to start anew. He'd been here two weeks now, and he planned on staying longer if all worked out.

The mornings were his favorite. He got up with the sun, brewed some coffee, and sat out on his front porch. It was quiet on the ranch. It made him realize just how noisy the city was, and now that he got to experience both, he found he had a preference, and that was the country.

Rex went up to the house that morning upon request from David. As he walked across the yard, he spotted Amanda, who was sitting on a wooden swing hanging from the thick branch of an old oak. She was barefooted and dressed in blue jeans and a faded flannel shirt.

Amanda waved at him and smiled. Rex nodded in return, picking up his pace in case she decided she wanted to engage him in conversation. Once she got going, there was no turning her off. He didn't mind her company, but he liked his peace and quiet; he wasn't a conversationalist, neither was he that good at keeping up with her.

Rex entered through the back door, letting the screen slam shut behind him. Margaret was in the kitchen making breakfast.

"Dave will be in shortly," she said. "Why don't you take a seat. Would you like something to eat?"

"No, ma'am, but thank you," said Rex. He ran splayed fingers through his thick, black hair and waited in silence. The aromas coming from the stove were mouth-watering. He'd already eaten a dull breakfast, though, and didn't want to stay too long.

David entered the room and greeted him with a cordial smile. "Good-morning, Rex."

"Good-mornin', sir. You called for me?"

"I did. I need you to run into town for me. I have a list of things I need from the hardware store, and I'm too tied up today to do it myself. You can take the truck."

"Oh, and I need some groceries," Margaret added. She grabbed a slip of paper and passed it to Rex. "Amanda will take care of that. She loves going into town. You don't mind, do you?"

Rex tried to smile. "No, ma'am. I don't mind at all."

He prepared himself for half-an-hour of constant chatter as he stepped out onto the patio and gazed across the lawn to where Amanda still sat on the swing. She looked up, a hopeful expression on her face. Rex sighed.

"I'm runnin' in to town and could use some company," he called. "Care to tag along?"

Amanda's face lit up like a ray of sunshine. "I'd love to."

Amanda was uncharacteristically quiet on the drive into town. Rex cranked the window down and let in the cool Wyoming air, enjoying the feel of it against his face. The nice thing about these back roads was that no one was ever on them. He drove a bit fast, but not recklessly fast; he had a lady in the passenger seat.

Rex spared Amanda a glance, wondering how she could be so chatty one minute, but so shy and reserved the next. He never really did understand women all that much. They were unpredictable, sometimes even emotional. But Amanda, she was different. She was as sweet as they came but he sensed she hid a temper somewhere underneath that innocent smile of hers. He wondered what it took to ignite this temper.

Rex took the unpredicted silence to sort his thoughts. He was wary about venturing into town, but he didn't believe he had to worry much about the authorities coming after him. With any luck, they thought him dead, swept away by the perilous tide of the San Francisco Bay.

He thought of somehow getting a letter sent to his mother, but it was too soon. As much as he hated the image of her being wrought with sorrow over his presumed death or disappearance, it was better this way. Perhaps in a few weeks when the excitement died down, he would let her know he was alive and well. By then, the news would find something else more exciting to report on and his escape would be yesterday's thrill.

Rex ought to have been smug about his escape from a prison that was known for being inescapable, but he wasn't. There were more important matters to him, like staying alive and making a new life for himself. He couldn't return to the old one. He'd betrayed his Family and that was enough to merit his death by their hands if he ever showed his face again.

Sorry, Ma, he thought, feeling an ache in his throat. He'd never meant to hurt her. Perhaps someday she would forgive him, but right now the wounds were still raw. It could take years—maybe never—to heal.

Rex pushed aside his thoughts and centered his mind elsewhere. He immediately thought of Amanda and wondered why she was being so quiet. Not that he minded, but he had to admit that he liked the sound of her voice. She could soothe a screaming child with her gentle soprano, which was probably good in her line of work, being a teacher and all.

Out of the corner of his eye, he saw Amanda turn slightly towards him. *Ah, hell. Here it goes,* he thought, but couldn't help the smile that tugged at his lips.

"Rex, I have a confession to make."

Rex raised a brow. "About—?"

Amanda blew out a breath. "David told me to be on my guard around you," she said, sounding embarrassed. "He doesn't trust very easily, you understand. But I'm not like him at all."

"Do *you* trust me?" Rex asked. He wouldn't blame her if she said no. There was much he hadn't told the Chandlers, his intentions being honorable, but also selfish. He wanted to protect them but also himself.

"The funny thing is, I do. I trust a complete stranger we found half-dead on the side of the road. What does that say about my character?"

She sounded upset by this. Rex sighed, deciding she made him feel dizzy with the whirlwind of emotions that was her.

"I see your point. For all you know, I could be a serial killer, or maybe just an all-around shady fellow with bad intentions. But I'm flattered you trust me." Rex took his eyes off the road for a quick moment to flash her a grin. Amanda smiled back.

And just like that, the spell of silence was broken and Amanda filled it with chatter. She told him about Crowley County, about the people that lived in it, and how she knew almost everyone. The beauty, Rex mused, of small town life.

"The sheriff is Joe Chandler. He's my uncle," Amanda said, much to Rex's dismay. "Do you mind if we drop by the sheriff's station to say hello on our way back?"

Rex didn't think that was a good idea. He never got along with lawmen, even the small town sort, and he wasn't about to start now. It would be wise to stay far away from the eyes of anyone who held that kind of authority.

"If we have time," he said, as a compromise.

"It's all right if we don't. He's coming for supper tomorrow night, that's why Peggy asked me to run into town to pick up a few groceries from the grocer."

"I see."

"Would you like to come? To supper, I mean." Rex heard a blush in her voice and found it to be endearing. She sure did get embarrassed by the smallest things.

"I don't think that's a good idea. I'm not good company."

"Sure you are. Besides, I want you to come. Would you think about it?" Amanda asked, sounding hopeful.

"What's the dress code?" Rex wanted to know.

"Casual. It's nothing fancy, but Margaret *does* require you to wash behind your ears." She laughed. "She's strict about that sort of thing."

"No kidding?"

That prompted Amanda to launch into a story about an incident her brother had with his wife one evening when he forgot to wash properly before dinner. Rex listened with half an ear, the other half of him thinking about the sheriff, wondering if the man would be a problem. Rex was just getting settled down and he didn't fancy running again.

Up ahead appeared the sign for the town limits. Rex drove through and started seeing signs of population as they went through a small neighborhood dotted with picturesque little houses with neat front lawns. A few miles further sat the town. It was your average small town, with a Main Street and shops on either side. At the heart of the town was the square, a patch of green lawn centered by an impressive statue of a soldier riding a horse, and neatly-kept flowerbeds.

Folks went about their daily lives, some strolling along, a few old men sitting in front of the barber shop trading stories. They passed mothers with small children, a couple of teenagers trying to find excitement, and a lot of folks who waved at Amanda in greeting. She really did seem to know everyone.

Rex found a place to park the truck in between the grocer and the hardware store. He got out and ran around to open Amanda's door for her. She seemed pleased by his courteous act.

"I'll meet you back here in an hour," Rex said, then headed off in the direction of the hardware store.

He consulted the list David had given him. There wasn't much on it, just a box of nails and a couple of other essential items one might require on a ranch.

Rex was about the only one in the store, except for a middle-aged fellow manning the counter and chatting away with a customer. He kept a wary eye on them out of habit as he went through the store, gathering up David's requested supplies. He couldn't help but see everyone as suspicious. Being a fugitive of the law was enough to make any man edgy, and for good reasons. It was only natural that he looked at every stranger as someone who might recognize him, or who might be affiliated with the law.

Rex waited until the customer left before bringing the items up and placing them on the counter.

"You must be Dave's new hand," the cashier said. "I'm Fred, the owner of this here place, by the way. Is this all you need, sir?"

News apparently spread quickly in a small town. Rex didn't know if this was a good thing or a bad thing, but it sure did succeed in making him feel like his privacy was no longer his.

"Yes, thank you." Rex pulled out the money David had given him for the supplies and handed it over.

"David stopped by the other day," Fred informed him. "Said you were a hard worker. You're not from around here, are you?"

Rex became wary. "No."

"Thought not. Your accent gives you away." Fred counted out the change and handed it back. "My missus is from back east. I assume that's where you hail, son."

"Sure is," Rex said, pocketing the change. He gathered up the supplies. "Have a nice day, sir."

He still had half an hour before meeting Amanda, so he dropped the supplies off at the truck and took a walk, hands stuffed in the pockets of his pants. It was pleasantly cool for summer. The sun warmed him, but a gentle breeze offered relief.

Rex paused at the antique store window and looked at the display. Behind him was the grocer, its reflection clear in the glass. He watched a moment until he saw Amanda come out with her arms laden down with paper sacks of groceries.

Rex turned on his heel and ran across the street to give her a hand. Amanda beamed him a grateful smile.

"I got everything on Peggy's list," she said breathlessly. "She's going to be pleased. Are you still thinking on my offer to join us for supper tomorrow?"

"I haven't decided," Rex admitted.

"That's all right. I got a little extra, just in case. Even if you don't say yes, I'll understand."

"It sounds like you'll be disappointed if I decline."

Amanda looked sheepish. "A little, yes. But only because I think it's good for you to meet new folks."

"I like being alone," Rex said. "I've never been what you'd call a social butterfly."

They reached the truck and got in, putting the sacks of groceries on the floor between them. Rex was about to start up the truck when he felt Amanda's gaze on him. He turned to glance at her, confirming that she was indeed staring at him.

"Rex, would you mind terribly if I drove home?"

Rex blinked, caught off guard. "You want to drive?"

"Yes. I don't have much experience, but I'm sure I'd do fine if you instructed me."

Rex didn't think this was a good idea, but he shrugged and got out so they could switch sides. Once Amanda was sitting in the driver's seat, he started giving her instructions, starting with the clutch and how to use it. Amanda drank in his every word like a student eager to learn. But when it came time to start up the engine and drive, Rex suddenly had regrets.

At first, Amanda did all right, but the moment they were free from the town limits and she had to accelerate, he discovered she had a lead foot. She hit the gas and the momentum caused him to jerk backwards into his seat.

"Jesus Christ!" Rex swore.

Amanda laughed like she was thoroughly enjoying herself. With the windows down, the wind whipped through her hair, blowing it into her eyes. The truck swerved precariously and would have gone off the road had Rex not leaned over and grabbed the wheel, bringing them back on course.

"Slow down," he yelled. "Get your foot off the gas!"

Amanda slammed on the brakes instead. Rex lost his balance and landed in her lap. It took him several moments to recover, as his heart was pounding in his chest. After the scare he had, he'd probably aged a couple of years, maybe more.

"I'm sorry," Amanda muttered, sounding contrite. "Rex, are you all right?"

"I'm fine," Rex reassured her, sitting up. "I think it's best if I drive the rest of the way home."

"Good idea."

Amanda scrambled out and ran around. Rex scooted over to the driver's side to retake his role as driver, thinking he'd have to give Amanda some proper lessons in a nice, big field. She certainly could use them.

"You're not mad, are you?" Amanda asked, pulling the door shut once she got in.

"No. Who taught you to drive, anyhow?"

"No one. I taught myself."

That figured. Rex shook his head and started up the engine again. "Sweetheart, you may be good at teachin' kids, but you sure as hell can't drive to save your life."

"I know. But David won't teach me." Amanda fell silent a moment, then spoke in softer tones. "See, our parents died in an automobile accident. Ever since then he's been real protective of me."

"That makes sense," Rex said gently. "He doesn't want to see you get hurt, or worse."

"I know, but I'm a grown woman now. I ought to be able to make my own decisions."

Rex didn't respond, afraid anything else he said might hurt her feelings. He didn't have little sisters, but he had a little cousin, and he had no trouble agreeing with David on being protective. Amanda was just a girl. She was naive and had tender feelings. David was right in wanting to keep her safe, even if she didn't like it.

Rex pulled back onto the road and headed in the direction of the ranch.

It was Saturday morning the next day, and it dawned bright and clear. Rex was sitting on the front porch of his cabin, enjoying a cup of coffee, when a scrawny little boy carrying a fishing pole and a tackle box walked up. Rex didn't have to ask his name. It was Billy, Ellen Sue and Solomon's son.

"Howdy, mister," the kid said.

Rex saluted in greeting. "You goin' fishing, kid?"

"Yep. Miss Amanda and me are goin'. Amanda sent me to ask if you'd like to tag along. Mister David said it was okay."

Rex should have known. He sighed, thinking there was much more important things he had to attend to than babysitting, but he didn't want to disappoint Amanda. Her feelings sure did get bruised easily.

"All right," Rex conceded, getting to his feet. He joined Billy and they headed off down the stretch of dirt road.

"I'm Billy, and I'm seven," the kid said. "What's your name, mister?"

"Rex."

"You have a funny accent."

Rex shrugged. "So do you."

Billy laughed and swung the arm holding the tackle box, making the contents rattle. "Amanda says there's lots of folks in this world with different accents. Just like there's black folk and white folk."

Rex looked down at him. "Is Amanda your teacher?" he asked.

"Yep. She teaches me all sorts of things. I like history the best, but I don't like math too much. It makes my brain hurt."

"You mean it gives you a headache," Rex said, and Billy nodded.

"Sure does. You wanna know somethin' else?"

Rex sighed. "What?"

"You're not so bad. For a white man, I mean. You remind me of my daddy."

Rex bit back a retort. Billy was just a child. "Thanks, kid. I'll take that as a compliment."

Amanda was waiting for them up at the house, her back against the truck. The dog, Grazer, lay at her feet. She had her long, blonde hair plaited in two braids today. Rex nodded to her in greeting.

"Good-morning," he said. "Guess I decided to tag along."

Amanda beamed. "That's good. You can drive." And with that she promptly handed him the keys, appointing him driver of this little venture.

It was certainly a lovely day for fishing. Rex hadn't been fishing in a while, not since he was a teenager and his father took him and his twin brother to a lake up in the country. He remembered that memory with fondness. Those were the days before everything changed, before the war, before everything took a tumble down-hill and he nearly lost his dignity.

Rex liked to think he was a changed man, but he knew by experience that change was something that never came easy. Sometimes he wondered if he'd made the right decisions in life.

But here was his chance to be a different man. Taking Amanda and Billy fishing would remind him of the good old days, before life took his youth from him and turned him into a hard, bitter man.

Amanda gave Rex directions to go down a dirt road. It was an old logger's road that nature had reclaimed, making it a nice, reclusive spot. Up ahead was an opening in the trees. Beyond that was the lake, its pristine waters reflecting the bright sunlight.

Rex stopped the truck and everyone hopped out. Grazer leapt from the bed and took off for the water like his life depended on it, a blur of brilliant golden fur and infinite energy.

"When it's especially warm, I like to come here and go swimming," Amanda told Rex.

"It sure seems like a nice place," Rex agreed. He grabbed the tackle box and followed her to the bank. Billy was already there, baiting his hook with freshly-dug worms.

"Grazer's gonna scare all the fish," the kid said, but he didn't sound upset, only amused. "Have you ever been fishing before, Mister Rex?"

Rex kneeled down and worked on baiting his own hook. "It's been a while. I haven't fished since I was a teenager."

"That must have been a very long time ago," Billy decided.

Rex was amused. "Yeah, it sure was, kid. It sure was."

Amanda impressed him. She didn't seem at all opposed to handling the slimy worms or baiting her own hook, which she did as if she'd been doing this her entire life. Most females would have gotten squeamish over the mere thought.

They fished in companionable silence for an hour. Billy caught a big one and declared he was going to have himself fried fish for supper. When noon came around, Amanda doled out sandwiches from the picnic basket she had packed; for dessert, they had homemade oatmeal cookies.

Amanda sat down beside Rex, having given up fishing after catching a few small ones that weren't worth keeping. She drew her knees up to her chest.

"Have you thought about my offer to join us for supper?" she asked.

Rex had, but he didn't think she was going to like his answer. He averted his gaze to the water that lapped gently at the shore.

"Not tonight, Amanda," he said. "Maybe next time."

"That's all right." She sounded crestfallen to him. "Just so you know, the invitation still stands. We always have room at our table."

Billy whooped excitedly as he reeled in another fish. He seemed like such a cheerful kid to Rex, always happy and unconcerned, perhaps because he lived a sheltered life. He didn't seem to know what the outside world was like. Rex hoped he never did, at least until he was old enough to understand, and cruel reality didn't break him of his spirit.

Rex looked up at the sky. It was getting late, and they all had chores to attend to. Amanda helped him gather up all their supplies and carry them back to the truck. In ten minutes, they were leaving the pond behind, a bounty of plump fish to take home. It had been a successful trip.

When they arrived back at the ranch, Rex did his chores, then returned to his cabin. He had the strongest urge to write to his mother, to let her know he was all right, even a little content despite the constant trepidation that hung over his head.

He grabbed a notepad and a pencil and went to sit on the porch step. *Dear Mama,* he wrote.

Rex never finished it. He crumpled the letter up in his fist and gazed out at the dawning night, his heart aching, regret tearing him up inside. But he couldn't cave to his desires. If his brother found out he was here, Rex would be jeopardizing everyone's lives. He didn't want that on his conscience.

It was best if his mother continued to believe he was dead.

Chapter Three

The pounding at the door pulled Rex from a deep, dreamless sleep. Rolling over, he consulted the clock on his bedside table and decided whoever had disturbed him at this hour could go to hell. He wasn't going to get up just to answer the door because first, the sun hadn't even risen; second, it was his day off; and third, he hadn't intended on getting up until eight.

The knocking persisted.

"In a minute," Rex grumbled, getting out of bed and pulling his pants and suspenders on. He went to the door and opened it, immediately regretting his previous thought when the early visitor turned out to be Amanda.

"Goodness gracious," she gasped, giving him the once over. She was dressed, he noticed, in a fancy blue dress and her hair was pulled into a tidy bun. She carried a clutch purse in one hand. The other flew to her chest in an aghast manner.

A blush crept across her cheeks.

He realized why and couldn't help but smile. He was shirtless. He noticed her eyes unashamedly admiring his toned, lean torso, his sculpted arms, and the dozens of deep, visible scars earned from the war and his years as his father's second.

"What brings you here this early in the morning?" Rex asked, folding his arms across his chest.

"It's Sunday," Amanda answered.

"And—?"

"And..." she trailed off, looking flustered for a moment. "Well," she continued, looking him in the eyes, "I was wondering if you might like to go to church with us."

"Is it a Baptist church?"

"Yes."

"Then you must excuse me."

"Why?"

"I'm Catholic."

She seemed bewildered for a moment as his words sunk in. Then, as if being Catholic was a mortal sin and his soul must be cleansed, she began to beg him to come, her tone desperate.

"It's dandy, Rex. We sing hymns and read passages from the Bible and… You must come. Everyone is welcome, even sinners."

"Are you suggesting I'm a sinner, sweetheart?" Rex asked, amused. He was the worst kind, in fact, but she didn't need to know that.

"Of course not." She looked peeved at him.

"Well," Rex sighed, uncrossing his arms, "If it means so much to you, I'll go."

Her eyes sparkled with glee. "We'll pick you up at eight," she informed him before turning on her heels and darting down the pathway to the dirt road. The truck waited for her there, David at the wheel. As it roared away in a cloud of dust, Rex vanished inside the cabin and went to the bathroom for a shave. He dressed in a suit and combed his hair. Before going out the door, he plopped a fedora on his head.

"Well," he muttered to himself, "here goes nothing."

It was a big white church with green shutters and green roofing. Surrounding it were ancient oak trees that cast welcoming shadows across the green, well-manicured lawn. Folks chattered amicably to one another as they made their way across the gravel parking lot to the church. Children chased each other, giggling. It was a gay atmosphere, one that made Rex rethink his religion. Not that he had plans to convert. It was just nice to see smiling faces instead of dour ones.

The preacher, Reverend Daniel Etlam, greeted each of his parishioners as if they were his family as they flooded in through the double doors. While David and Margaret went to find seats, Amanda introduced Rex.

"Reverend, this is Rex Moretti, our new hand. He's Catholic."

Rex wanted to shrink into the shadows as Reverend Etlam fixed him with dark brown eyes that clearly said: *A Catholic, eh? Well, we'll see about that when I'm through preaching to him!*

"How do you do?" the good reverend said, putting on a friendly smile.

"Lookin' forward to hearing your sermon, Reverend," Rex replied nervously, not knowing what else to say.

Once he and Amanda were making their way down a narrow aisle towards David and Margaret, he let Amanda know exactly how he felt about her spilling the beans that he was Catholic.

She merely smiled, a twinkle in her eyes. "Reverend Etlam welcomes all. Catholics, Protestants, Methodists…"

"Okay, I get the picture."

They sat down.

Rex allowed his gaze to wander about. He observed families in their Sunday best, bachelors and bachelorettes, elderly couples, teenagers…

That's when he noticed her. The woman. She was sitting alone with her hands folded daintily in her lap, her eyes downcast. Her hair, a stunning amber brown, shone in the soft sunlight streaming through the tall, ornate windows. He couldn't tell what color her eyes were, but he made a guess they were a mysterious brown.

He touched Amanda's shoulder to get her attention.

"Who is that?"

"Who?"

He subtly pointed her out. The lovely dame with amber brown hair.

Amanda snorted. "Oh, that's Beverly," she said in an offhand way. "Beverly Lind."

"Is she…"

"Married?"

"Yes."

"No. She was engaged once. The poor fellow died in the war."

Rex nodded thoughtfully. He continued to ogle Ms. Lind until the service started.

Reverend Etlam led them in prayer, then they sang a few hymns. Afterwards came a long-winded sermon about salvation for the damned Rex felt was aimed at him. But seeing as he had just been introduced to the good reverend, such a thought was ridiculous and he quickly banished it from his mind and focused instead on the woman he was smitten with.

As soon as the service was over, he sought her out, and intercepted her in the parking lot. She was tall, he quickly realized. In fact, she was perhaps an inch taller than him, but he credited that to the heels she wore.

"Hello, mister," she greeted in a honeyed voice.

"Uh, hello. I couldn't help but notice you sat alone through the entire service," he pointed out as a conversation starter. "Why is that?"

"Oh, I don't know. I haven't got a husband nor children, and my parents live in New York. I suppose that answers your question?"

"New York? You don't say. I'm from there myself."

A smile ignited her face and made her that more beautiful. "Really? What a coincidence! My name is Beverly Lind," she introduced.

"Rex. Rex Moretti. Say, can I take you to supper sometime? Tomorrow night, perhaps?"

"I'd like that, Mr. Moretti."

"Rex. Call me Rex."

"Then I give you permission to call me Beverly."

Rex was on top of the world. He said good-bye and raced to catch up to Amanda and her family. Amanda playfully shoved him as a little sister would. He grinned at her, then told her about his date. She frowned for a moment, looking upset all of a sudden, but quickly cheered up and said she was happy for him.

"Thanks, kid," he said, kissing her cheek.

* * *

"So you goin' a-courtin'," Billy said as they sat on Rex's front porch whittling wood.

"Yep," Rex answered, working his knife expertly. Another trade his father had taught him. "Tonight."

"With who?"

"With *whom* not *who*. And her name is Beverly Lind."

Billy was silent for a good deal of time as he worked at shaping his piece of wood to look like Grazer. He was an amateur, but with time and patience, Rex reckoned he might become a professional.

"I don't like Ms. Lind," Billy said after a while, frankly offering his honest opinion.

"Why not?" Rex wanted to know.

"She ain't nice to us colored folk."

"Oh."

Rex continued whittling away, thinking. He liked Billy. His father not so much, but that was because Rex was still sore that Solomon was the foreman and thus his boss—when David wasn't around to give orders, that is.

Once he added finishing touches to his wood, Rex presented his masterpiece to Billy, who grinned and nodded approval.

"Miss Amanda'll like that very much," he decided seriously. "She likes hummingbirds."

"How did you know it was a hummingbird?"

"Easy. It looks an awful lot like one. You ought to give it to Miss Amanda."

"It was supposed to be for Beverly."

"Aww, shucks, don't be givin' it to her! She hates birds."

Rex frowned. Well, so much for that. Beverly would just have to suffice with a bunch of wildflowers. He gave Billy the hummingbird and told him to run along and give it to Amanda instead. Happy to comply, Billy snatched the carving and was off in a blink of an eye, stirring up a cloud of dust in his wake.

Rex got ready for his date. He was to meet Beverly at the little Italian restaurant in town at seven sharp, and left early so he could collect a bouquet of wildflowers. He tied the ends together with a piece of twine and hoped Beverly liked his gift. Why wouldn't she? She was a good old-fashioned country girl with a beautiful smile and he couldn't wait to see her again. He was smitten.

A little after seven, he and Beverly were seated in a comfortable corner booth getting to know one another. Rex, as always, was evasive about his past. He was a man of honor, and as such, he did not, under no circumstances, speak of his Family and who they were to outsiders. Trust must be established first, and then, just maybe, he would tell her, but only a scant few details. He was still afraid of what people—particularly the Chandlers—might think if they discovered he was a man of Tradition, a *Mafioso*.

Beverly told him stories of her youth while they dined on good old-fashioned spaghetti and sipped glasses of fine Italian wine. When she prompted him to tell of his past, Rex selected a few innocent memories hidden in the depths of pain, violence, and bloodshed. He recalled a time he was seven and oblivious to what he was to become. He remembered going on adventures with Stefano, the trouble they managed to get themselves into.

Reminiscing the good old days brought on a fond sense of nostalgia, and for a moment, Rex also experienced a pang of sadness. Those days of complete innocence had been before Dad got it in his head that power was wealth. Soon after he was poisoned, Stefano followed. The five Families had almost been torn apart all thanks to the father and son duo who declared war on the remaining peace-loving Families. The brutality lasted four years—until Vincenzo Moretti, Father of the Moretti Family, killed Rex's father. Rex remembered that day like a bad dream. He and his best friend, Al, had tried their damnedest to stay out of the war, but were ultimately swept into it and as a result received scars inside and out. The battles waged on empty streets, in restaurants and barber shops, in their own homes, had been violent and merciless. Dozens were killed over the span of four years, all because Dad had wanted power. In the end, he had lost.

After dinner, Rex took Beverly on a leisurely stroll through town. He pointed out constellations in the sky. He told her more stories of his youth. When it was time for the both of them to go home, he walked her to her automobile and kissed her innocently on the cheek before saying farewell and seeing her off.

They had made plans to see each other again soon. Rex had a good feeling about this blossoming romance, and hoped that perhaps, someday, Beverly might be his wife. He liked that idea. He could just picture his life years from now: Beverly would be Mrs. Alexander Armati and they would live on a small ranch and raise chickens and cows and pigs. They would plant a garden and harvest fresh vegetables in the summer and fall. Their children would giggle and shriek as they ran around in pretty pink dresses and faded blue jeans...

"What a fantasy," Rex grumbled, starting the truck he'd borrowed from David. He cruised on down the road at a leisurely pace. He liked it here. In fact, he wanted to lay his roots here, start a family, officially change his name to something other than Moretti. He didn't think the Moretti family would appreciate him using their surname to start over, but then, when he thought of Al, he decided they might actually approve. Alberto Moretti was his best friend. In fact, he was almost like an older brother to Rex. If he knew Rex was using his name as an alias, he would grin and say, "Rex, old pal, the name suits you better than Armati." And then he would say Rex was welcome in the Moretti Family anytime.

Rex heaved a sigh. He felt lost and alone. If only he could write his mother. He made up his mind.

As soon as he got home, he sat down and penned a short letter to Mama. He told her he was alive and well. He told her he'd gotten a job on a ranch, but he left out where. He also told her he had possibly found love. He finished with a warning that as soon as she finished reading the letter, she must burn it.

Once he'd signed his name, he sealed the letter in an envelope and addressed it. He didn't put a return address on it. Rex was confident that, should Stefano happen to intercept the letter, he would have a difficult time tracing it.

As usual, Rex got up early, ate breakfast, and spent the rest of the day keeping up the ranch with Solomon and the hands.

Rex got along well with his peers. There were eight hands in all, not including himself. Their names were Arthur, Walker, Stan, Oscar, Zachariah, Tom, Joe, and Hunter. Out of all of them, Rex most got along with Arthur.

Arthur was tall, with a muscular frame and a friendly albeit brooding disposition. He didn't talk much and got his work done effectively and without fail. He was also a victim of a dark past, and although he didn't speak of it often, Rex got the feeling it troubled him greatly.

On this particular day, David was in charge. During the violent storm last night, a tree had fallen on a section of the fence in the north pasture. He gave the job of removing the tree and fixing the fence to Rex and Solomon. Rex couldn't help the hostility that rose up in his belly and threatened to overwhelm him at this unwise decision-making. Unfortunately, if he opened his mouth to argue, it might cost him his job, so he put all hostilities aside and climbed in the passenger seat of the truck alongside Solomon. They drove to the far end of the north pasture where a small tree had fallen through the fence. First things first was to cut the tree into pieces with a saw. Solomon and Rex worked together, sweat perspiring on their skin as the hot sun beat unmercifully down on them.

"Billy thinks very highly of you," Solomon said as they worked. "He has it in his head that you're some gangster."

Rex laughed nervously, swiping a hand across his forehead. "Does he now? How do you like that? Well, just because I'm Italian doesn't mean I'm a… *gangster*."

"Mhm. That's what I told him."

"He's a good kid."

"That he is."

Rex fell silent. The cold tension between the two was enough to freeze over a lake. Rex tried to get along with this man, but it was difficult. Their differences were numerous and sometimes Rex found himself wondering why he was the only one who had a problem with Solomon as the foreman. The other hands were happy to take orders from the negro in David's absence, and not once did they cast him a look that suggested they bore inward hostilities.

When the tree was removed and stacked in the bed of the truck, they set to work on mending the fence. They were a good team, Rex admitted to himself—hardworking and silent. Not one word of conversation passed between them.

When all was done, they returned to the farmhouse. Amanda came out and handed them each a glass of cold sweat tea.

"Your lady friend called," Amanda informed Rex in a tone he thought sounded an awful lot like she was mocking him. He frowned.

"What did she want?" he asked.

"She wouldn't tell me. She simply told me to tell you to call her back."

"Thanks for the message. May I borrow your phone?"

"Be my guest."

Rex went into the house. He thought it rather inconvenient that there were no telephones installed in the cabins at Bachelors' Row. If one wanted to make a phone call, one must traipse all the way to the farmhouse where the only telephone on the entire ranch was installed in the kitchen. And if you wanted to make a private call, then too bad.

The lines, unfortunately, were party lines. There was no telling who would be listening in on your call. It might be the eavesdropping operator Doris, or Mrs. Payton, a widow who lived in town and had nothing better to do than listen to folks' conversations, which she would then gossip about to the entire town first chance she got. If you were engaged in an illicit romance, she was the first to know. If you were planning a robbery, she was the first to know. There was no privacy when it came to making a phone call. As far as Rex was concerned, that was the only major issue with this town.

Rex dialed Beverly's number and waited for her to pick up. When her voice sounded out a quizzical hello, his heart began to race like a lovesick teenager's.

"Hi, Bev, it's me. Rex."

"Rex! Hi," she greeted enthusiastically.

"What's new?"

"Oh, nothing much."

"What did you want to ask me?"

"I know we had plans to go to dinner on Sunday night, but I just can't wait until then. Would you like to go to the movies with me tonight? Devon Emond is starring in a new picture called *An Affair in the Shadows* and I'm just dying to see it!"

Rex had to smile in amusement at the giddy, girlish way she spoke the actor's name—as if she was a lovesick teenager.

"I figured you for the Clark Gable type," he teased. "I didn't know you were so smitten with old, washed-up British actors."

"Devon Emond is not old and washed-up," Beverly argued defensively. "He's charming, elegant, and he has an oh-so-lovely voice. So does Carey Grant."

"What time shall I pick you up?"

"Six sharp. And don't be late. Until then?"

"Until then."

Rex hung up the phone, grinning like a fool.

"Going to the movies, are we?"

Rex jumped and clutched his chest when he realized Amanda was standing behind him, arms folded stiffly across her chest.

"Jesus, kid, you almost gave me a heart attack!" he accused hotly. "How long have you been standing there?"

"Not long," she answered with a shrug. "Would you like to go fishing with me this afternoon?"

"No thanks. I've got a date to prepare for. Perhaps we'll go some other time."

Amanda looked crestfallen, but she accepted his refusal and allowed a smile to curve her lips to hide her disappointment.

"So long then, Rex," she bid him. "Have a good time at the movies."

"Thanks, kid."

* * *

Amanda heaved a soft sigh as she headed to the pond with Grazer and Billy. The sun was hot, but the numerous trees surrounding the pond cast welcoming shadows in which to sit while they fished. As they were baiting their hooks, Walker, one of the hands, came whistling down the pathway, a pole in one hand.

"Howdy," he greeted with a wide, endearing smile. "Mind if I join you?"

"Not at all, Walker," Amanda consented, waving him over.

"Much obliged."

Walker wasn't much of a heartthrob, Amanda thought as she watched him bait his hook. He was short with skinny legs, a lean frame, and coarse black hair that framed a homely face. He was kind, though. She supposed looks didn't matter when a man was considerate and tender, and treated a woman with respect.

They fished in companionable silence for an hour, just listening to the pleasant sounds of nature. Amanda would miss this come fall when it came time to return to her teaching job at Crowley Elementary. Gone would be the pleasant fishing trips until spring, when school would let out and summer vacation would begin. Amanda loved summer. She loved the heat, the sky, the sun.

"There's a dance next week on Saturday," Walker spoke, and Amanda nodded.

"I know. Mrs. Payton keeps us well informed don't you forget."

Walker laughed, a pleasant sound. "She's a character, that old woman." He smiled at her, then frowned as if the next words he wanted to say refused to come easy. "So … Um … Would you … Would you like to go? With me?"

Amanda shrugged. "Why not?"

The smile returned. "I'll pick you up at six?" he offered happily.

"Fine."

Uncle Joe came over for supper that night. As always, he spoke of how easy his job was because the crime in Crowley County seemed to be nonexistent. He complained how dull and uneventful it was to be sheriff. Amanda loved her uncle, but sometimes, she found his grousing to be vexing and unpleasant. So what if there was a lack of criminal activity in their humble little town? Amanda preferred it that way, because she felt safe and at ease.

Uncle Joe smoothed back his messy, sandy blonde hair and fixed David with a stern, accusing look as if he had done something wrong.

"Speaking of criminals—or a lack thereof, anyway—how come I haven't been acquainted with your new hand yet?" he asked. "I have a right to assess his character to determine whether he's trustworthy or not."

"I trust Rex more than I trust my other hands," David answered easily. "He's a good man."

"I'll be the judge of that, David. Remember Harvey? I judged that he harbored a dark past. You didn't believe me. As a result, he robbed you and fled."

"Don't remind me, Uncle Joe," David grumbled sourly, attacking his green beans with a vengeance.

"I like Rex," Amanda spoke up. "He's kind."

"Don't get any ideas, young lady!" Uncle Joe warned.

"Rex is already spoken for. Besides, I'm sweet on Walker."

"Ah! Now there's a fine young man."

"Walker?" Margret repeated, wrinkling her nose as if she'd tasted something sour. "Why, just two days ago you told me he disgusted you!"

Amanda shrugged nonchalantly. "Well, Peg, I guess I changed my mind," she murmured half-heartedly.

Grazer rested his muzzle on Amanda's lap. She snuck him a chunk of biscuit and scratched behind his soft, golden ears. She wished supper would be over and the dishes washed so she could retire to her room, because she had much to think about in terms of her love life and she wanted to think in private. For some strange reason she couldn't quite comprehend, she now regretted saying yes to Walker. He wasn't her type, she reasoned, picking at her meatloaf. He certainly was no Gregory Peck!

Sighing a miserable sigh, she realized the only reason she had agreed to go to the dance with Walker was because she was getting on in years. At twenty-three, she was single and childless. Most of her friends from high school were either married or engaged. Her married friends all had children. She was beginning to feel like an old maid, and that was exactly what she would be unless she found a husband soon. She was tired of watching David and Margret go through life in wedded bliss, tired of listening to them talk of the babies they planned to have.

Grazer gave a mournful whine and Amanda gave him another biscuit.

Walker was a nice fellow, she thought, deciding to give him a chance. He would treat her with respect and honor. He would also allow her to keep her teaching job, and for that, she most certainty would welcome his attempts to woo her.

Perhaps soon, she too would be in wedded bliss.

Chapter Four

Rex rose at dawn, ate a quick breakfast, and headed up to the barn to saddle his horse. It was his turn today to ride fence. He was looking forward to having a bit of time to himself, perhaps to do a little thinking, but he was more interested in the peace and quiet. It would be just him, nature, and his horse. It didn't get much better than that.

Esther nickered warmly when Rex entered the barn. He took the time to feed her her morning grain and lavish her with a bit of affection. Their relationship as horse and man had started off strong, and now Rex admitted to himself that he was fond of the old mare. She seemed to like him, too.

As Rex was saddling Esther, he heard someone enter the barn and assumed it was one of the hands. He turned to offer a greeting, only to find Amanda standing there, looking up at him.

"Good morning," she greeted.

Rex nodded. "Mornin'. What are you doin' up so early?"

Amanda scuffed the toe of her boot in the dirt. "I was up an hour ago. I couldn't sleep." She paused. "Rex…"

Rex sighed, already knowing what she wanted. Why she was so attached to him he didn't know, but what he did know was that his plans for a quiet day to himself had just gone up in smoke.

"Yes, Amanda," he said in resignation. "You may join me."

Amanda ran off to get her own horse ready. She joined Rex outside a few minutes later, beaming at him like he'd just made her day. He mounted his horse and waited for her to do the same before coaxing the mare forward with a nudge from his heels.

They rode through the gate of the south pasture and went from there, riding close to the fence line. Blessed silence ensued for a good long while. The only sounds consisted of the steady *clomp-clomp* of the horses' hooves on the damp ground, the distance calls of birds, and the gentle song of the wind.

Rex kept his gaze on the fence, keeping an eye out for damage or places that needed a bit of repair. He'd brought a few tools just in case. Solomon had informed him always to be prepared, as life on a ranch merited it. You never knew when something needed mending, and that included the animals, who had a tendency to get themselves injured, especially when they became spooked.

Rex found it ironic that, in a few short weeks, he'd gone from being a man born and raised in the city to one who now rode horses and mended fences. Not only that but he'd discovered a different part of himself that had just now been uncovered by the recent events.

He wouldn't call himself a changed man. A man didn't change, nor was it easy to rid himself of old habits. But he'd come a long way since his escape from Alcatraz, and the results pleased him.

Rex and Amanda rode for an hour before they discovered a damaged section of the fence caused by the forces of nature. It was an easy repair, Rex decided. He dismounted Esther and fished the tools from the saddlebag.

"Would you care for any help?" Amanda offered, jumping down from her own horse.

Rex crouched down in front of the fence. "Sure, kid."

Amanda sighed despairingly as if he'd said something to offend her, but didn't remark upon it. Instead, she crouched next to him and held the tools in her lap, watching silently a bit as he fixed the small tear in the fence.

"You know, I'm not a kid," she finally said, giving Rex a hint as to what was bothering her. "I'm a woman. I thought you'd notice by now."

Rex turned slowly and took all of her in, deciding after his once-over that the loosely-fitted flannel shirt and ragged jeans sure didn't help her figure. He turned back to his work to hide the smile that tugged at his lips.

"Sweetheart, I've noticed a lot of things about you," he said.

"Really? Like what?"

"First, you talk too much. Second, you've got dirt on your chin."

"Oh."

Out of the corner of his eye, Rex saw Amanda lick her thumb to moisten it. Then she scrubbed furiously at her chin, missing the dirt entirely, which amused him. He pulled his handkerchief from the pocket of his pants and spit on it.

"I've noticed a lot about you, too," Amanda said as Rex leaned over and wiped away the dirt.

"Good things, I hope," said Rex.

"Why wouldn't they be? I've noticed that you're quiet, but if the moment presented itself, you would speak out. You're kind to children and animals, and even if I got on your nerves, you wouldn't say so because you're too polite."

Rex stuffed his handkerchief back in his pocket and returned his attention to finishing up the repairs. "Where'd you get all this?"

"From observing. You learn more that way than asking questions."

He wondered if she'd seen more in him than, say, the burdens he carried on his shoulders from his past, but even if she did, he didn't think she'd bring it up. He didn't know how he felt about this. To be frank, he didn't want her to see the side of him he kept hidden if only to keep her safe from the truth.

Rex finished up and stored the tools back in his saddlebag. They still had a lot of fence to go, and he wanted to get it done before mid-morning. They mounted their horses and continued on.

Today was going to be a hot one. It had been cool enough as of late, but every once and a while there were days when it heated up. Rex was sweating and it wasn't even nine o'clock.

"Did you hear about the dance that's coming up?" Amanda asked, out of the blue.

Rex swatted away a pesky fly that was buzzing around him. "Yep. I invited Beverly."

"Oh. Walker is taking me."

Walker? Rex tried not to think too badly of the kid, but failed miserably. Walker was flighty. He was the sort of man who could be depended on, but as soon as his feet got itching to go, he'd be gone in the blink of an eye.

Amanda was observant all right, but she only saw the good in people. Sooner or later her heart was going to get broken. Rex had the fiercest urge to protect her, but she already had an over-protective brother, and that, he knew, was why she so easily trusted. He was always there to protect her when she needed him. That had been all fine and good when she was a child, but now she was a woman, and it was time David stop shielding her from the bad things that existed in the world.

The sun was beating down steadily and hot by the time Rex finished checking the fence line. Amanda suggested they go swimming.

"I know a swell place," she told him. "We used to go there as children and spent all day swimming to our hearts' content."

Rex thought of dunking his sweaty head in cold water and agreed. Amanda led the way.

They soon arrived at a cluster of trees. Nestled inside was a mountain-fed watering hole that looked too inviting to pass up. A thick rope hung from one of the trees, telling of days gone by when daring children swung from it to fly briefly before dropping into the deep water below.

Amanda dismounted her horse and scuffed her toe in the dirt. Suddenly, she looked embarrassed.

"I overlooked one little detail," she said. "I, uh … I usually swim alone … without my clothes."

Rex couldn't help but smile. "I figured you didn't swim with them on."

"I suppose if you don't mind seeing me in my slip…"

"Sweetheart, I'm a man. Why would I mind?" Rex almost laughed at the mortified expression on her face, but he didn't. "If it makes you feel better, I won't look until you're in the water."

"Promise?"

"Cross my heart."

Rex looked away when she undressed down to her slip and drawers. He heard a splash and turned in time to see her head come up out of the water.

"The water feels wonderfully cold," she called. "What are you waiting for?"

Rex made quick work of pulling off his shirt and pants until he wore nothing but his boxer shorts. Amanda, he noticed, had turned away and refused to look at him. Her innocence was refreshing.

He took off running and cannon-balled into the water. It was a shock when he found out just how cold it was. He came up sputtering, much to Amanda's obvious amusement. She laughed with glee at his predicament.

"Why didn't you tell me it was this cold?" he growled.

"Not telling you and seeing your reaction was worth it," Amanda said, eyes twinkling in merriment. She floated on her back, the sun filtering through the trees causing the water droplets on her skin to shine. Without the flannel shirt and jeans, dressed only in a flimsy slip, Rex finally noticed the womanly curves of her body, the strain of her nipples against the thin fabric. He had to look away. It didn't feel right staring, especially when his body reacted. Amanda was his employer's sister and he wasn't going to forget it.

Disgusted with himself, Rex swam to shore, deciding he'd had enough time of leisure. There was work waiting for him back at the ranch that he had to tend to before the day was out.

"Rex?"

Rex turned. "Yes?" he said, a little too brusquely. Thankfully, Amanda didn't seem to notice.

"Would you save a dance for me?" Amanda asked softly, as if she were afraid he might say no. Rex suddenly felt bad for being cool with her. It wasn't her fault she had kindled within him the reaction of a healthy man who'd noticed an attractive woman.

"As long as Walker isn't the jealous sort, then yes, I'll save a dance for you."

Amanda smiled at him. Rex turned and walked back to his horse, not wanting to spare her another glance, afraid she'd spark within him feelings he didn't want to ignite.

* * *

"Ellen Sue?"

"Yes, sugar?"

Amanda was sitting on the top porch step putting the finishing touches on the dress she was making for Saturday night's dance. Ellen Sue was sitting on the swing shelling beans. She was a robust woman with a deep voice as warm as honey and a smile that rivaled the sun in brightness. She was the nicest woman Amanda knew, and she was also her friend, whose advice she very-much needed at this very moment.

"How do you capture a man's heart?" Amanda asked, quite serious. It seemed a difficult task to her, something she had always struggled with because of her demure nature, even if certain individuals had pointed out that she talked too much.

Ellen Sue looked thoughtful a moment, then smiled as if reminiscing a fond memory. "A tried and true way is indulgin' their sweet tooth, honey," she said. "It certainly worked with my Solomon, and he's a tough one to please."

Amanda put her sewing aside and rested her chin on her knuckles. "I'm just curious, is all. Perhaps I'll do some baking this afternoon before supper."

"For Walker, I assume. That boy'll eat anything."

"Mmm," Amanda hummed in response, not really wanting to answer the question. She got up and went inside to put her nearly-finished dress away.

If the way to a man's heart was through sweet things, she knew a few good recipes to try. They were from her mama's favorite cookbook, the one she had turned to when she wanted to please. It was an old leather-bound yellow-stained collection of recipes from three generations of bakers. Amanda had inherited it after her mother's death.

It was times like these where the pang of loss tended to rear its ugly head. Amanda was taken aback by the pain a moment and had to sit down, her eyes blurring as she held the leather notebook to her chest. She really missed Mama. She missed their long conversations on the front porch, and the many hours spent in the kitchen together, baking and laughing.

Amanda brushed away a tear that escaped her lashes. Right at this very moment, she wished for the sound of her mother's voice, telling her everything was going to be all right. All they needed was a little sweetness and a dash of cinnamon.

Amanda chose her mother's oatmeal cookie recipe and got to work. David came in as she was taking the first batch out of the oven. His hair was damp with sweat, his hands dirty. He considerably washed them at the sink before reaching for a cookie.

"What's the occasion?" he asked, tugging at one of her braids like she was a child again. His eyes twinkled. "I don't recall there being any church socials, and it certainly isn't a rainy day … Are these for a certain young man?"

Amanda felt her cheeks go red. "How did you know? Did Ellen Sue—"

"No. I assumed all on my own. These are delicious, by the way. Walker is going to be pleased you thought of him. He's been working like a dog all day and a few sweets delivered by the pretty girl he's sweet on will be a nice reward."

Amanda turned away and attacked the dirty dishes in the sink with a sponge and soap. "I'm a woman," she muttered under her breath. "Why does no one ever notice?"

David sighed and rested a hand on her shoulder. "I apologize if I've offended you," he murmured. "You have to see it my way, though. I'm your big brother. You will always be my little sister to me."

"I understand that, I suppose." Amanda blew out a breath and changed the subject.

"David, are you and Peggy going to the dance this Saturday?" she asked.

"It depends on how Peggy feels. She's been feeling under the weather, so she's gone to see Dr. Johnson this afternoon."

Amanda became worried. "Do you think she's going to be all right?"

David grabbed another cookie. "Sure she is. My Peggy is strong." He winked at her, then left the kitchen, the screen door clacking shut behind him.

Amanda finished the dishes and put them away in all their assigned places. Margaret liked to keep the kitchen organized and was very specific where each pot and pan went, down to the spices and sugar. After that, she wrapped the rest of the cookies in a clean cloth, her plans to deliver them later after supper.

An hour before the evening meal, Margaret came home with a bag of groceries. Amanda helped her unpack. They made dinner together, Margaret avoiding talking about her trip into town, making Amanda worry all the more. She feared something was wrong. But she didn't ask, because if Margaret wanted to tell her, she would. Margaret told Amanda everything. They were like sisters.

After dinner, Amanda collected the basket and her shawl and left to deliver the sweets. It wasn't quite dark yet, giving her enough light to go by. Even so, she didn't like walking down this road in the dark. When they were children, David had scared her with tales of ravenous animals coming to eat children, and ever since then she had never quite gotten over the childish fear.

Amanda went right by Walker's cabin and down to the next. A warm light glowed from the porch, blanketing the ground in soft light. Rex was sitting on the porch swing with Arthur, one of the hands, both men drinking cups of coffee and no doubt swapping stories.

"Amanda," Arthur drawled in a southern brogue. Amanda didn't know the tall, quiet man with the dark shoulder-length hair and the gray eyes very well. He was always aloof, never one to talk much. But it seemed he and Rex had found common ground.

Amanda felt shy suddenly. She hadn't been expecting Rex to have company. "If this is a bad time…" she began.

Rex stood and came down the steps. "It's not a bad time," he said.

"I made you cookies." Amanda pressed the basket into his hands. "They're oatmeal."

"My favorite. Thank you." Rex smiled down at her, and Amanda's heart fluttered in her chest like butterfly wings.

"It's dark," he murmured. "Would you like me to walk you back up to the house?"

Amanda backed up a step. "No, that's all right. You've got company and all, and I assure you, no wild animal is going to come after me."

Rex blinked. "Who gave you that ludicrous idea?"

"My brother," Amanda said. "Good-night, Rex."

She turned and started walking back up the road, not expecting Rex to follow. He appeared beside her, his hands stuffed in the pockets of his pants.

"My mama would be disappointed in me if I didn't walk you home," he supplied when she looked at him. "She raised me to be a gentleman."

Amanda was curious. She'd never heard him mention his mother before, or any other family, for that matter. He was as private a man as Arthur.

"What's your mother's name?" Amanda asked.

Rex was silent for a long moment. Amanda thought he wasn't going to answer.

"Maria. Her name is Maria."

Amanda smiled. "That's a lovely name. She must be a wonderful woman."

"She is," Rex said, a note of sadness in his voice that Amanda didn't miss. She decided not to probe any further, afraid the subject was painful for him.

They walked the rest of the way in silence. By the time they arrived at the farmhouse, it was dark, inviting the shadows to come and play on the lawn. Warm light shone from the windows, beckoning Amanda inside where she knew it would be warm. A chill permeated the night air.

Rex walked Amanda to the back porch steps. Amanda climbed the first step and turned to face him.

"Thank you," she murmured. "For walking me home."

"It was no trouble at all," said Rex, smiling. "Good-night, Amanda." He turned and started back the way they'd come, the dark swallowing him whole.

Amanda stood there in silence for several long moments before the chilly breeze finally chased her inside.

***

The next day, a buzz of excitement circulated around the ranch when a truck hauling a trailer pulled up. Inside it was a magnificent stallion with a coat the color of coal. He was unbroken and spirited, and he was the ranch's newest addition.

The hands gathered around the corral next to the barn to watch the stallion be unleashed. The stallion was wary and alert, and as he burst free from the trailer, he made for the center and stood there, snorting and pawing at the ground.

Rex was leaning up against the fence when Amanda came over and leaned beside him. He was pleased by her show of loyalty. She could have stood with Walker, but she'd chosen him instead, something that wasn't missed by Walker. The man was indeed the jealous type. If looks could kill, Rex would be dead this instant.

Amanda leaned in close. "What's happening?" she asked.

"Looks like if one of us manages to break this stallion, he's all ours," Rex answered, just as Arthur slipped into the corral.

The hand approached slowly, one palm upward, murmured words coming from his lips. A rope was hidden behind his back. The stallion flinched and took a step back.

Arthur was patient. When the stallion became anxious, he would stop in his tracks and wait for the animal to calm down enough to continue his approach. Finally, he decided to make his move.

The hands and Amanda watched with bated breath. In the blink of an eye, Arthur threw the rope over the stallion's head, but this only served to further agitate him. He jerked his head away, trying in desperation to free himself of the rope tightening around his neck.

Arthur looked almost triumphant until the stallion charged him. He scrambled up and over the fence to safety, landing hard on the other side.

The men all laughed at his misfortune.

"I'll tame this devil," Walker boasted. He slipped under the fence to accomplish just that.

Rex couldn't help but be amused. Walker was only trying to show off for Amanda, and this never ended well for anyone. He watched as the young hand made a complete fool of himself by moving in too soon and reaching for the rope. The stallion spooked and bolted away.

Walker left the corral in disgrace.

Solomon took his turn. He impressed Rex by being the first man to successfully mount the stallion, but his triumph was short-lived when he was bucked clean off, not even lasting two seconds.

"City boy, why don't you give it a go?" one of the hands called. It was more of a taunt than an invitation, and Rex almost bristled. But he didn't.

"Go on, Rex, ol' boy," Arthur said, more encouraging. "Show us what you got."

Rex felt Amanda grab his shirt and tug. "Hold out your hand," she whispered.

Rex did, and she dropped something into the palm of his hand. He closed his fingers around a couple of sugar cubes. How this would help his chance of success he wasn't sure, but he trusted Amanda and decided sweetening the stallion up first seemed a better idea than anything else he'd had in mind.

Rex went carefully into the corral. After several attempts at being handled, the stallion wasn't going to be easily approached. He'd become even more wary and frightened.

"Steady now," Rex murmured soothingly. "I'm not gonna hurt you. That's it…"

The stallion watched him, ears twitching in uncertainty. Rex inched a little closer, one small step at a time, speaking softly all the while. He finally got close enough to offer one of the sugar cubes. He was expecting to be rejected, but was surprised when the stallion lipped the cube from his palm. Rex gave him another.

He was aware of the tense silence, but most of his focus was on the stallion. One wrong move and he'd set the horse off. Rex reached tentatively to give the stallion a pat on his neck, being cautious but calm. The stallion allowed this show of affection.

Rex lavished murmured words and gentle pats. He finally felt confident enough to reach for the rope that was still around the horse's neck. The stallion jerked his head back, but quieted down when Rex reassured him with a neck rub.

"We're gonna do this nice and easy," Rex muttered, for the horse's ears only. "Steady now…"

He slid his hand along the stallion's spine, feeling nervous but trying not to let on that he was. His heart was pounding in his chest. This was a first for him, but he was determined to see it through, even if he ended up on the ground, with a wounded pride and a bruised backside to show for it. If only the Family could see me now, he thought. They'd think he'd gone mad.

Rex blew out a breath and rested his hands on the stallion's withers. When the horse didn't tense, he thought that a good sign. Perhaps now, when he had his trust, he would attempt to mount.

The hands were beginning to get impatient, but several looked curious as to how Rex would fare. Rex hoped good. He wasn't looking for their admiration, nor their respect, but it would be nice for a change if they treated him like one of their own and not an outsider.

Rex propelled himself off the ground and onto the horse's back. He grabbed a handful of mane and held on for dear life as the stallion attempted to buck him off. But the attempt was half-hearted, and after tossing his head and making a few dashes around the corral, he settled down.

Rex was amazed. He hadn't expected this, but he suspected his patience and the sugar cubes had made him a new friend. He dismounted and offered the stallion the last bit of sugar.

Shocked silence had fallen. Rex didn't care to look at the faces of the other hands. Instead, he looked to Amanda, and found her smiling at him. She looked pleased by his success.

"Well, it looks like he's all yours, partner," David said, coming in. He clasped Rex on the shoulder. "I must say I'm surprised, no offense to you, but I think we all ought to take a page from your book."

"Patience and kindness goes a long way," Rex said.

"Yes. That and sugar cubes." David winked at him, then walked away.

The other hands left one by one to get back to their chores. Amanda slipped under the fence and came up. The stallion greeted her with a soft nicker as if they were long-time friends. Curious, that.

"I take it you two know one another," Rex decided when the stallion nudged her shoulder.

Amanda rubbed his forehead affectionately. "A few years ago, my father gave Mr. Sanders—he owns the ranch a few miles from here—his prized stallion to breed with one of Mr. Sanders's mares. After the foal was born, I went over every day to see him. His favorite snack is sugar cubes."

"I see. Well, since you two seem so close, I think it's only fair that I give you the honor of naming him. I ain't too good at names."

Amanda's eyes lit up. "You mean it?"

Rex couldn't help it. He reached for one of her braids and gave it a gentle tug. "'Course I do, sweetheart."

"In that case, I already have a name for him. It's Prince."

Rex closed his eyes a moment. Of all the names in the world, why on earth did she have to choose a name like Prince?

He didn't ask. He simply smiled and said, "All right. Prince it is."

Chapter Five
New York

Alberto "Al" Moretti surveyed the angry face of Stefano Armati. They were seated in a secluded booth in an empty bar in a small town near Lorenville where Al lived. It was midnight. Al wanted to go home, but he'd come to hear Stefano out and he intended to stay right where he was until the poor old bastard spilled what was on his mind. Stefano trusted no one, except perhaps Al, as they had grown up together.

"I've got a hunch, old pal," Stefano said, looking around as if he thought there might be someone eavesdropping. The bar was nearly empty, save for the table up front which was occupied by a group of factory workers getting soused on cheap whiskey after a hard day's work. Al doubted they would be interested in what a troubled man from Sicily had to say.

"I ain't got all night, Stefano," Al muttered impatiently, on the verge of losing his temper. He was tired. He'd had a long day.

Stefano took a sip of his drink, then wiped a sleeve across his mouth.

"Mama's been acting funny," he divulged, leaning in close. Al could smell the cheap whiskey on his breath. "She says she thinks Rex survived his escape from Alcatraz."

"That's impossible."

"Is it? Rex is a strong swimmer. He always was."

"So what if he did survive?"

"I'd kill him."

Al didn't like where this conversation was going. He loved Rex like a brother. They had been inseparable as kids, their bond thus unbreakable. If Stefano were to even attempt to find Rex so as he could kill him, then Al would have no choice but to kill Stefano.

Stefano was destroying the Families and everything they stood for. He set a bad example for the young ones of their Tradition, and created chaos in his wake. He was attracting the attention of the cops and the press. The press, which liked to refer to men of honor as mobsters, had a field day with Stefano's dangerous, uncalled-for antics.

Al realized something must be done about Stefano, as did his Family. But did the other Families recognize the danger in which Stefano was putting them all? Possibly, possibly not. Peace was dwindling. In its place, an evil was rising.

Al got to his feet, said his good-byes, and left the suspicious Stefano to wallow in thoughts of murder and chaos.

He went home.

The next morning, he retrieved the paper from the edge of his driveway as he always did, and sat down in his comfortable little kitchen to read it. He sipped coffee and nibbled on stale doughnuts.

"That son-of-a-bitch!" he snapped when he read the front-page headline. He picked up the phone and dialed his brother Lorenzo "Luke's" number.

The second eldest Moretti picked up on the second ring.

"Yeah? It's six o'clock in the mornin'. What the hell do you want?"

"Is that any way to talk to your big brother?" Al said, slightly amused in spite of the anger festering inside him.

"Oh. Hi, Al. I didn't know it was you. What's new?"

"Did you read the paper yet?"

"I didn't get a chance. The dog ate it."

"I'll read you the headlines: 'Mob boss responsible for death of police officer.'"

"How do you like that character?!" Luke growled. "I'm not defending Stefano or anythin', but who wrote that article? I'd like to throttle him for referring to the bastard as a mob boss."

"It's a dame, actually," Al corrected. "Nancy Payne of Sunrise Times."

"Sunrise Times, eh? You read *that* rag?"

"Never mind. I know it was Stefano who killed the cop. His name's written all over the article."

"Somethin' must be done about him."

"It don't matter much to me what we do to Stefano. He needs to be stopped."

"Yeah. He called me up last night to inform me he's got a sneakin' suspicion Rex is still alive."

"Oh, he gave you that bit too?"

"For an hour. Listen, I'll call you up later. I've got a doctor's appointment at nine."

"Sure thing, Luke."

Al hung up the phone. He downed the rest of his coffee, polished the rest of his doughnut, and decided to pay a little visit to Mrs. Armati, who lived in an apartment in the city.

Two hours later, he was seated in Mrs. Armati's living room listening to her drone on about trivial matters not concerning him. He waited patiently for her to cease talking, and once she was through, subtly brought up Rex.

"Rex? What about him?" she said evasively, fiddling with a loose thread on her neat, freshly-ironed dress.

"Your other son thinks he's alive," Al said, folding his hands in his lap. "And he got that idea from you."

"Rex was always a good swimmer," Mrs. Armati allowed with a fond smile. "And…" she trailed off when there was a knock at the door. Excusing herself, she rushed to get it, seemingly grateful for the distraction.

Al sighed. Something wasn't right. Mrs. Armati was hiding something from him, and he intended to discover exactly what it was she was concealing.

"Hi, Mrs. Armati. I've come to see about that leaky faucet in your bathroom," a male voice said pleasantly.

"Oh!" Mrs. Armati gushed, sounding flustered, "I forgot to expect you! Do come in, Mr. Steinfeldt."

"Gabriel," the landlord corrected.

"You know I find it rather strange to call you by your first name."

Moments later, Mrs. Armati returned after directing Gabriel to the leak. She seemed happy and at ease. Last time Al had paid her visit, she'd been mourning the loss of a son. This new behavior had suspicion written all over it.

Al knew enough. Rex was alive, and he was quite obviously corresponding with his mother. If Al could find a way to contact Rex, he'd reprimand him for his stupidity. Stefano was intelligent. He could find a way to intercept the letters before they reached Mrs. Armati and discover his brother's location, thus sealing Rex's doom.

He told Mrs. Armati this.

Mrs. Armati flushed. "Well! I knew you were smart, Al, but I had no idea you were *that* smart."

Al was offended. "Gee, thanks a lot."

"Yes, my darling boy is alive," she finally confessed, two identical sparkles in her eyes. "But I am not telling you where he is."

"Fair enough. Listen, Mrs. Armati, write to Rex and inform him to stop all correspondence with you. I mean it. I'll post the letter in Lorenville to be sure Stefano don't intercept it."

Mrs. Armati's lip quivered as if she were on the verge of tears. She gave a feeble nod, told Al to wait while she quickly scribbled out a note, and bustled away. Five minutes later, she returned and presented to him a sealed envelope. Al tucked it in an inner pocket of his jacket. Plopping his homburg on his head, he bid Mrs. Armati good day and left the apartment.

A woman loaded down with a paper bag of groceries was struggling with the entrance door. Al rushed over to hold it open for her.

"Thank you," she murmured, flustered, brown eyes meeting his.

Al paused a moment to tip his homburg and offer a friendly smile. "My pleasure, ma'am."

Her cheeks flushed crimson and she hurried away. For a moment, her golden hair was caught in the glow of the sunlight streaming gently through the open door, and it shone in lovely, silky waves. Al found himself admiring the curvy figure and the wonderfully graceful way this young dame walked. As she disappeared into the landlord's apartment, he finally stepped outside into the cool, morning air and decided it was going to be a swell day.

But not, he reasoned, until he posted this letter. He felt as though a target had been painted on his chest and back, and that if he didn't post the letter very soon, he was going to be whacked. Call it superstition, but in Al's world, anything was possible.

When Al got home, he realized too late that the envelope was addressed to a Mr. Armati but didn't contain an address. He wanted to curse aloud, and did so freely. Trust Mrs. Armati to do a thing like that. He assumed Rex hadn't supplied an exact location to his mother, but that didn't mean the letter didn't contain a stamp providing which state it had come from.

Al called Mrs. Armati up and asked her where the letter had originated.

"Wyoming," she answered.

Al thanked her and hung up, after which he promptly called the consigliere of the Moretti Family, Rosario "Oliver" Benevoli. Oliver was an expert at finding folks who didn't want to be found. Al quickly explained the situation, then assigned Oliver the task of discreetly discovering where Rex was laying low.

After all that was accomplished, Al found a safe place for the letter until he could post it.

* * *

Amanda sighed softly as she gazed at herself in the floor-length mirror in her bedroom. The dark blue dress flattered her figure and brought about a womanly look to it. It was too bad Rex wouldn't take notice. He would be too busy ogling Ms. Lind to pay any mind to her.

"Walker's here!" Margaret called from the kitchen.

Amanda gave her appearance one last sweep, then walked slowly and half-heartedly to the kitchen. Margaret sat at the table knitting what appeared to be socks, except they were small and unsuitable for an adult. Perhaps she was knitting socks for Billy, but it was too early. She didn't usually begin knitting gloves and socks for cold hands and feet until the fall, when the weather began to drastically cool.

Lately, Margaret's mannerisms had been strange. She appeared to be glowing and happy. Amanda couldn't quite figure out why, and wished Peggy would tell her. She was tired of the smiles exchanged between her sister-in-law and David as if they shared a secret between them. As if…

Walker's voice cut through her thoughts like a knife through a loaf of bread.

"Howdy, darlin'!"

"Hi," Amanda muttered, forcing a smile. She was beginning to realize something about Walker: he was possessive. If a fellow even looked sideways at her, he threatened to fist fight them. If they said an innocent howdy, he glared at them. It was embarrassing, but Amanda decided it was a better trait to have than the other poor ones she could think of that some of the men in Crowley possessed.

Walker was a good man despite this one fault. If Amanda needed help, she could trust him to come running to her aid. He would also be faithful, and would never leave her for another woman. That, Amanda decided, was worth staying with a man for.

"You ready?" Walker asked, offering an arm.

"Yes," Amanda said with a nod, looping her arm through his.

"Have fun, kids," Margaret called as they headed out the door.

The dance was being held in town at the town hall. Amanda was pleased by the turnout. She waved to friends and acquaintances, all the while sweeping her gaze through the crowd in search of Rex. He had promised her one dance, and she intended to make sure he kept that promise.

The band on the small stage was playing a pleasant little love song Amanda enjoyed hearing Frank Sinatra croon on the radio. A table was set up in one corner with refreshments and desserts. Children ran around, giggling and high on sugar, weaving in and out of the small groups of people mingling about chatting.

Couples were dancing and having a good time. Amanda discovered Rex in the throng, looking like a lovestruck fool as he held Ms. Lind close, the hand on the small of her back too low to be appropriate. Ms. Lind looked as though she'd swallowed a lemon whole. She always looked like that. Amanda didn't know what Rex saw in her.

"I don't mind if you spare Rex that dance he promised you," Walker said, subconsciously tightening his grip on her waist. "But seein' as you're *my* date, it's only fair I get the first dance."

Amanda nodded. "Of course, Walker."

"Shall we, then?"

He guided her into the sea of couples and took her into his arms. He was a clumsy dancer, Amanda was quick to learn, and more than once throughout the song, he managed to step on her toes. Amanda would have to give him a lesson on how to properly dance. He was definitely no Fred Astaire.

When the number was over, they stepped off to the side. Walker excused himself to go to the men's room, leaving Amanda to watch Rex longingly. She couldn't help but recall the day they'd gone swimming; the image of Rex clad only in his boxer shorts made her feel warm and achy inside. Margaret and David would have her head if they found out she'd gone swimming with a half-naked man.

"Having fun?"

Amanda's heart quickened when she saw Rex approaching.

"I don't know," she admitted, shrugging. "Are you?"

"Beverly ain't much of a partner."

Amanda was surprised at his confession, but also very pleased. She hid the smile that threatened to reveal her true feelings and shook her head in feigned sympathy.

"I'm sorry. Walker isn't much of a partner, either."

"I promised you a dance. I've come to make good on that promise." He held out his hand. "I won't step on your toes, sweetheart. I give you my word."

"How did you know Walker stepped on my toes?" Amanda asked breathlessly, willingly surrendering her hand to Rex.

"It was an educated guess. Come on. I'll show you how a man ought to conduct himself when he's got a dame in his arms."

Amanda followed Rex into the sea of waltzing couples. He took her in his arms good and proper, and guided her in time to the old-fashioned tune played beautifully by the band. There were those pleasant feelings again, like she was running a fever except she felt wonderful. She tilted her head and gazed adoringly into Rex's beautiful, mysterious brown eyes. She never wanted the song to end, never wanted his arms to leave her body.

But the song did eventually end, and his arms unwound from her body. As Walker came to fetch her, those arms were soon around Beverly, and the lovers were sharing smiles. Amanda gazed across the room where Rex danced with his date to a Bing Crosby tune. With a sad sigh, she subjected herself to another dance with the man she was supposed to love but didn't.

Walker smiled at her and kissed her cheek.

He managed to step on her toes four more times the remainder of the night.

* * *

Rex felt like hell, and the hot sun was making matters worse. He had woken up feeling refreshed after the dance last night, but gradually throughout the day, he'd begun to waver. He wondered if he was catching that virus going around. Or perhaps it was something else, something much worse. Whatever it was, he wasn't longed for this world.

After a long day of work, he rubbed Esther down and turned her out into the pasture behind the barn. He had plans to retire early, but before he could set a course for his cabin, Amanda called his name and he turned to acknowledge her. He wanted to curse, but as she giddily grabbed his hand and tugged him into the barn where the milk cows were kept, he decided whatever had her smiling so wide must be worth seeing.

"Look!" she whispered, pointing into an empty stall beneath the manger.

Rex looked. Lying nestled in the straw was Milly the cat, five little newborn kittens snuggled into her belly. Despite that he wasn't very fond of cats, Rex had to grin.

"Well, I'll be damned," he murmured in awe.

"Aren't they precious?" Amanda asked, squeezing his hand.

"Well..."

At that moment, Ellen Sue rushed into the barn, frantic and pale. Rex rose to meet her as she came flying into his arms, hysteric and wide-eyed.

"My Billy! He's gone missing," she cried, clinging to him with all her might.

"Woah, ma'am, calm down." Rex patted the woman awkwardly on the back. "Are you certain he ain't down at the pond fishin'?"

"I looked. Solomon and Arthur are out searching as we speak. Oh! What if someone done kidnapped him?"

"Don't worry, Mrs. Elwood. I'll ride out and help."

"I'll come, too," Amanda offered, shooting Rex a nasty look when he opened his mouth to protest.

"Fine," he growled, grabbing her hand and yanking her along behind him.

They saddled their respective horses and rode out.

Dusk was falling fast, and nasty, dark grey clouds were rolling in from the east. The wind, as usual, was blowing hard and increasing in power by the minute. Rex glared up at the sky, hoping to God it didn't rain until they found Billy.

"Where do you suppose he went?" he asked Amanda.

"There are caves up near Wildwood Creek. Billy likes to explore there."

"Lead the way, then."

Esther snorted nervously as distant thunder moaned softly. Rex knew for a fact that she hated storms.

At the caves, there was no sign of Billy. A raindrop splashed Rex's cheek and made a wet trail down his neck. Amanda suggested the old abandoned homestead next, the one her great grandparents had built and lived on in the early eighteen hundreds. By the time they arrived, the sky had opened up and unmercifully dumped rain on them. They were soaked to skin, but there was Billy, huddled on the rotting front porch looking frightened. Amanda dismounted and ran to him, scooping him up in a tight hug.

"Billy Solomon Elwood! You gave us a fright!" she scolded.

Rex dismounted and nearly stumbled. His vision swam and his legs refused to work properly, but he managed to herd Amanda, Billy, and the horses into the safety of the barn just the same. They would have to hole up here until the storm was over.

"I knew there was a storm a-comin'," Billy explained for his long absence, plopping himself on an overturned bucket. "I decided to wait it out here."

"Good thinkin', kid," said Rex, swiping a hand across his forehead to wipe the sweat and rain away. He seated himself on a crate. "I would have done the same thing."

He scooted over so Amanda could join him. As her hand accidentally brushed his, she retracted it as if she'd touched a hot poker. She stood and faced him, her palms going to frame his cheeks.

"Rex, you've got a fever," she said as if they were discussing how long he had to live after a diagnosis.

"So what if I do?" he retorted, hating the way his body responded to her touch. He was supposed to be in love with Beverly, damnit.

"Well—! If you want to take that tone with me, Rex Moretti, then *I'm* not helping you."

"I'm sorry. I just feel like shit."

"Don't you dare you use that language around Billy!"

"I ain't no kid," Billy argued, leaping to his feet in protest.

Amanda whirled on him. "Yes, you are! I don't want you repeating anything this man says. Do you understand me?"

Billy shrugged as if he didn't give a damn. But just to appease Amanda, he said, "Yes'm."

"If this is how you treat your students," Rex joked, trying to grin, "then I'm sure glad I ain't one of them."

"She don't," Billy defended Amanda. "She just don't want us children learnin' bad language, is all."

Amanda plopped herself down next to Rex and refused to speak to him even when the storm ended and they were able to head back to the house.

Ellen Sue and Margaret rushed out to meet them. Billy flew into his mother's arms, and she cocooned him in an embrace fit to choke the life out of him.

Rex went home after stabling his horse. He took a shower, dressed in a pair of boxer shorts, and went to bed.

In the morning, he could hardly move for the fever that wracked his body like a violent storm. His head pounded, and he could hear his heart pounding in his ears. Funny. Since arriving in Crowley, he'd suffer a cold here, a twenty-four-hour virus there. In New York, he'd been as fit as a fiddle, never once catching a single ailment.

The front door slammed, making him jump.

"Rex?" Amanda called.

"Shit," he cursed, trying to sit up.

Amanda appeared in the doorway moments later wearing a frown. "Oh, dear! I knew it."

"Let me guess. David sent you up here to ask why the hell I'm not at work."

"Of course not. I told him last night you were out of sorts and wouldn't be able to work today. You're welcome."

She approached quietly and flattened a cool, soft palm against his forehead. Nodding as if she'd come to some conclusion, she turned and disappeared out the door. She returned momentarily with a bottle and a spoon.

"What is that?" Rex demanded, watching in horror as she poured a healthy dose of syrup onto the spoon.

"Elderberry," she replied. "My mama believed it was good for all sorts of ailments. Now open your mouth."

Rex obeyed, and she fed him the medicine. It was surprisingly good, and he swallowed it down easily.

Next, Amanda made him lie down so she could pull the covers to his chin.

"I'm not going anywhere," she promised tenderly, "so if you need me, I'll be in the kitchen making you a pot of chicken soup."

"Thanks, Amanda."

"Oh. Before I forget, your sweetheart called. She made plans to visit with you today, but when I told her you were sick, she changed her mind. She said she didn't want to come in contact with your germs."

Some sweetheart, Rex thought bitterly, closing his eyes. *What sort of a wife would Beverly make?* he found himself pondering. Not a very good one if she refused to take care of him when he was sick. But, he reasoned, it was only one fault, and he wouldn't judge her for it.

Still, he pondered.

He fell asleep and suffered feverish nightmares.

Chapter Six

"We'll only be gone a few days," Margaret said breathlessly. She was bustling around her and David's bedroom, grabbing things she thought she might need and placing them neatly in the big, brown suitcase.

Amanda sat on the bed, her cheek pressed against the bedpost. She was nervous about spending a few nights at the homestead alone while David and Margaret traveled to Marbeck County to visit the latter's sister, Jenny, who had just had a baby. At least she had the comfort of the shotgun that hung above the back door.

Margaret finished packing and snapped the suitcase shut. She brushed a wisp of hair from her eyes. "There. Did I forget anything?"

"I don't think so," Amanda said helpfully. "You certainly packed enough for a two-week stay."

"I'm always prepared," Margaret said, smiling. She sat down beside Amanda and rested a cool hand on her arm. "Are you going to be all right? You've been acting awfully nervous."

Amanda feigned a smile. "Of course I'll be fine. What makes you say that?"

"For one, you only nibble on your lower lip when you're worried. I realize it must make you uncomfortable being here on the ranch alone."

"It isn't that. I have Ellen Sue, and I have Solomon. Rex is here, too." Amanda swallowed the lump that had formed in her throat. "You have to understand something, Peg. I … the last time I was here alone was after the accident."

Margaret's expression softened. "I understand. Is there anything I can do? If it makes you feel better, David and I won't go—"

"No." Amanda shook her head. "Please don't cancel your trip on my account. I'll be fine. I know how badly you want to see Jenny and your new niece."

Margaret heaved a soft sigh and patted Amanda's arm. "It's only a few days," she reminded her. "We'll be home before you know it."

After that, Amanda watched from the top porch step as David loaded the suitcase into the trunk of the Oldsmobile. Margaret was already waiting in the passenger seat for them to depart.

David slammed the hatch and came up to the porch. He glanced at Amanda with concerned blue eyes that reminded her so much of Daddy's.

"Just go," Amanda urged, making a shooing gesture with her hand. "You'll be late for supper. You know how Belinda is…"

Belinda was Margaret's mother, a stern middle-aged woman who detested tardiness. David winced, no doubt remembering the last time they had been late to a family gathering for supper. She had called him out on it in front of the entire family.

"If there's any trouble, Solomon's in charge until I get back," David reminded her. "And Amanda … I love you."

Amanda smiled. "I love you too, Dave." She watched him get into the car, then saw it off, waiting until it had disappeared up the driveway before turning to go back inside.

There wasn't much to do around the house. It was spotless, every square inch of it, a testimony of Margaret's habit of taking a rag and dusting off each surface every morning after the kitchen was cleaned of the breakfast dishes.

It used to bother Amanda that Margaret had taken over the homestead. This had been Mama's domain, where she had cooked and cleaned and lovingly sewed the children's socks and hats for the chilly winter months. This was where she had lived for twenty-four years after marrying Daddy, their love bearing two children, and nearly another, had the accident not taken the three of them.

But Amanda was content. Mama would have been pleased by Margaret's devotion to the homestead. And someday, there would be the patter of little feet again, when David and Margaret finally had children of their own. It would be complete.

Amanda wandered out on the back porch and leaned up against the rail. It was nearing afternoon, the sun beating down hot, but the ancient oak tree provided cool shade. She suddenly regretted coming out when she saw Walker coming up to the house from the barn. He had spotted her, and was waving.

Amanda sighed warily. She wasn't in the mood to be sociable right now. What sounded enticing was to saddle up her horse and go for a ride, perhaps to her favorite swimming hole to take a dip in the refreshingly icy waters.

"Amanda!" Walker called. He jogged up to the front porch and gave her a smile. "I'm glad I caught you. I've been meanin' to ask if you'd like to go out with me tonight."

Amanda became uncomfortable. This was the first time he had asked to take her out alone, and she wasn't sure how she felt about it.

"Why now?" she asked. Why had he asked now, when David and Margaret weren't here?

Walker shrugged noncommittally. "Just 'cause. I want to spend some time together, is all. I know a swell place off Piney Road. We could go dancing and get a drink."

Amanda worried her lower lip with her teeth, thinking. She wanted very much to reject him, but knew he would never give up pestering her until she finally gave in. Besides, the thought of doing something new excited her. She had never gone on a date alone before.

"What time would you come for me?"

Walker grinned cheekily, clearly pleased. "Swell! I'll swing around at seven to pick you up." He turned around to go, but changed his mind and turned back. "Oh, and wear that pretty little blue dress, the one you wore to the dance. You look mighty pretty in it."

Amanda frowned at his retreating back, suddenly regretting her agreement to go. She was beginning to see another side to him that made her uncomfortable. Not only was he possessive, but he was cocky, and she disliked that trait immensely. He was nothing like Rex.

But Rex was already taken, and he had expressed on multiple occasions he thought of her as a child. It was true she had a bit of a childish nature, but that was due to her lack of experience in worldly matters. If only she was brave enough to tell him she cared.

But not today, not tomorrow. Tonight, she was Walker's girl, and she would get dolled up and enjoy herself. It wasn't everyday she got asked on a date. This was the very first time, and she wanted to drink it all in.

Amanda was restless the remainder of the afternoon. She baked for an hour, did a little work in the garden, and counted down the hours until the time came to get ready for her date. When five-thirty arrived, she spent a good hour in the tub, hoping the hot water would soothe her frazzled nerves. During her soak in the tub, her thoughts were at first on whether she wanted to wear her mother's single strand of pearls, or the sapphire teardrop pendant David had gotten her for her sixteenth birthday. Then they irrevocably shifted to Rex. They always did that, ever since the day she met him, and forever would his smile be etched into her mind.

Amanda became frustrated. She didn't understand why she cared so much for a man she had met only a month ago. Rex was a man who harbored a past he didn't want known. She knew because he was guarded; although, it seemed each time they were together, she was able to see through the cracks.

Rex was a troubled soul. But even so, Amanda saw an honorable man behind the gruff exterior, and it was this she was no doubt drawn to. He was a man, who, despite the burdens he no doubt carried, would give her the world should she only ask.

But I don't want the world. I only want Rex.

Wishful thinking, that. Amanda lost the spark of excitement she had felt earlier. She dressed half-heartedly in the blue dress and decided not on the pearls, nor the sapphire pendant, but a simple gold crucifix passed down from her grandmother to her. She was no longer in the mood to seek excitement; she only wanted to get the evening over with. It was funny how one thought could ruin the moment.

Seven came, and Walker was there on the dot, bearing a bouquet of wildflowers as a gift. He commented on how lovely Amanda looked tonight while she put the flowers in a vase. After that, they left for their destination in the Chevy truck he'd borrowed from Joe.

Their destination was a bar just off Piney Road. When Walker pulled into the crowded lot, Amanda got the feeling they weren't going to a reputable restaurant to have a nice dinner and share a few dances. She suddenly became nervous; this was unexpected.

Walker found a place to park and got out, running around to open the door for her. Amanda accepted his arm as they started in the direction of the building. Loud music and the murmur of conversation drifted out from the open doors. Amanda caught a glimpse of couples dancing closely to one another through the smoky air.

"I'm gonna show you how to have a good time, sweetie," Walker drawled, snaking an arm around her waist. "You spend too much time in that little world of yours."

Amanda became defensive. "I know how to enjoy myself."

"Sure you do. How 'bout a drink? You look like you could use one."

They entered the building, the music and loud conversation engulfing them, making Amanda's ears ring. She tried not to feel her lack of confidence but failed. This was a new experience for her and she felt strangely out of place.

Walker went to the bar and ordered two beers. The bartender slid two full glasses over. Amanda took a small sip of hers, but was repulsed by the unusual taste, and was unable to take another sip.

"Let's dance," Walker suggested, taking her by the hand. He led her to the dance floor and swept her into his arms. The band was playing a fast, swinging rhythm, one that Amanda let Walker take the lead on. He swung her around, clearly enjoying himself. He pulled her close against him until they were cheek-to-cheek, their bodies swaying as one, Amanda almost finding excitement, but uncertainty marring the moment. Walker's hand slid down her back in an intimate caress that startled her.

Amanda pushed him away. "Don't do that," she hissed.

Walker grinned as if finding her discomfort amusing. "Come on, baby. Lighten up, will you?"

"If you had any ounce of dignity, you would respect my wishes. I don't want you touching me like that."

Walker shrugged carelessly. "If that's what you want, sweetheart."

Amanda bristled. When Walker called her sweetheart, she felt only revulsion, not the warm pleasure that filled her when the word came from Rex's lips. Walker made it sound like it was devoid of any meaning.

Walker left her on the floor and went to get another drink. Amanda stood by herself near the back wall, watching him. He joined a group of other men, who he appeared to know, and they burst out in raucous laughter as they clanked glasses and spilled their beer. She was beginning to become frightened. If he became too muddled, he would be unable to take her home. There was no one at the house to pick up the telephone if she called.

Amanda hugged herself to stave away the chill she suddenly felt. This was not an environment she was used to. It was all so different and alien to her that she could find no comfort, even in the familiar face of Walker, who was beginning to totter precariously. He stumbled over to her, his feet uncertain from the effects of the multiple drinks he'd consumed. Amanda was disgusted with him.

"How 'bout another dance, baby?" Walker slurred, reaching for her.

"You can barely stand, let alone dance," Amanda said coolly, pushing his hands away. "How do you suppose we get home now? I don't believe you ought to get behind the wheel."

Walker settled his hands on her hips and pulled her against him. "One dance, baby. The night's still young."

Amanda placed two firm hands on his chest and pushed him away. The look in Walker's eyes suddenly changed. He became angry and grabbed her shoulders hard enough to cause pain. Amanda became frightened. Walker, sweet, mild-mannered Walker, who'd never hurt a fly, looked as if he'd very much like to throttle her at this very moment.

"You'll not speak to me like that, woman," Walked hissed. "I won't have it." And he slapped her hard across the cheek with the back of his hand, an action that startled her more than it stung.

"Walker!" Amanda gasped, stunned.

Walker grabbed her wrist and gave a firm tug. Amanda had no choice but to follow him outside, fearing he'd do something rash. She yearned to take the keys to the truck from him but decided against it. He was unpredictable in his current state.

Amanda finally had enough of being handled like she was nothing but a rag. She planted her feet firmly into the ground and stopped, preventing Walker from taking another step. He spun around and made to strike her again, but Amanda quickly stepped back, out of harm's way.

"This ain't fun anymore," Walker slurred petulantly. "I'm goin' home."

"Well, then, you can go on without me," Amanda declared fervently. "I'm not getting in a vehicle with you, Walker. You're soused."

Walker stared at her a long moment as if warring with himself, then shrugged his shoulders, turned unsteadily, and stumbled away. He got into the truck and managed to somehow get it out of the lot without hitting another vehicle.

Then he was gone.

Amanda's shoulders slumped. A cool breeze brushed against her bruised cheek, but nothing pained her more than the realization that Walker wasn't the man she'd thought him to be. A few drinks had turned him into an abusive drunk with a nasty temper, and she couldn't soon forgive him for this.

Amanda had no choice but to find a telephone and call home in hopes that Solomon or Ellen Sue would have come to check on her and would hear the ringing of the phone. She went inside and asked the bartender if there was a phone she could use. He was kind enough to let her use the one in the office.

Amanda shut the door for privacy and sat down on an old leather sofa to get off her shaky knees. She set the base in her lap and picked up the receiver to dial home, praying fervently that someone would pick up.

* * *

Rex was restless that evening. He decided to take a walk to clear his head and sate his restlessness. Today had been the first day he'd felt better since falling ill, and now he wanted nothing more than to drink in the invigorating Wyoming air, which smelled fresh and clean after a recent rainstorm.

Rex went up to the wood shed near the house, thinking a little strenuous activity would be good for him. He picked up the ax and started to chop wood to add to the growing pile. David had begun this chore that morning, but hadn't finished it before leaving with Margaret on their trip to visit her sister in Marbeck.

The activity proved to be just what he needed. In no time, Rex's shirt was soaked with sweat, his muscles aching from the three days he hadn't used them. It felt wonderful. He kept up at the task, swinging the ax, splitting the wood, adding it to the pile.

Rex paused to wipe sweat from his brow. In that moment of silence, he heard the phone ringing from the house. There was no one there to answer it. He knew because he'd seen Walker and Amanda leave two hours ago. Where they'd gone, he didn't know, but he wasn't liking the thought of sweet, innocent Amanda being alone with flighty Walker. The picture it painted left a bitter taste in Rex's mouth.

Biting back a curse, Rex tossed the ax aside and jogged up to the house. The phone call could be important. As always, the back door was unlocked, giving him entrance. He got to the phone just in time. "Hello?"

"Rex?" It was Amanda. She sounded relieved. "Rex, thank God it's you."

Rex was suddenly worried. "Amanda, is everything all right?" he demanded. If Walker had done something to her, he was going to see to it that he got what was coming to him.

"Rex…" Amanda's voice broke. "Would you mind coming to get me?"

Rex fought hard not to lose his calm. "Where are you, Amanda?"

She gave him the address, her voice trembling as if she were trying hard not to cry. Rex had to take several deep breaths to suppress the fury that welled up inside him.

"I'll be there as soon as I can," he promised. He hung up and grabbed the keys to David's truck. In another few minutes, he was pulling out onto the main road.

Rex couldn't stop hearing the frightened edge in Amanda's voice. He couldn't even begin to imagine the look on her face, because he'd never seen her scared before. All he knew was that she needed him.

I'm going to kill that son of a bitch, Rex vowed, thinking of Walker. A man who was capable of hurting a woman wasn't a man at all, but a coward and a fool. There was no honor in him.

Rex was no stranger to taking another man's life. He'd done it once before in self-defense, but this time it wasn't going to be that way. If he chose to give into his fury and take Walker's life, he would only be asking for trouble.

So he tried to calm himself once more. Walker wasn't worth it. Rex slowly inhaled, then exhaled, until his heart slowed and his vision cleared. Amanda didn't need to see him this way. What she needed was for him to take her home, perhaps even to provide a bit of comfort, although Rex didn't know if he was good at that sort of thing or not.

When Rex arrived at his destination, he saw Amanda waiting for him outside, her back pressed against the wall of the building. She had her arms folded over her chest as if hugging herself. Rex saw not a child then, but a woman who was uncertain and insecure in this unfamiliar world she'd stepped into.

Rex stopped the truck and got out. It was clear what Amanda needed when she rushed towards him, pressing herself into his embrace, her arms wounding around his neck. Rex held her against him and tried to soothe her with murmured reassurances.

"It's all right, sweetheart. It's all right…"

Amanda was trembling uncontrollably. Rex got her into the truck and started towards home. The entire way there, she sat close to him, her head resting on his shoulder. The trembles had ceased. In their wake came the aftermath, which he knew from experience was exhaustion; but she wouldn't sleep tonight. He knew that, too. There would be too much thoughts to sort, emotions to swallow back.

Rex wanted to know what happened, but now wasn't the appropriate moment to ask. When Amanda was ready, she would tell him. Until then, she seemed content with their nearness, and he wasn't going to deny her that.

Grazer came bounding out to meet them when the truck pulled up to the house. The dog was happy to see Amanda, but he wasn't his normal exuberant self, as if he sensed her distress. He followed them quietly into the house.

It was when Rex turned on the lights that he saw the bruise forming on her cheek, and he nearly lost it then and there.

"Please don't get angry," Amanda pleaded when she saw the look on his face. He never could hide it when he was angry.

Rex sighed gustily, releasing the tension. He tried not to show he was mad. She was already frightened enough, and it wasn't hard now to piece together what had happened.

Rex took her chin in gentle fingers and ran the pad of his thumb over the bruise. "Does it hurt?" he wanted to know.

Amanda closed her eyes. "No." He could tell she was lying, but didn't press her. "It doesn't hurt at all."

"Walker did this."

Amanda opened her eyes and looked at him through the tears that glistened in the light. "You can never really know who a person is, can you?"

"No." Rex let go of her chin and dropped his hand. "No, you can't."

Amanda hesitated. "Rex..." Her eyes became imploring. "I don't want to be alone tonight. Would you..."

Rex understood. "I'm not going anywhere, sweetheart."

"Good." Amanda got down on her knees and threw her arms around Grazer, no doubt feeling comforted by him. Her face disappeared in the thick golden fur on his neck.

Rex stood there in silence for several long moments, foolishly wishing it was his neck she was crying into and not the dog's.

Amanda finished her cry and got to her feet. "I'm going to get a hot bath," she decided.

Rex followed her in case she decided she needed him. Amanda would no doubt have another cry in the privacy of the bathroom where no one could see her tears, except maybe the dog. She let Grazer come in with her before shutting the door.

Rex looked around him at her room and found it to be very much like her—feminine, with a touch of the child she'd once been. There were flowers everywhere—on the drapes, along the boarder, on the bedspread. He took a seat on the widow seat, resting his hands on his knees and trying his damnedest not to entertain the tempting thought of smashing Walker's face into a brick wall.

The bathroom door creaked open. Rex stood as Amanda came out, dressed in a nightgown, her blonde hair falling loose down her shoulders. Her face was red and puffy from crying.

"I'll be all right," she murmured as if to reassure him. "Rex?"

"What?"

"Is your promise still good? Are you going to stay?"

Rex couldn't say no. "I never break my promises," he said.

"Good." Amanda sat down on the bed and patted the edge. "I sure could use someone to talk to."

Rex sat down on the edge of the bed. "Talking helps."

"I know, but I have the nastiest things to say, and I don't really want to say them. I might break one of the Ten Commandments."

Rex tried to keep a straight face. "Sweetheart, if it makes you feel better—"

"It won't." Amanda sighed softly. "Besides, this is bad enough, sharing my bed with a man."

Rex guessed this meant he was staying here—in her bed—tonight. This was going to be a long night for sure.

"You're not the first person to break one of the Commandments," he said dryly. "Folks have been doin' it for years."

"That doesn't reassure me," Amanda muttered. She got under the covers and pulled them up to her chin.

Rex kicked off his boots and laid beside her, his hands folded behind his head. The sound of her steady breathing was a comforting one. He listened and heard her shift, then felt her body heat as she rested her hand on his chest. His heart began to pound under her touch.

"Amanda—"

But she was already asleep, exhaustion taking its toll. Having him close must have put her mind at ease.

Rex was surprised when he drifted to sleep. When he awoke, dawn was peeking over the horizon. It reminded him that he had chores to do, but that wasn't foremost on his mind, only secondary. What filled his primary urge was to find Walker and beat some sense into him.

Rex carefully extracted himself from Amanda's arms and went quietly down the steps. Grazer followed, his nails clicking on the hardwood floor. Dog and man slipped outside into the cool morning air.

Rex paused on the top step to reflect on the night before. Something had changed between him and Amanda, and he wasn't sure what it was, but he knew he wasn't ever going to look at Beverly the same. He could try, but it would be pointless.

Lying beside Amanda last night had awakened within Rex a feeling of content and purpose, as if finally he had found what he'd spent his entire life looking for. Perhaps it had happened much earlier, but he'd been too blind to see it.

Rex scuffed the toe of his boot on the rough wooden boards of the porch. Sooner or later, he was going to have to tell Amanda the truth about his past, but not now. He wasn't even going to tell her how he felt about her. She was hurting right now, a hurt that would take a long time to heal.

Solomon was coming up the road. Instead of heading for the barn, he came up to the house, a steely expression on his face. But it wasn't meant for Rex.

"Walker didn't bring Miss Amanda home, did he." It wasn't a question but an assumption.

Rex shook his head. "No. What do you suppose we do about it?"

Solomon spat on the ground. "I reckon we grab that shotgun and run that son of a bitch off the ranch. He's trespassin'."

Rex went inside and grabbed the shotgun that hung above the door. He wasn't planning on shooting Walker; scaring him would be much more satisfying. Someday the kid would get what was coming to him, but Rex wasn't going to be the one to do it.

Rex and Solomon walked side-by-side up the two-mile drive to Bachelors' Row. For the first time, they put their differences aside, bound by the one thing they shared, and that was their deep fondness for Amanda.

They ran into Arthur along the way.

"You goin' to pay Walker a visit?" he drawled. News traveled fast on the ranch.

"Yep. Wanna come along?" Solomon invited.

Arthur socked his fist into the palm of his hand. "Count me in, gentlemen." He came in step with them until they formed a line of three. They looked a formidable sight, the three of them, with their steely looks of determination and purpose on their faces.

When they arrived at Walker's cabin, they didn't knock, but went in uninvited. Walker scrambled up from his bed with a high-pitched yelp. When the light hit his face, he moaned and covered his eyes with his hands, no doubt suffering a hangover from his drinking.

Arthur grabbed him by the scruff of his shirt and hauled him to his feet. "Do you know what you did, son?" he said softly, but with an icy edge.

Walker tried to bat his hands away, but it was a clumsy attempt. "Leave me alone," he grumbled.

Rex passed the shotgun to Solomon. With his hands free, he swung his fist back and hit Walker one in the nose. Walker gasped in surprise, reeling back. Arthur let go of him and smiled in satisfaction when Walker fell on his rear with an audible *thump*.

"That's for Amanda," Rex growled.

Solomon stepped forward. "As David's foreman, I have the right to throw any unwanted persons off the ranch," he said. "That includes you. Get your things. It's 'bout time you left."

Walker sat there, looking stunned, blood trickling down his nose and staining his shirt. "Are you sayin' I'm fired?"

"Yeah. Would you like me to spell it out? Get your worthless hide up off the ground and start packin'!" Solomon made a point of shifting the shotgun to his other hand. "I could put this to use, if you still ain't gettin' the message."

Walker scrambled clumsily to his feet. He gathered up his meager belongings and stuffed them in a worn travel bag. All the while, Solomon kept a steely glare on him, letting Walker know he wasn't playing around.

"Now," Solomon said calmly. "It's time for you to leave. Not unless you want Mister Rex here to give you a coupla bruises on that ugly mug of yours."

Walker grabbed his hat and shoved it on his head. He was smart enough not to try and have the last word. With a murderous look directed at Rex, he spun on his heels and stomped out the door.

"Good riddance, I say," Arthur muttered.

"Yeah. We won't be seein' his face 'round here no more," Solomon said. He turned to Rex and gave him a nod, then left the cabin.

Rex went back up to the house to check on Amanda after doing his chores. Ellen Sue was there, sitting at the kitchen table with her, their heads bent close as they spoke in murmured tones. Amanda looked much more composed. The only evidence of her rough night was the bruise on her face.

"Rex!" Amanda stood and smiled shyly. "Rex, I forgot to thank you for bringing me home last night."

Rex waved it off. "No need. Are you feelin' all right?"

Ellen Sue got up and left the room, but not before Rex saw the smile on her lips. Whatever that meant.

"I'm fine, thank you," Amanda assured him softly. "Rex, about last night…"

Rex came over to her and put his hands on her shoulders. "It's all right. I understand." He gave her a smile meant to reassure. "You worry about feelin' better."

Amanda blew out a tremulous breath. "I'll try, Rex. I'll try."

Rex knew she was in pain—not physically, but mentally. There was nothing he could tell her that would help speed up the healing process. This was something that would take time, and perhaps a good dose of understanding.

On impulse, Rex leaned forward and pressed a kiss to her forehead. "I'll be back later," he promised.

He tried not to notice the tears that suddenly shone in Amanda's eyes. Instead, he smiled, plopped on his hat, and left the house by way of the back door.

Chapter Seven

"A letter has arrived for you."

Rex sat on the Chandler's front porch with Billy, showing the latter how to carve a horse out of a chunk of cedar wood. He looked up when Amanda made her announcement, and stretched out a hand to receive the envelope she was extending to him.

"I believe it's from your mother."

"I'll be damned," Rex murmured, examining the tidy cursive scrawl and determining it to in fact be his mother's. He would recognize that elegant scrawl anywhere.

"Need I remind you not to speak that way in front of Billy?" Amanda said crossly as she settled herself on the front porch swing.

Rex mock saluted her. "My apologies, ma'am."

She glared at him half-heartedly, then indicated to the letter. "I couldn't help but notice you sounded surprised that your mother sent you a letter," she observed.

Damn her shrewd observations.

"I wasn't expectin' her to reply," he said evasively, tucking the letter in his breast pocket.

"Oh. I'm sorry."

He turned and cast her a quizzical look. "Why?"

"You have one of those for a mother. So does Margaret, you understand."

"What's that supposed to mean?"

"Never you mind."

If only Rex could tell her his mother was the best mother a man could have. He pushed that aside for now in favor of dwelling on what now would preoccupy his mind until he could get answers: how his mother had gotten the Chandlers' address. He decided she could easily have asked someone to discover his location, but who? Al? Possibly.

As he was wondering all these things, Beverly's Ford Convertible rumbled down the drive and came to a stop beside the truck. Rex ought to have leapt up to get her door, but the thing of it was, he didn't want to. Not when Amanda was sitting behind him.

Grazer didn't move, either, the lazy sod. He merely lifted his head, released a half-hearted growl, and laid it back down.

"Yoo-hoo!" Beverly called, waving.

"Oh brother," Billy muttered under his breath.

Rex waved back, allowed a smile to curve his lips. "*Buon pomeriggio*," he greeted.

"What is that? French?" Beverly asked.

Amanda snorted. "It's Italian, Ms. Lind. Or haven't you noticed where Rex's roots lie?"

"The greeting was in fact Italian. But I'm Sicilian," Rex corrected just to be clear.

Beverly cast Amanda a cool look, which darkened into a glare when she saw Billy seated next to Rex. Billy returned the glare as boldly as you please.

"What brings you here, Bev?" Rex asked.

"I made you a pie."

Rex smiled in appreciation as Beverly gingerly handed to him a tin pie pan covered with a checkered cloth. He peeked underneath and was pleased to see it was blueberry, his favorite. The aroma of it made his mouth water.

"Thank you, doll," he said in gratitude. "Blueberry's my favorite, you know."

Beverly beamed. "You're very welcome, sweetie."

Rex passed the pie into Billy's care and instructed him to take it inside. Billy, eager to help, did as he was asked, and disappeared into the house. Rex had no doubt the lad would dip eager fingers in and help himself to a taste.

"I must be going now," Beverly announced, bending low and offering a cheek to Rex. He dutifully kissed it, and it surprised him to realize he felt no love for Beverly, only obligation.

As her Ford rolled peacefully down the road whence it came, Billy rejoined them and reclaimed his seat next to Rex. He took up the cedar wood and began to work at it, silent and thoughtful.

Then, "I wouldn't eat that pie if my life depended on it," he blurted, looking directly at Rex when he said it. "Miss Lind ain't a good cook."

"And how would you know that, young man?" Rex wanted to know.

"Easy. I tasted the pie."

"That figures."

"Are you mad?"

Rex touched the boy's bony shoulder. "'Course I ain't, son."

"The way I see, I done spared you a sour mouth."

Amanda laughed, a melodious sound that got Rex's heart going. He looked over his shoulder and beamed her with a tender smile, which she returned while a blush crept into her cheeks and made her that more beautiful.

"Oh, good Lord almighty!" Billy exclaimed, causing the two of them to look at him.

"Billy!" Amanda gasped, shocked.

"Mama gonna whup me if I don't skedaddle. She said I had to help her shell beans for supper. See you later!"

Rex grinned as he watched Billy take off at a run up the road that led to Bachelors' Row. The kid was a fast runner. Rex wouldn't be surprised if he could outrun an adult male.

"We still got plenty of daylight left," he announced, shifting so that he faced Amanda. "I say we teach you to drive good and proper."

Amanda's eyes lit up. "Really?"

"Sure. Come on."

Grazer barked excitedly as they headed for the truck; Rex lowered the tailgate so the dog could jump into the bed. He climbed into the driver's side, intending on driving to a secluded back road before he allowed Amanda behind the wheel.

When he arrived at said backroad, they switched seats and he began to instruct her on the basics.

"See those three pedals down there?" he asked, indicating. "From left to right, we have the clutch pedal, the brake pedal, and the gas pedal."

Amanda nodded to show she understood.

"This here is the gear shift knob. And on the dashboard, we have the tachometer, which is very important as it helps you to determine when you ought to shift gears."

"This all sounds rather complicated," Amanda observed, looking nervous.

"Relax, sweetheart. I'll be with you every step of the way."

"Promise?"

"I'm a man of my word."

Amanda heaved a shaky sigh. "I'm ready," she said, and Rex nodded.

"Okay. To start the truck, you're gonna push down the clutch with your left foot, and the brake with your right. Shift into first gear, then start the truck."

Amanda did everything she was told and the truck roared to life. Next, Rex instructed her to take her right foot off the break and slowly release her left foot off the clutch as she pressed down on the gas.

The truck stalled with a lurch, and she tried again. This time, she got the truck rolling forward. After that, Rex had her go through the motions of upshifting and downshifting, and pretty soon, she had mostly mastered the art of driving the truck. She learned quickly, and Rex was proud of her.

"Rex?" Amanda asked after a while.

"Hmm?"

"You're such a mysterious man. Won't you tell me a little more about yourself?"

Rex considered her request for a long time. He watched the trees pass by, observed a doe and her fawn picking their way through the brush on the side of the road. He was at war with himself. Should he tell her the truth and nothing but the truth or give her the glorified version he'd given Beverly?

He cranked open his window to feel the cool breeze on his face and decided he ought to allow her just a tiny taste of who he was.

"I ain't the man I seem, Amanda," he said, steadily and surely. "Make a right up here."

"Go on," she urged, turning as he instructed.

"Well … stop here and I'll tell you what I'm ready for you to know."

Amanda pulled the truck off to the side, stopped, and killed the engine. She turned to face him, ready to hear what he had to say.

"My father immigrated here at a very young age from a little village in Sicily," Rex began, "and my mother was born in New York into a family that immigrated from the same village. They grew up together and eventually married.

"Dad became a very prominent leader of the … Moretti Family at a very young age. A year after his rise to power, my twin brother, Stefano, and I were born. Years later, I joined the war. When I returned home, the Family was in turmoil. Dad had fallen fast and he'd dragged Stefano right along with him. At first I stood with them, then I began to realize the corruption, the chaos.

"A brutal war waged for years, and Dad was killed towards the end. Finally, I went to the police, but they scarcely listened to me. Stefano managed to frame me for all of it and I was tried and sent to Alcatraz."

"You went to jail?" Amanda breathed, eyes wide as saucers.

"Yep. Does that surprise you?"

"Yes. Very much. Rex, you sound like a gangster."

Rex bristled at the word *gangster*. It was an insult to his Tradition, but he wasn't going to correct Amanda.

"I ain't no gangster," he said, and it was the truth.

"I must say, you were very brave and gallant to escape Alcatraz," she said softly. "Is Rex Moretti your real name?"

"Rex is. But Moretti ain't." He became somber. "No one can ever know what I just confessed to you. Do you understand me, Amanda?"

"Of course I do."

"Do you still trust me in spite of my confession?"

She nodded slowly. "Yes."

Rex felt relieved. He felt as though a great weight had been lifted from his shoulders.

Amanda reached cautiously forward and traced the deep scar beneath his right eye with gentle fingers. "Did you receive that from the war?" she asked.

Rex couldn't help but notice how soft the tips of her fingers were. He gently took the hand boldly tracing the scar before she could withdraw it and wove his fingers through hers.

"Rex—"

At that moment, Rex happened to look in Amanda's wing mirror and see the police automobile pulling up behind them. As it came to a stop, he muttered a curse, and Amanda looked behind her to see what had provoked him to utter such a foul word. She frowned.

"It's my uncle," she said, withdrawing her hand from his so that she could crank down her window.

Sheriff Joe Chandler wandered over and peeked in, frowning when he saw Rex. He gave Amanda a look that suggested he was disappointed in her. Rex could tell he wanted to ask what his niece was doing on a secluded backroad with a man, but out of respect for her feelings, he didn't. Instead, he asked, "Havin' 'mobile trouble?"

"Rex was teaching me how to drive, Uncle Joe," Amanda offered in explanation.

"Oh?" He looked at Rex again. "So *you're* the mysterious Rex Moretti."

"Yes, sir," Rex confirmed with a nod.

"Aren't you the fella going steady with Ms. Beverly Lind?"

"Yes, sir."

"Polite and to the point," Sheriff Chandler noticed. "I like that in a man. Son, you just make sure my niece doesn't drive into a tree."

"I will, sir."

"Rex never breaks his word," Amanda pointed out, and her uncle merely grunted.

"Oh, I'm sure. Be on your way now. If anyone else besides myself were to see you two stopped like this, they'd think you were neckin'. You know how quickly gossip spreads 'round here."

"We sure do," Rex muttered knowingly under his breath. That was the only thing he hated about this town: the gossipers who had nothing better to do with their time.

Amanda started the truck and waved to her uncle as she accelerated forward. When he was out of sight, Rex slumped in his seat and blew out a sigh of relief. That was a close one, although he didn't think Sheriff Chandler recognized him. In a small backwater county like this, who would recognize a notorious criminal who had escaped from jail? Not that Rex was a criminal. The world might consider him one, he realized, but that was because they were blind to who he really was.

"Your uncle's a friendly guy," he said, and Amanda looked at him and smiled. "Keep your eye on the road, honey," he instructed.

"He is," Amanda agreed as she reverted her gaze to the road.

"I admit I was afraid he'd recognize me."

"Don't be silly, Rex. This is a small town and around here, we're oblivious as to what goes on in the outside world. I suppose that's a good thing."

"Crowley is a swell place to lie low when one has successfully escaped prison."

"I'm glad you came here," Amanda confessed, a blush creeping into her cheeks. "If you hadn't, we would never have met."

Rex couldn't help it: he reached for her long, golden hair and ran his fingers through it. It felt like silk. He noticed the goose flesh rising along her arms and realized he invoked within her desires she was probably forbidden to feel. She had been raised with old-fashioned standards. Rex had been raised in such a way, too, but he was no stranger to breaking those rules Mama had drilled into his head. Nevertheless, he respected Amanda's beliefs, and besides, he didn't want to give her the impression he was a cad.

He withdrew his hand. He was still in a relationship with Beverly despite that his feelings for the self-centered dame were dwindling by the day as he came to realize she wasn't all he'd thought she'd be. He saw something in Bev he didn't like, and although he hadn't quite figured it out yet, he had a sneaking suspicion his lady friend was nothing more than a Jezebel.

Amanda?

Boy, Amanda was something. She was tender-hearted and put others before her; she was soft-spoken and sweet. And although she talked too much, Rex adored her.

"It's going to be dark soon," he said, indicating to the setting sun. "We ought to start headin' back before folks start to realize we're missing. I don't want your reputation marred."

"I'm a grown woman, Rex," Amanda argued ardently.

"So I've noticed."

"There's still plenty of daylight."

He gazed at her suspiciously. "What're you drivin' at?"

"I want to go swimming."

"What about David and Margaret? I'm sure they'll have plenty of things to say about you—our—staying out late."

"David and Peggy aren't here. In fact, they'll be gone for five more days. I know a perfect place to go swimming. Please, Rex?"

Rex shrugged in a go-ahead gesture, and she smiled a smile he couldn't resist. He sighed. He would never know what possessed women to decide to do such crazy things out of the blue. He just hoped he'd be able to control himself. Last time they'd gone swimming…

He tried not to picture the way her nipples had strained against her slip, but failed and suffered as a consequence. Moving closer to his window, he breathed in the cool mountain air and managed to half-heartedly erase her image from his head.

"Where are we goin'?" he asked Amanda without looking at her.

"Deer Meadow Lake," she replied. "No one ever goes there."

"Why?"

"Ghosts."

Rex looked at her this time. "I beg your pardon?"

"Ghosts," she repeated. "Legend has it, renegade soldiers—North and South—started their own little war over the lake because there was rumored to be treasure buried at its murky bottoms."

"Let me guess—they all died as a result of their stupidity."

"Two brothers survived. Years later, one killed the other in a saloon fight. He buried his brother here at the lake, then killed himself."

Rex was slightly disturbed by this story, and chose not to believe the dead soldiers now haunted this Deer Meadow Lake as ghosts. It was a preposterous idea.

"Did I give you the spooks?" Amanda asked, amused.

"I don't scare easily," Rex muttered, not about to admit that the story had somewhat given him the creeps. He had never been overly fond of ghost stories; Stefano, however, loved them. He'd most likely get a kick out of the legend associated with Deer Meadow Lake.

Amanda pulled onto a rutted dirt road and soon, they arrived at a large lake surrounded by picturesque scenery commonly found on the postcards Rex's mother used to send to relatives in Sicily. From Rex's vantage point, he got the illusion the lake stretched on for miles. Wyoming was a place of wonder and beauty, he decided as he climbed out of the truck. He let down the tailgate so Grazer could jump out; the dog raced towards the lake, galloped across the old wooden bridge, and took a flying leap. *Splash*.

Amanda began to unbutton her blouse. Rex assumed they'd swim in their underthings like they had done last time.

"Rex? Have you ever gone skinny dipping?" she asked shyly.

"Nope," he replied candidly, shrugging out of his jeans so that only his boxer shorts remained. "Why do you ask?"

"We're friends, aren't we?"

He turned curiously towards her. "Of course we are."

"Then you won't mind if we go skinny dipping."

Before he could reply and tell her what a terrible idea that was, she was taking her slip off and tossing it with the rest of her cloths. She now stood gloriously naked before him. He knew he ought to turn away, but he was too captivated by what he saw to avert his gaze. He trailed Amanda's every movement as she headed to the bridge and sat down at its edge to test the water with a toe.

Rex wasted no time in completely ridding himself of his boxer shorts. As he walked out onto the bridge, Amanda lowered herself into the lake and waded out until the water was up to her belly. Now, she turned, and her eyes widened in captivated awe as she beheld him. Rex determined by the lovely blush creeping into her cheeks that she'd never seen a naked man before.

He got into the water and was taken aback by how cold it was; he refrained from cursing at the shock of it, and swam over to Amanda.

"When my parents took us to the beach in the summer when we were younger, the water was always warm and pleasant," he said.

"I've always wanted to go to the beach," Amanda confessed with a sigh of longing.

"Maybe I'll take you someday."

Her eyes brightened. "Would you?"

After a brief consideration, he nodded. "Yes."

"Promise?"

"Promise. How would you like to seal that?"

She wrapped her arms around his neck and his body reacted to her touch as she pressed herself to him. Spurned by the fire ignited within him, he took her chin gently between thumb and forefinger and inclined his head to capture her lips. Her soft moan of pleasure vibrated through to his very soul.

When they parted, he framed her face between his hands and caressed her cheeks with the pads of his thumbs. He was expecting to feel guilty for kissing a woman when he was involved with another, but he didn't. Instead, he felt a tenderness and a love so strong, his heart ached.

"Amanda," he began, but she pressed a forefinger to his lips to silence him.

"I know what you're going to say," she whispered, eyes misting. "And I don't want to hear it."

"I was going to say I love you," he responded, moving his hands to her back and flattening them against her smooth, soft skin.

"You love me?" she repeated, voice breaking.

"Yes, Amanda. Yes."

"I love you, too."

"I know. And this lake is freezin'."

She laughed, a lovely sound that made him want to kiss her again. They waded to shore and dressed in their clothes. Grazer jumped into the bed of the truck and barked as if to tell them he wanted to go home. Rex shut the tailgate, tried not to wince in disgust when the dog gave him a big smooch on the cheek. He casually wiped a hand across his wet skin and climbed into the driver's seat.

He drove home.

"Won't you join me for supper tonight?" Amanda asked as they walked to the farmhouse. "I'm a good cook, honest."

"I know you are, sweetheart," Rex agreed, holding the screen door open for her.

"Is that a yes?"

"As long as you allow me to help you wash the dishes afterwards."

She looked over her shoulder at him in surprise. "If you'd like."

"I'd like that very much."

Rex sat down at the kitchen table and Grazer lay his head in his lap. He scratched behind the soft golden ears as he watched Amanda get out pots and pans and set them on the stove. He was pleasantly surprised the moment he realized she was making his favorite, spaghetti. He got up to ask her if he could be of any assistance, but she shooed him away and he reclaimed his seat.

"Rex, tell me more about your family," she requested, and he obliged, glad for something to do.

With supper just about ready, Amanda allowed him to set the table, and as they sat down, requested him to say the blessing. Despite that he never knew what to say when it came to saying grace, Rex did it anyway because Amanda asked him to.

Once the blessing was said, Rex helped himself to a generous helping of spaghetti. Grazer whined mournfully beneath the table, his big brown eyes imploring and huge. Feeling sorry for the dog, Rex fed him a piece of buttered bread and instantly regretted it when his hand was nearly snatched right along with the morsel.

Amanda talked about her family and her job throughout supper. She talked about her desire to travel and explore the world, and how she wanted to visit New York, the city that never slept. Rex would have gladly taken her to his birthplace had it not been for his brother, who would without a doubt kill him on the spot if he ever stepped foot in New York City again.

After supper, he helped Amanda do the dishes. She was strangely silent as she washed and he dried. Rex knew there was something on her mind, and asked her about it.

"Rex? Is what you said earlier … is it true? Do you really love me?"

Rex had never met a more insecure woman. He waited a moment to answer her, drying two more dishes before he spoke. "It's true," he said as she handed him another dish. "Why do you doubt me?"

"I don't. Do you still love Beverly? Are you still going to court her?"

Now he set aside the dishcloth he was using to dry the dishes so that he could take Amanda's shoulders between his hands.

"Amanda, I'm a man of tradition. I'm honorable. Does that answer your question?"

He realized the mistake he'd made by saying those words when her eyes flashed and she tugged free from his grasp.

"I think we ought to put a stop to all this right now," she suggested to him in a voice so full of sorrow, his heart nearly shattered into a million pieces.

"Amanda—"

"No!"

She turned and began to flee the room, but he caught her elbow and swung her around to face him.

"Amanda! Wait. You misinterpreted my words." He heaved a frustrated sigh as he saw the tears moistening her cheeks. "I ought to have been more specific. I meant those words for you." He relaxed his grip on her shoulders and moved his hands to frame her face. "Amanda, I want to make love to you."

Amanda nodded silently and took his hand. "I'm yours, Rex," she consented softly.

She seemed confident and sure of herself as she led him into her room, but as Rex closed the door shut behind them, he realized she was trembling. The terrified look in her eyes as she turned to face him spoke of an innocence so profound, Rex knew that tonight, he would be a tender and gentle lover. He flattened one hand to her chest and could feel her pulse racing beneath his palm.

"There's nothing to be afraid of," he crooned as she shivered in pleasure beneath his touch.

She responded by leaning up and pressing her lips to his own. His arms encircled her waist while hers entwined about his neck. She moaned softly into his mouth, the sound vibrating through his body. He desired to feel her bare skin against his own, to explore every inch of her with his lips, to make her his.

They undressed one another in a careless abandon, but once they were beneath the covers of her bed entwined in one another's arms, Amanda began to tremble again. Rex murmured words of reassurance into her ear until she relaxed.

He trailed his lips up the soft skin of her neck while she lay beneath him, hands splayed over his hard, muscular chest. She gently framed his face and coaxed his lips back to her own. A fire consumed them both, heating their bodies and creating a sheen of sweat on their skin as they joined as one.

Amanda squeezed her eyes shut against the brief pain that consumed her body, a pain that was soon overcome by an overwhelming pleasure. She felt Rex weave his finger through her left hand and she opened her eyes to gaze lovingly into his beautiful brown eyes.

"Amanda," he groaned, the last half of her name sounding muffled as he buried his face in her neck.

She felt his warmth spill forth into her body. Sweat saturated them both, and as he collapsed beside her, the loss of his heat was immediate. She quickly rediscovered his warmth when he encumbered her in his arms and held her against him. She could hear the rapid beating of his heart and listened intently as it slowed and found an even pace.

"I love you," he murmured breathlessly.

Amanda closed her eyes and smiled. "And I you."

Chapter Eight

When Rex next opened his eyes, it was dawn. Amanda was curled up against him sleeping soundly. He felt her warmth and took comfort from it, something that felt like contentment falling over him. He stroked her soft hair under his work-roughened hands, smiling tenderly when she stirred.

Amanda's eyes fluttered open. "Rex? Is it morning already?" she asked sleepily.

Rex chuckled. "Sure is, sweetheart."

Amanda became shy despite their intimacy the night before. Rex touched the tip of her nose with his index finger, eliciting a smile from her, and the shyness was suddenly gone, replaced by the same contentment Rex felt.

"How are you feeling?" Rex asked.

"I have no regrets, if that's what you're asking," Amanda murmured.

Rex was glad of that. Considering her devotion to the Ten Commandments, he had thought she'd react differently, but there was none of that. Amanda stretched out beside him, her legs brushing against his.

She sat up, clutching the sheet against her chest. "David and Margaret are coming home today. I want to tidy up the house and make them a nice supper."

Rex cupped her chin in his hand and skimmed his thumb over her cheek. "I've also got chores to see to. But they can wait a moment longer."

He saw Amanda's breath catch. He leaned in and kissed her, firmly but gently, and she melted against him, her arms coming to drape about his neck. Rex knew it was too soon to make love to her again, but he was content with stealing a kiss or two.

They both got up and dressed, then parted ways. It was Rex's turn to muck out the stalls in the barn. He spent the morning doing that, working up quite a sweat until his shirt stuck to his back. The cool breeze that drifted through the doorways and the windows was his only respite. He thought of Amanda while he worked. Thoughts of her helped the time pass, and he finished the chore in less than two hours.

The rest of the day went as any normal day, except today Rex had something else to look forward to. He spent most of his time sorting his thoughts and looking forward to seeing Amanda again. They hardly saw one another that day, but they managed to snatch a moment in the barn to steal a few kisses. After that, it was nearly supper time and Amanda had to finish up preparing a welcome-home meal for David and Margaret.

Rex was planning on staying in that night, but Arthur had other ideas. He dropped by and invited Rex to go get a drink at Harley's, a joint located half an hour from the ranch, a place in between here and town. Rex accepted, thinking a drink or two would do him good.

Arthur, Rex, Solomon, and a few of the other hands piled in the former's truck and they were off to Harley's. They had all gotten paid last Friday but had been too busy to go out and spend it.

Rex only planned on having one drink, but the night had other plans. When they arrived at Harley's, the bar was packed. It was Friday night, and folks just wanted to have a good time. David's hands were among them.

With Arthur leading the way, David's hands filed into the bar, ready to have a drink, the single ones hoping to find a pretty girl to practice their charms on. Rex went up to the bar with Solomon and Arthur.

"I'll have a beer," Arthur said. "No, make that a whiskey on the double."

"What he said," Solomon told the bartender.

The bartender hesitated, a look of uncertainty on his face. Rex saw his eyes flicker to the right and curiosity made him look, too. A middle-aged man dressed in a three-piece suit was glaring at Solomon with obvious hostility.

"Who's that?" Rex asked casually, leaning up against the bar.

"That's Mr. Harley," the bartender muttered. He nodded in Solomon's direction. "He don't take kindly to *his* kind drinkin' at his establishment."

Rex saw Solomon bristle.

"Is that so?"

Harley straightened and ambled over, a slight limp to his stride. "Mr. McGregor, I thought I made it clear to you the rules I keep," he drawled. "We don't serve negroes here."

This time, Rex found himself bristling, too. He might not have seen eye-to-eye with Solomon when they'd first met, but now he respected him, and a friendship had kindled between them. No one was going to insult Solomon without dealing with Rex first.

"That's my friend you're insulting," Rex said calmly.

Mr. Harley turned to acknowledge him. "And just who might you be? I've never seen your face 'round here before."

"I'm the fellow who's gonna ruin your night."

And Rex hit him, right in the nose. Mr. Harley reeled back and fell on his rear with an audible thump. The room went deadly silent, all eyes on Rex and Mr. Harley—who was being helped to his feet by the flustered bartender—waiting to see what was going to happen.

Arthur brushed past Rex. "I'm the other fellow who's gonna ruin your night," he said, before giving Harley the same treatment Rex had.

As if a chain reaction went off, all hell broke loose. Bottles sailed across the room, hitting the wall and the floor and raining bits of glass. Chairs were picked up and smashed into heads. Men wrestled, curses flew in all directions, and Rex was so amazed by it all, Arthur had to yank him out of the way before a beer bottle could hit him in the face.

David's hands left the bar before the sheriff could arrive, because if Uncle Joe knew who'd started the fight, he'd tell David, then they'd all be in hot water.

"Some mess you started back there, son," Arthur drawled, giving Rex a playful punch on the shoulder. He started up the truck and pulled out of the lot.

Solomon was very quiet for several long minutes. Rex was afraid he was upset, but Solomon wasn't a man who was easily moved by much.

"Ain't no one ever stuck up for me like that," he said finally. "Thank you."

Rex stuck out his hand, and the two men shook.

"Here's to friendship," he said, meaning it.

"To friendship," Solomon agreed. "I guess we'll just have to find a new place to get a drink."

"We ain't gonna be welcome there no more," Arthur agreed. He snorted. "Mr. Harley's gonna have a hell of a bill when all that's over. Do you think he'll sue?"

"Nah. That's what insurance is for, ain't it?"

The men shared a laugh.

Rex was lying in bed that night, thinking of Amanda, when he heard a knock on his door. He wondered who'd be at his door at ten past midnight until he opened it and saw Amanda standing there in her nightgown, looking up at him with a shy smile on her lips. She was barefooted.

"I missed you," she murmured.

Rex didn't think this was a good idea, but he didn't want to send her away, either. Instead, he swept her up in his arms and kissed her, becoming intoxicated just from her nearness. He had missed her, too. There hadn't been one moment that day that she'd been absent from his thoughts.

Despite still being tender, Amanda wanted him to make love to her, and Rex didn't refuse her this. He made careful, considerate love to her until they were both spent and fulfilled. After that, they were content to lie in one another's arms, legs tangled.

"Rex? Where did you get this scar?" Amanda asked, tracing an old, jagged scar on one of his biceps.

Rex knew what scar she was taking about, but was hesitant to tell her. He'd been young, and picked a fight with a boy much older than he and who'd been armed with a knife.

"An accident, I think," he lied. "It happened when I was a kid."

"What about this one?" She lightly touched a puckered scar on his shoulder.

Rex decided he couldn't lie about that one. "I was shot by my brother."

"Oh. Did you make him mad?"

Rex wanted to laugh, but he didn't. "No," he said. "We were both fourteen at the time, and decided it would be a swell idea to play with our father's guns. Stefano accidentally pulled the trigger."

Amanda gasped. "You could have been killed!"

"I'm still here, aren't I?" Rex winced. "But thinkin' back, my brother probably did it on purpose. I was Ma's favorite and I bet he wanted to get rid of the competition."

"There's nothing like a bit of sibling rivalry," Amanda agreed, laughing softly. She traced the scar on his face with her fingertip. "You sure do carry a lot of scars, Rex."

"That one's from the war," he supplied, but said nothing more. Memories of the war still haunted him.

Amanda nestled her head in the crook of his neck and pressed her lips against his skin in a gentle kiss. She fell asleep not a moment later. Rex held her the remainder of the night until dawn arrived, then he had to wake her. It was best if she went on home before the ranch started to wake. Rex offered to walk her home, and they started out into the cool morning air.

"I was thinkin'," Rex said.

"About what?" Amanda murmured.

"About the future. About settlin' down, and havin' a place of my own."

Amanda took his hand in her small one. "Am I a part of your future?"

Rex squeezed her hand. "There's no one else I'd rather share it with."

Amanda squeezed back. They arrived at the house, and he was expecting her to go through the back door, but she didn't. Rex watched in amazement as she climbed the old oak tree as nimble as a monkey and slipped in through her open bedroom window.

"That woman is going to be the end of me," he muttered, shaking his head. He stuffed his hands in his pockets and headed for the barn to begin his chores.

The day started early, because that afternoon was the start of the Crowley County Fair, and some of the hands were planning on going after the work was done. Amanda invited Rex to come along and he couldn't disappoint her despite being wary about being around such a large crowd. He put his fears aside, deciding to enjoy himself for once.

They left at noon and arrived on the fairgrounds half an hour later. There were indeed a lot of people present, come to enjoy the festivity and the many activities to do and see. There were livestock showings, games for the children, a plethora of vendors selling funnel cakes, hotdogs, and popcorn, a handful of carnival rides, and much more.

Rex was only interested in one thing, and that was pleasing Amanda. She took him by the hand, dragging him off to see the animals first. Amidst the bellowing cows, and the baahs of sheep, and the flies, Rex discovered that Amanda adored rabbits. What woman didn't? She would have remained there all day if Rex hadn't suggested they go get something to drink.

While Rex was purchasing two lemonades, Amanda saw a few folks she knew and went over to greet them. Rex brought her her drink and couldn't help smiling when he saw her crouched down, holding a conversation with a boy about Billy's age.

"Rex, this is one of my students, Ben," Amanda said, making introductions. "And these are his parents, Matilda and Howard Winchester."

Rex gave her one of the lemonades and stuck out a hand. Ben shook it, grinning wide, showing off a missing front tooth.

"Nice to meet you, kid," Rex said.

"You have a funny accent, mister," Ben remarked.

"Ben!" his mother gasped. "You ought to apologize. That wasn't a polite thing to say."

Rex waved it off. "It's alright, ma'am. I'm used to it."

Matilda smiled at him and placed a hand on her round abdomen, which Rex couldn't help but notice. She was with child, and he wondered for a minute what it would be like if Amanda were to have his kid. He sure wouldn't mind being a dad. Not only would he be a better father than his old man had been, but he'd give his child a secure life where he'd never have to be scared of anything.

Ben tugged on his father's arm. "Pa, can we go ride on the merry-go-round?" he begged. "You promised."

"I know that, son," Mr. Winchester said. "But one last ride, all right? Your mother's getting tired."

"I'll be fine, Howard," his wife insisted.

Mr. Winchester nodded at Rex. "It was nice meeting you, sir."

Amanda sighed as she watched the Winchester family leave, and Rex slid an arm around her waist and gently squeezed. He didn't have to guess hard to know that her thoughts had something to do with children.

"You want kids, don't you?" he said.

Amanda looked at him. "Of course I do. Do you?" She looked hopeful he'd say yes.

"Sure I do." And he meant it.

"Good. I want three, and I don't care if they're all sons, just as long as I have one daughter."

Rex was amused. "You don't want sons," he said.

Amanda looked confused. "Why not?"

"Because sons break their mother's hearts. Trust me, I know."

They started off arm-in-arm, Rex content just to take it all in with Amanda by his side. He wished they were alone but she seemed to be enjoying herself, and he didn't want to spoil her fun. They viewed a bit of the 4H show, then they each had a hot dog before heading back to the automobile to rendezvous with David and Margaret.

It was late now. Because they had an early morning, they left for the ranch and arrived home at eight. Grazer came out to greet them.

"I'm pooped," Margaret said with a yawn. "Did everyone have a good time?"

"We sure did," Amanda agreed with a smile.

Rex gave David a nod. "I'm gonna head down Bachelors' Row and hit the sack," he said. "Good-night, folks."

He didn't care if David was watching. He leaned over and gave Amanda a kiss on the cheek, then turned and left, but not before he saw the blush that crept up her neck.

Rex wasn't tired. He stayed up for another hour, sitting on the front porch and enjoying the cool night breeze. He knew Amanda wasn't going to come tonight, but he looked forward to the next time he got to hold her in his arms again. She made him feel fulfilled.

Of course, there was still the matter of telling Beverly he no longer wanted to see her. He didn't think she'd be too upset. She'd proven to him that they could never be a pair on countless occasions, and he hoped by letting her go that she might find the man right for her. He just wasn't it.

Rex finally went to bed, but he barely closed his eyes before there was a loud pounding at his door. He shot up in bed with a curse, then pulled himself together and went to answer it.

Solomon was standing there, a shotgun in his hands. "There's been trouble out at the Winchester ranch," he said gravely. "Sheriff wants a search party out and lookin' for Howard Winchester."

"Did he say why?" Rex asked, pulling on a shirt.

"Mrs. Winchester is dead. So is her baby. Mr. Winchester took off, makin' himself look guilty as hell."

Rex was disturbed by this news. He'd met the Winchesters earlier and thought them to be nice folks. Mr. Winchester didn't seem like the type to commit such a monstrosity.

Rex left his cabin and followed Solomon up to the barn. Several of the hands were there saddling their horses, including David. Rex saw Amanda leaning up against the door. She looked upset, but she had a right to be. He knew she was worried about Ben.

Rex took Amanda's hand and squeezed it gently as a reassuring gesture, then went to saddle Prince. He would have preferred to use Esther, but she had been turned out to the pasture for the night.

"All right, men," David called. "Let's go."

They all led their horses outside and mounted.

The Winchester ranch sat just behind the Chandlers'. The last anyone had seen Howard Winchester, he'd taken off through the woods.

David split them up into two groups. "Solomon, take Arthur and Rex and go south. Stan, Oscar, Zachariah, and I will go north. Tom, Joe, and Hunter will stay here just in case Mr. Winchester shows up. Got it?"

"Yes, sir," came the unisonous reply from all the men.

They all started off in their respective directions. Solomon took the lead. He knew the land better than Arthur and Rex, and he had the shotgun. If things got messy, which Rex hoped they didn't, it seemed best if at least one of them were armed.

Arthur had an extra pistol on him. He handed it over to Rex. "You're gonna want this," he said. "Right now, Mr. Winchester is unpredictable. He might be armed."

Rex accepted the gun with a muttered thanks and tucked it into the waistband of his trousers. They continued on, picking their way through the dark woods, where the shadows danced and owls hooted. Each man had a lantern to light their way, paired by the light from the full moon.

They searched for an hour until they reached the line that divided the two properties. Solomon suggested they turn back until Rex saw something dart through the trees. He motioned to the two men, and Solomon waved for him to lead the way.

Rex urged Prince forward. The horse was suddenly nervous, his ears twitching in uncertainty. Something was bothering him. Rex was alert, looking around cautiously, keeping his ears peeled for sudden noises. It was then he picked up the sound of boots crunching on leaves.

Rex decided to dismount and continue on foot. He hurried forward when he saw the shape of a man through the trees. His instincts proved to be right when he emerged and found Mr. Howard.

The man was on his knees, a gun pressed to his temple. "Don't come any closer," he warned. "Just don't."

"Howard, take it easy," Arthur said soothingly, coming to stand beside Rex with his hands raised in a placating gesture. "Put the gun down."

"No!" Mr. Winchester began to weep. "I didn't kill my wife and baby. God took them from me."

"We can settle this nice and easy," Rex said soothingly. "Think about your son, man. Think about Ben."

"Ben," Mr. Winchester echoed. "Ben … he's in good hands. Miss Amanda will take care of him."

"Howard, don't do this to him," Solomon growled. "The kid needs his pa. You're gonna take that away from him if you pull that trigger."

"I already made up my mind. Ben's better off without me. Tell him I love him, won't you?"

"You tell him yourself, you ungrateful son of a bitch!"

Mr. Winchester smiled serenely, then pulled the trigger. *Bang.* His body slumped over as he died, the gun slipping from his grasp and falling harmlessly to the ground.

Joe pulled the automobile up to the Winchester house. Amanda sat in the passenger seat, trying hard not to let on that she was badly shaken. There were two other vehicles parked nearby, one belonging to Joe's deputy, the other to Reverend Etlam.

"Brace yourself, honey," Uncle Joe said softly. "This ain't going to be easy."

"I know," Amanda whispered. "But Ben needs me."

"The kid's badly shaken up. His mother's dead, and now his pa up and ran off on him. That's bound to leave mental scars."

Amanda got out of the car and went slowly towards the house. Joe was right behind her. Inside, she heard the sound of voices and followed them to the living room. Reverend Etlam was there, along with his wife, Sylvia. Ben sat on the floor with his knees drawn up to his chest.

"Sheriff," Reverend Etlam greeted solemnly. "Any word?"

"No," Joe said regretfully. "No word on Winchester yet."

Ben sprang up and ran into Amanda's arms, burying his head in her stomach with a loud sob. Amanda hugged him tight, her eyes burning. She couldn't stop the tears from falling.

"Shh, it's going to be all right," she murmured, rubbing soothing circles into his back.

"I don't wanna stay here no more, Miss Amanda," Ben cried. "I wanna go home with you."

"And you will. Uncle Joe, I think it's time we took Ben home."

Joe understood. He nodded a farewell to the reverend and his wife, and escorted Amanda and Ben back to the car. The ride home was utterly quiet. Ben cried softly, his tears soaking the sleeve of Amanda's dress.

They arrived back at the Chandler ranch half an hour later. Margaret was waiting for them on the back porch, wringing her hands anxiously.

"Is Ben all right?" she asked as Joe carried the exhausted child up the porch steps.

"I don't think so," the sheriff said. "Do you mind lettin' him stay here until we can locate his next of kin?"

"No, not at all. He can stay here for as long as he'd like."

Joe took Ben to Amanda's room and set the now-sleeping child on her bed. Amanda pulled off his shoes and covered him with a quilt. She brushed her fingertips over his flushed face.

"I'll be back shortly," she promised in a whisper.

Downstairs, Margaret was making a big pot of coffee. The men would be needing it when they arrived back from the search for Mr. Winchester.

"I best be going," Joe said, turning his hat around in his hands. "If there's anything you ladies need, don't hesitate to call."

"We won't, Uncle Joe," Amanda promised.

The back door opened and Solomon came in, looking grave. "Sheriff, we found Howard Winchester," he said quietly.

Amanda had a sinking feeling in her stomach. "He's dead, isn't he?" she said, and Solomon nodded a confirmation.

"Took his own life. Said he didn't kill his wife, but that's all we got outta him before he pulled the trigger."

"Shit," Joe cursed, then muttered an apology to Amanda and Margaret. He sighed and ran splayed fingers through his head of gray hair. "Guess we'll never know what really happened, will we?"

He followed Solomon out the door.

Amanda walked outside onto the back porch and hugged herself. All she could think about was Ben, whose life would be greatly affected by this. She wanted to weep for him.

"Amanda?" Rex stood there on the bottom step, gazing up at her in concern. Amanda threw herself in his arms and wept. She found consolation in his embrace, and was suddenly filled with the familiar fear that she'd lose him, too. Everything she held dear was always being taken from her. First her grandmother, then her parents. She couldn't bear the thought of Rex being next.

"Rex? Promise me you won't leave me," Amanda pleaded, gripping fistfuls of his shirt.

Rex framed her face in his hands and stroked her cheeks with his thumbs. "Sweetheart, you have nothing to fear. I'm not gonna leave you," he assured her.

"Just promise."

"All right. I promise." Rex leaned forward and pressed a gentle kiss to her forehead. "What's got you so shaken? Hmm?"

"I don't want to talk about it right now," Amanda said. "You understand, don't you?"

"I do." Rex dragged her into his embrace and hugged her again, and Amanda stood in his arms a moment longer, not ready to part. It was only after she realized her responsibility to Ben that she regretfully pulled away and said a murmured good-night before going back inside.

She went upstairs to her room to check on Ben. He was fast asleep, but that failed to erase the lines of sorrow etched on his face. Amanda smoothed his hair from his eyes and sighed softly. She didn't have to imagine what he was going through. His pain was familiar to her, because not long ago her parents had perished too, and never would she forget that day. The pain was always present, never to fade. It would lessen, as it did every day, but Amanda clung to it because it was all she had left of her parents beside for her memories of them.

Chapter Nine

Stefano wavered drunkenly towards the apartment building his mother lived in. His mind was swirling, his vision as well, and he felt on the verge of losing it. Revenge was like an ever-present hunger, or even a cancer, gnawing at him, eating his soul to pieces. All he could hear echoed over and over in his mind was *kill, kill, kill.*

He reached for the door, pulled it open, and slipped inside.

Mama knew where Rex was. Stefano had no doubt in his mind. She wasn't expecting him tonight, but that was all right. It would make his job that much easier.

He arrived at her apartment, hammered on the door, and decided that if she didn't answer, he would barge in uninvited. He was a master at that sort of thing. He was also a master at interrogation. Mama would willingly tell him where Rex was or else he would have to force her to. Stefano didn't want this little visit to turn sour, but he wasn't opposed to getting ugly.

The door open, and there stood Mama dressed in a fancy evening gown, her black hair in rollers. Stefano had to grin. It appeared she was preparing to go out for a little much-needed fun. With a man, perhaps? So soon after Papa?

His mother looked surprised by his visit. "Stefano?"

Stefano invited himself in and shut the door. For good measure, he locked it. He took Mama by the shoulders and guided her to the small living room, then made her be seated on the sofa.

"Stefano, what is the meaning of this?" she demanded shrilly.

Stefano clasped his hands behind his back and began pacing. How to phrase what he desired to say without the words coming out harsh? He eyed Mama calmly.

"Mama, I know Rex is still alive," he began, and put up a hand to silence her when she opened her mouth to protest. "You must tell me where he is."

"Well—! I never!" Mama gasped, one hand flying to her slim neck in shock. "How dare you defile your brother's memory in such a callous manner?"

She began to rant to him in Italian.

Stefano's patience was failing like a spluttering motorcar engine. He tried to remain cool, relaxed. Mama's shrill voice would surely attract the neighbors and he didn't want that.

He lunged at her and curled his fingers around that skinny little neck, pulling her to her feet so that they were eye-to-eye.

"Where is he, Mama? I don't got the time nor the patience to listen to your berates!"

Mama's eyes widened in fear, and tears welled up in her eyes. She clawed at his hands in a desperate attempt to free herself and replenish her vastly diminishing air.

He squeezed harder.

"All … right!" she gasped, and he let her go.

He waited patiently for her to catch her breath.

"Your brother is alive," she confessed in a raspy voice. "He resides in Wyoming."

Stefano smiled. "Thank you, Mother. Now, you will tell me *where* in Wyoming."

"I will not!"

"You will!" he growled, temper rekindled.

"I don't know where your brother is in Wyoming and that is the truth!"

Stefano backhanded his mother for her defiance; she stumbled and fell, and becoming even more enraged, he grabbed her arm and jerked her painfully to her feet. She cried out in pain.

"Tell me, Mother!" he ordered, raising his voice. "*Tell me!*"

※ ※ ※

Gabriel Steinfeldt was having a pleasant supper with his sisters Lydia and Nancy, and Nancy's husband, Calvin, when the commotion five doors down disrupted it. At first, he brushed the raising of voices he'd heard as the always arguing middle-aged couple in apartment A12, but when he heard the shriek, he realized the commotion was in fact coming from A10.

Mrs. Armati lived in A10. Gabriel thought her a sweet old Italian woman whose cooking was to die for. She always brought him cookies, or *pizzelle*, as she called them, and he liked to dip the waffle-like dessert in a glass of cold milk. He wondered what was the matter. Her high-pitched screaming in her native dialect was a cause for concern. Mrs. Armati never raised her voice, even when the folks in A12 stayed up past midnight having one of their famous arguments.

"What's all that ungodly noise?" Calvin grumbled, looking towards the source. "It sounds violent."

"I don't know, but I'm going to go put a stop to it," Gabriel decided, pushing back his chair and getting to his feet.

Nancy got up, too. "I'm coming with you," she insisted.

Gabriel let her despite that her coming to check on Mrs. Armati with him made no sense at all. Calvin and Lydia tagged along, too.

"No, Stefano! Stop!" they heard Mrs. Armati cry.

"Stefano?" Lydia asked, grabbing a fistful of Gabriel's shirt. "Is that her husband?"

"Mrs. Armati's a widow. No, I think it's her son."

"I think her son is beating on her," Calvin remarked, shoving his way to the lead. "*That* is unacceptable. A son ought to respect his mother."

"What are you going to do, Cal?" asked Nancy, eyes brimming with worry as her husband knocked on the door.

"I'm going to put a stop to it, that's what I'm going to do, Nance."

"How—?"

"Hey! Open up!" Calvin shouted, hammering a little harder on the door.

When that didn't work, he told them to step back.

Gabriel had a sneaking suspicious Calvin was about to break through the door. If he did, and there was damage done, he would not hesitate to demand that his brother-in-law pay for the destruction of his property.

"Ooh, I'm so nervous," Lydia moaned, digging her nails into the fabric of Gabriel's shirt.

Nancy rushed to cling to his other arm, her nails actually puncturing his skin. He winced. In spite of the situation, he was glad his sisters felt the need to cling to him in a time of crises, even if he was the middle child and not the eldest.

Calvin angled his shoulder and lunged at the door, slamming into it with what Gabriel assumed was the equivalent of a charging bull's brute strength. It certainly appeared that way when the door gave, splintered wood and all. Calvin, the ungraceful fool, lost his balance and went flying head-first into the apartment.

"Oh, heavens!" Nancy gasped, rushing forward to help him up off the floor.

"Damn," Calvin groaned, rubbing his head, "that hurt."

"I'm sure it did, dear. Oh! Calvin, look out!"

An enraged Stefano lunged at Calvin and Nancy. Calvin pushed Nancy out of the way and met the Italian head-on. A violent fistfight ensued.

Gabriel sprang to Mrs. Armati's aid and helped her up off the floor. She clung to him like a lifeline as he guided her to safety.

"Shall I call the police?" Lydia asked, wincing when Stefano slugged Calvin in the nose. A brief crack was heard, an indication the bones had been broken.

"No! Do not call the police," Mrs. Armati pleaded.

Stefano delivered one good sock to Calvin's belly and with an *oof* and a foul curse, Nancy's husband crash-landed on the expensive-looking coffee table and lie still, groaning. Stefano fled the scene and disappeared out the front entrance.

Nancy ran to Calvin's side. "Cal! Oh, heavens! Are you all right?"

"Jesus Christ," Calvin responded with a groan. "My nose! Oh, Lord! My nose!"

"Hush now. Up we go. There. Let's get that nose of yours fixed, shall we?"

Gabriel led the group into the apartment he shared with his sister and instructed Nancy to sit Calvin down on the sofa. Mrs. Armati he guided to an armchair. Now, he awaited orders from Lydia, who was a nurse and had fixed many a broken nose in her time.

"Is he all right?" Lydia asked Nancy, gesturing to a moaning Calvin.

"I think he's dying, by the sound of it," Nancy said seriously, but Gabriel knew her well enough to know that she was only joking.

Lydia finally issued those orders. "Gabriel? Will you make tea for Mrs. Armati?"

"Right away."

Gabriel hurried to the kitchen to prepare a pot of tea. While the water was boiling, he got a tray out and set upon it a bowl of sugar, a little pitcher of cream, some spoons with which to stir the cream, and a plate of freshly baked ginger snaps.

Once the tea was ready and steeped, he carried the tray out to the living room and set it on the coffee table. He served Mrs. Armati a steaming cup, and she thanked him gratefully.

The loud, audible crack of bones being swiftly set made Gabriel wince.

Calvin screamed.

Mrs. Armati became startled and sloshed some of her tea on the skirt of her dress. "Madonna," she uttered, grimacing. She accepted the handkerchief Gabriel gave to her, and meticulously dabbed at her skirt. "I must make a phone call," she announced when she was satisfied her skirt wasn't soiled. "May I use your telephone?"

Gabriel nodded, accepting his handkerchief back. "Yes," he consented, "by all means do. Here—I'll fetch it for you."

He took up the entire telephone which sat on the lamp table next to the sofa, base and all, and carried it to Mrs. Armati. The cord barely allowed for the distance, but it was long enough not to strain and disconnect from the base.

Gabriel collected his pipe, sat down on the armchair in front of the fireplace, and carefully pressed a pinch of tobacco into the chamber. He struck a match and lit the fragrant leaves, puffing on the pipe to get the flame going.

Mrs. Armati dialed a number and put the phone to her ear. She waited a moment, troubled and white-faced. A bruise was forming on her cheek, as well as her neck. When she spoke into the receiver, her throat was hoarse.

"Al? This is Mrs. Armati. Yes. There has been trouble. How did you guess? He is a disappointment. How could the Lord have given me such a son?"

Gabriel assumed she was referring to Stefano. He tried not to listen in to the conversation, but it was difficult.

"Al, you must warn Rex. Stefano knows. He shall surely kill his brother if he finds him. Do you understand? Good. You will meet me at the Iris, yes? I have something to give you. Yes, tonight. Until then, Al."

She disconnected the call.

Gabriel leapt up to take handset and base from her. Once replacing these on the lamp table, he reclaimed his seat and continued to smoke his pipe.

A dead, awkward silence hung in the air. The only sound was Calvin's labored breathing, which began to irk Gabriel. For something to do, he offered to escort Mrs. Armati back to her apartment and she gratefully excepted.

"I'll fix the door in the morning," he offered sheepishly, and she smiled tenderly at him.

"You are too kind, Mr. Steinfeldt. The world is in dire need of men like you, men like my son Rex and his friend Al."

"Do you need me to do anything else for you?"

She nodded. "Yes, as a matter of fact. Would you be so kind as to call me a taxi? I must go out. I must meet Al."

"Sure thing, Mrs. Armati."

She pinched his cheek in an affectionate manner and thanked him.

* * *

The Iris was a nightclub in a swanky part of town, owned by a gentleman by the name of Arnold Braden. Al knew Arnold and his family well. In fact, he would go so far as to say he would trust the Bradens with his life. He knew when he walked into the Iris, he would be given a private corner booth where he could see everything going on in the room and where he could talk with Mrs. Armati without the fear of being overheard.

Dressed in a tuxedo, Al sauntered into the Iris, feigning a calm he didn't feel. Rex was in danger. Every minute spent here was a minute wasted, a minute Stefano could use to formulate a plan of attack. Al had plans to leave for Wyoming as soon as this meeting with Mrs. Armati was concluded.

Al was escorted to a table despite his lack of reservations. He seated himself and in moments, his eyes were drinking in everything from the fella crooning love songs on the large stage to a waiter serving a man and a woman glasses of fine champagne.

A young woman bounded gracefully up to his table and slid into the booth across from him. Her brunette hair was bobbed, giving her the appearance of a teenager. A wide smile graced her ruby red lips, further lending to the illusion that she was much younger than her twenty-some years. This was Iris, daughter of Arnold and Vivian Braden. Iris adored Al like a little sister would a big brother, and liked to listen to him tell stories of his Tradition.

"Al! How marvelous! You came on the night I'm to make my debut." she gushed gleefully. "You will stay, won't you, and listen to my performance?"

"The ol' man finally allowed you to go up on stage and sing, eh?" Al said, pleased. Iris had a lovely voice, and Al was always baffled as to why Arnold never allowed her to use her gift to entertain others. He supposed the old fool had finally given in.

"Oh, yes! He said I was ready." Iris was momentarily startled when the band stopped playing and the current singer crooned his last note. "That's my cue," she gasped, getting to her feet. "Wish me luck?"

"Break a leg," Al offered, and she dashed away.

At that moment, a waiter escorted Mrs. Armati over, and out of respect for her, Al stood and waited for her to be seated.

Mrs. Armati looked like a wreck. Her hair was untidy and falling loose from her usually meticulous bun. Her eyes were bloodshot and drooping from exhaustion. The beginnings of bruises formed on her right cheek and her neck.

Al's blood began to boil. He knew exactly who had caused those marks, and it took every ounce of his will not to jump up at that very moment, hunt the bastard down, and kill him. Stefano never was a true man of Tradition. He had no respect for the opposite sex, even his own mother.

Iris began to sing the very old but sentimental tune, *What'll I Do*.

Al couldn't listen. He tried, but in the end, he was too focused on wondering why Mrs. Armati had wanted to meet him here. He watched her with patience and concern as she fished for something in her purse. Finding what she was looking for, she had Al hold out his hand. Presently, she deposited a ring in his palm.

"That was my husband's ring," Mrs. Armati explained. "The Armati family coat of arms is inscribed there, on the face. To wear this ring signifies one is the Father of one's Family. I would like for Rex to have it. He must be our Father."

"I'll be sure to give it to him," Al vowed.

"Thank you, Al. When will you be leaving?"

"Tonight. I ain't gonna dilly-dally."

And true to his word, he left for Wyoming from the Iris, a worn leather case containing an assortment of clothes from freshly starched shirts to ironed slacks in the trunk of his automobile.

The trip took him two days.

By the time he pulled down the dirt driveway and arrived at a quaint little farmhouse where two children were sitting on the porch steps carving wood, he was travel-worn. Sure, he'd stopped here and there to get a little shut-eye at a motor court or an inn, but he hadn't really slept a wink. What he needed was a fine, home-cooked meal and a nice, comfortable bed. Or even a sofa would do.

He got out of his black Cadillac convertible, wondering where Rex could be. The mountain air smelled good. One of the children, he noticed, had gotten up to investigate the newcomer.

"Howdy, mister," he greeted. "You ain't from 'round here. You lost?"

"I should hope not," Al said, taking off his homburg and wiping his sleeve across his forehead.

"Hey! Ain't that a fancy car you got there, mister! I bet it cost ya a pretty penny."

"Sure did, kid. Say, is Rex around?"

"Rex? Oh. Yeah. He and Miss Amanda are at the lake skinny dippin'. They like to do that a lot. I'm Billy by the way. And that's my friend over there, Ben."

"Nice to meet you, kid. I'm Al."

A negro woman came out onto the front porch, then, and shielded her eyes to gaze warily at Al. She was most likely wondering why Billy—probably her son—was talking to a complete stranger. A stranger in an expensive suit with an expensive automobile no less.

Billy turned to cast his mother a cursory look, then reverted his gaze to Al. "Oh, that's my ma," he explained, scuffing his bare foot in the dirt. "Her name is Ellen Sue. She and Miss Peggy are bakin' cookies."

"She don't look too happy to see you conversin' with a stranger," Al observed thoughtfully. "I ought to go introduce myself. Did you say Rex was at the lake skinny dippin' with some dame?"

"Sure did, mister."

Al shook his head. Rex had always been a favorite of the ladies. Al? He was too short and dumpy to be considered a ladies' man; the dames always steered clear of him.

"Now who might you be, Mr. Fancy?" Ellen Sue asked, placing two fisted hands on her hips.

"Al Moretti, ma'am," Al introduced politely.

"Ooooh," she gushed, seeming to relax. An easy smile graced her lips. "You must be Rex's brother!"

Confused, Al rubbed the back of his neck. "Brother? Yeah, I guess you could say that."

"Come inside, sugar. I bet you could use a glass of cold lemonade."

"Yes, ma'am, I sure could."

"I don't know where that brother of yours has run off to, so you make yourself comfortable until he returns."

"Thank you, ma'am."

Al followed Ellen Sue into a spacious kitchen. There, he was introduced to Margaret Chandler. As he sat down at the kitchen table, Margaret served him cookies fresh from the oven on a plate, and Ellen Sue poured him a glass of lemonade. Al had never felt so welcomed before. These women hardly knew him from Adam and yet they felt the need to spoil him! He was enjoying himself heartily.

Shortly after he was welcomed into the house, a looker of a dame entered and allowed the screen door to slam unceremoniously shut behind her. Her blonde hair was damp, as if she'd recently gone swimming. Al assumed this was Amanda, the little lady his "brother" had taken skinny dipping. She flushed when she saw him, apparently startled by the unannounced guest.

"Peggy?" she implored for an explanation, but Al beat her to it.

He stood, towering at least two inches over her. Usually, the women he became acquainted with were almost always taller than him, especially his little sister Vera who was nearly the same height as Luke, the six foot one giant.

"I'm Al," Al introduced, grinning. "Apparently I'm Rex's brother. You wouldn't happen to know anythin' 'bout that, would you?"

"Oh, so *you're* Al," Amanda said in a way that suggested he wasn't at all the way she'd pictured him. She had pictured, Al suspected, a tall handsome fella much like Rex with a slender frame and hard, ridged muscles. Instead, here stood a dumpy little man. Yep. That was Al. He wasn't bad looking though, if the ladies would just see past his general dumpiness.

"The one and only," Al replied, still maintaining that grin. "You must be Amanda. Say, where can I find Rex?"

"I'll take you to him," Amanda offered, going out the screen door. "Is that your car?" she asked, indicating to the ol' '47 Cadillac.

"She's mine all right. Ain't she a beaut? I'd take you for a ride, but Rex might not like that."

"If you take the children along, too, perhaps he won't mind at all."

Amanda led Al up to a section of cabins she called Bachelors' Row. Rex was seated on the front steps of one of them, reading a letter with furrowed brows. His hair was damp, too.

When he heard them coming up the path, he looked up. Recognizing Al, his face appeared to go ashen white. Al didn't blame him for not being pleased to see him. He probably knew why Al was here, and if that was the letter Al had sent weeks back, then he had more reason to recognize that his best friend wasn't here for a social visit.

"Al," he acknowledged solemnly, offering a nod in greeting. "How did you find me?"

"It was Oliver who found you. Stefano … he's comin' for you, Rex."

"Spare me the details. All I want to know is *when*."

"Who knows? It ain't tomorrow, that's for sure. Stefano likes to plan."

Rex scoffed. "Oh, I know that all too damn well."

Amanda sat beside Rex, her face pale, her eyes swimming with worry. Rex settled an arm around her waist and she lay her head against his shoulder. Al wished he had a woman to hold. Watching Rex and Amanda made him feel alone.

"What are you going to do?" Amanda asked softly.

"Wait," Rex decided.

"And then what?"

"My brother is predictable."

"He means since they're twins, they got a special bond," Al explained when Amanda looked appropriately confused.

"I wouldn't put it that way," Rex grumbled.

"Put it any way you want. Stefano's comin' whether you're prepared or not. I suggest you make it in your best interest to plan ahead."

"Easier said than done."

* * *

Stefano soon arrived in the humble little town of Crowley. It had been all too easy. Stefano thought Al had always been the smarter out of his entire family, but he had proved Stefano wrong by (unknowingly) leading him here. All it had taken was an associate overhearing a conversation. That associate had just so happened to be in the Iris the very night Mama and Al had decided to hold a little private meeting there between the two of them. The associate had been sitting in the booth directly next to Al's, and had overheard absolutely everything said. Every. Last. Detail.

Stefano was pleased with himself. He had friends and he had associates, all of them utterly loyal. Rex had always been wary of making new friends, because the poor fellow had trouble trusting folks. Therefore, he lacked power, and a lack of power was a most terrible thing, in Stefano's opinion, which he would freely give when asked. He wasn't afraid to speak his mind—no, sir!

Stefano was starved for a good meal. He located a diner situated between a beauty parlor and an antique shop. He paused in the doorway to look around, counting the individuals, making a mental note to keep an eye on the seedy fellow brooding in a back-corner booth.

Stefano took a seat at the bar. He ordered a burger and fries from the man at the counter. The woman seated four stools down looked up from her book and stared at him.

"Rex?" she said, a sultry smile playing at her lips.

"I'm not Rex, honey," Stefano corrected. He was pleased. Now, he had proof Rex was here in this very town. "I'm his brother, Stefano."

"Well, you are certainly far more attractive, if you don't mind me saying so."

Stefano admired the long, sleek legs and the lips that seemed to be perpetually pouting. He liked what he saw. Perhaps this little lady would be so kind as to supply him with the information he required.

"I don't mind at all," Stefano answered, smiling. "Mind if I join you?"

"Please do, Stefano. May I call you Stefano?"

"Yes, of course. But first, your name."

"Beverly."

"Well, then, Beverly. May I ask you a personal question?"

She pretended to consider him long and hard. Then, "Why, you go right on ahead, honey."

"Are you and my brother romancing?"

"We were. But I find you much more desirable."

That's all Stefano had wanted to hear. He could have left Beverly then and there, but he had gone too long without the flesh and comforts of a woman. What was the harm in having a little fun? Beverly looked like an experienced little lady who had gone to bed with all the single—perhaps even married—

men in town. She was no stranger to what went on between a man and a woman behind closed bedroom doors.

Stefano liked them experienced. Unlike Rex, he enjoyed the companionship of a woman, particularly a beautiful one. And unlike Rex, who was the type of man to seek a lifelong relationship, Stefano had a woman for every night of the week.

And that's just the way he liked it.

* * *

Rex had meant to tell Beverly they couldn't be together anymore, but he had never gotten around to it. He knew it was the honorable thing to do. But since Al arrived, it had once again slipped his mind.

It had been three days since Al's arrival. Since then, Rex had given him a tour of the ranch and taken him fishing in his spare time. Amanda had taught him how to ride Esther. Billy and Ben liked to sit on either side of him on the front porch of the Chandlers' house and listen to him tell stories. Everyone, Rex thought, loved Al. Especially the women, because he paid them flattering compliments.

Rex finally decided to go pay Beverly a visit. He went in the evening after supper. As he drove, he recited in his head how he was going to say to her they couldn't be together anymore. She would probably rejoice.

There had been many times Rex suspected Beverly had been unfaithful to him. Too many to count, in fact. But he had always refused to believe she was the sort of woman to sleep around with every man that crossed her path. Beverly was sweet and kind, and would go out of her way to help a person in need. Someday she would find the man she was destined to be with, but that man wasn't Rex.

Rex arrived at Beverly's house and parked at the edge of the driveway. He wanted to make this good-bye as quick as possible, as he knew it would involve tears on Beverly's part, and Rex hated to see a woman cry.

The driveway was a mile long, and he suddenly regretted parking all the way at the end. It was dark. Not to mention there was no moon to guide his way. He had to rely solely on the porch lights, and even then, they were barely visible through the thick trees. Solomon had warned Rex many times that mountain lions roamed the Wyoming wilderness, especially at night. Although they wouldn't attack unless provoked, Rex was still cautious.

Arriving at that house, he prepared to go up the little pathway leading to the front porch when he noticed the dark red Pontiac Coup parked next to Beverly's rundown Ford Convertible. He recognized that Pontiac. As he bent to read the numbers on the license plate, the front door opened and Beverly's high-pitched giggles floated out to meet his ears.

"Oh, Stefano! You dreamboat," she breathed, sounding a little tipsy.

Rex's heart seemed to accelerate at an alarming rate. He darted behind the closest tree as his twin brother stumbled onto the porch, red-faced and grinning like an idiot.

Rex peeked around the trunk. He became nauseated when Stefano pulled Beverly flush against him and kissed her in a way Rex wouldn't call passionate. Aggressive was more like it.

"Won't you stay with me tonight?" Beverly begged, pouting her lips. "You are marvelous in bed."

Rex wanted to leave at that moment, but there was no cover between house and driveway. He would be spotted if he attempted to sneak out, and Stefano would no doubt kill him then and there. So he waited, listening to the grossly sweet mush Beverly and Stefano were tossing back and forth at each other.

Beverly finally managed to coax Stefano inside. As the door slammed shut, Rex made a run for it.

His heart didn't slow to an even pace until he was pulling into the Chandlers' driveway. He stumbled up to Bachelors' Row and nearly scared Al to death when he burst through the front door of his cabin.

"He's here," Rex spluttered, collapsing in an armchair. "Stefano is here."

"How do you like that?" Al grumbled, brows knitting together. "He followed me here!"

"Not necessarily—"

"Ah, you don't need to defend me, pal. I was careless. I ought to have covered my tracks, but I was too intent on reachin' you."

"He's got Beverly under his skin."

"How do you mean?"

Rex told him the story.

Al made a retching noise. "I reckon they deserve each other," he remarked, making a face.

"I'm gonna get some sleep Al. I'll see you in the mornin'."

"'Night, Rex."

"Good-night, Al."

* * *

Amanda sat on her bed brushing the tangles from her hair in even strokes. She was fantasizing about Rex, and the children they might have. Someday, she prayed, he would propose to her, and they would get married. She was sure of it.

Smiling at the thoughts conjured by her desires, she didn't realize Margaret had come in until she spoke.

"Amanda, we've got something to tell you. May I sit down?"

Amanda patted the space beside her, and Margaret sat down. Moments later, David wandered in, piquing Amanda's curiosity. They obviously had something important to tell her; she could just see it in their eyes.

"Amanda, remember when I visited the doctor's?" Margaret asked, resting a hand on Amanda's knee.

"I sure do, Peggy," Amanda said with a nod. "Is something the matter?"

David and Margaret shared smiles.

"I'm expecting a child, Amanda," Margaret revealed.

Amanda hugged both David and Margaret, expressing her joy at discovering she was going to be an aunt. She was happy for them. They had been trying for years to have a child, and now, God had finally decided it was time to bless them.

Amanda hoped the child was a girl.

Chapter Ten

Rex was so busy worrying about his brother, he became preoccupied. He wasn't afraid for himself, but for Amanda, and everyone else on the ranch. When Stefano was ready, he wouldn't come alone, but with armed men to back him up.

Rex had come to a place where he could no longer lie about his past. The Chandlers had been so good to him and he didn't want anything to happen to them because of his brother. There was no keeping them in the dark any longer.

Rex warred with himself all day about what to do. He hated the thought of running again; he was done running. No, this time he had to face Stefano, and he had to come to terms that one of them was going to die. As much as he abhorred the thought of killing his own brother, there was no way around it.

That afternoon, Rex took Billy and Ben fishing, as promised. It had been three weeks since the death of his parents and baby sister, but Ben was holding up all right. Rex knew at that age the mind pushed all painful memories aside to make room for the more pleasant ones. Sometimes Ben cried himself to sleep at night, but he was trying to make the best of it.

"Mister Rex, what's got you so fixed?" Billy asked, breaking the silence. "You ain't fishin'—you dreamin'."

Rex smiled despite himself. "I suppose my thoughts are elsewhere," he admitted.

"My mama says it's good to think, so long as it don't distract you from the task at hand. Mama's full of good sayings."

"My mama used to say good dreams were from God," Ben remarked thoughtfully. "And that bad dreams were the work of Satan."

"That makes sense," Rex said.

"I know. So who's bothering you? God or Satan?"

Rex knew exactly how to answer that, thinking his brother to be the spawn of the devil himself. "Has to be Satan. What do you suppose I do?"

"Pray," Billy answered. "That's what I do when I'm scared. Ain't that right, Ben?"

"It sure is," Ben agreed.

Rex wasn't a praying man, but he thanked the kids for their sound advice and decided to let his thoughts go and focus on the task at hand. He caught a nice, big bass much to the delight of the boys. They both loved fried fish and potatoes. Ellen Sue made the best.

When the afternoon began to wane, Rex and the kids started home. There were chores to be done, and Rex had to get cleaned up for supper. Amanda had invited him to eat with them that night.

When they arrived back at the farmhouse, Rex saw Amanda sitting on the front porch with a young woman he'd never met or seen before. But Ben knew her, because she looked right at him, her expression going soft. Amanda, Rex noticed, looked upset.

"Benjamin?" The woman stood up and came down the steps. "Do you remember me?"

Ben scuffed the toe of his shoe in the dirt. "I sure do, ma'am," he said. "You're Cousin Mary."

"That's right. I've come to take you home with me. Would you like that?"

Ben looked at Amanda, who nodded in encouragement. He returned his gaze to the woman named Mary. "I'm not sure, ma'am. I like it here."

"I know, but I'm your family." Mary smiled. "I know you hardly know me, but it will be all right. You'll see."

Ben looked at Amanda again, tears welling up in his eyes. Amanda pressed a fist to her mouth as if to suppress her own tears.

"Ben?" Mary hesitated, then rested her hand on his shoulder.

Ben sniffed and wiped his sleeve across his face. "I'll gather my things, ma'am," he said, then bolted off into the house.

Mary looked upset. "I thought he'd be happy," she said. "My husband and I ... we're willing to give him all we've got to make him happy."

"Give him time," Amanda suggested gently. "Ben has been through a lot. It will take time for him to heal."

"You're right. Thank you for taking him under your wing, Miss Amanda. I am sure he'll always cherish this time he spent here on the ranch."

Ben came out with a bag slung over his shoulder. In it was everything he owned. He went to Billy and the two kids shook hands.

"Thanks for everything, Mister Rex," Ben muttered, looking up at him.

"You're welcome, kid," Rex said, ruffling his hair. "You be good for Cousin Mary, you hear?"

"I hear." Ben turned and walked slowly to Amanda. "I'll sure miss you, Miss Amanda," he said. "You're the best teacher a kid could ever ask for."

"Oh, Ben," Amanda murmured, her voice breaking.

Ben threw himself into her arms, sobbing softly. Rex had to look away. He felt himself choke up, but wasn't ashamed of this, only disturbed, because he hadn't gotten emotional in years. Not even when his father had died.

Mary didn't lose patience, but stood quietly until Ben was done saying his good-byes. Rex could tell she'd be good to Ben. This gave him reassurance and hope that Ben would be okay. He was a good kid.

Amanda stood hugging herself and watched until the car carrying Ben to his new home disappeared around the bend. Rex approached her and placed his hand on her shoulder.

"You all right, sweetheart?" he asked.

Amanda nodded. "I'll be fine. It's for the best, you know." She turned to look up at him. "Rex, I've been meaning to talk to you about something. It's important."

Rex led her up the porch steps and sat down on the swing. She sat beside him, hands coming to rest in her lap. They swayed gently in silence for several long moments.

"Rex, I'm worried about you," Amanda said at last. "You haven't been yourself since Stefano's arrival."

Rex contemplated his reply. He didn't want to upset her, but sooner or later he was going to have to tell her, anyway.

"Amanda, my brother is not here to make amends. He's here to kill me."

"Isn't there anything we can do to stop him?"

"No. I'm gonna have to kill him."

He expected her to protest, even recite the *thou shalt not kill* bit of the Ten Commandments, but she didn't. She simply took his hand and squeezed.

"You won't have to face him alone. I'll be right beside you."

"This is somethin' *I've* got to do alone," Rex told her firmly. "I won't put you or anyone else on this ranch in danger."

Amanda didn't respond for the longest time. Rex finally looked at her and discovered the tears spilling from her lashes. She wouldn't look at him, even when he squeezed her hand.

"Amanda, honey, please look at me," Rex said softly. When she did, he suddenly was at loss for words. He didn't want to hurt her any further than he already had.

"Amanda, what's botherin' you?" he murmured instead. Perhaps if he got her to open up to him, they'd both feel all the better for it.

Rex saw Amanda hesitate. Finally, she swallowed hard and said in barely a whisper, "I don't want to lose you like I lost my mother and father. Rex, I can't go through that again."

Her eyes once more filled with tears. Rex used his knuckle to wipe them away. He didn't fully understand her pain, but he'd seen first-hand the insecurity and the mental scars left behind by the death of her parents.

"Amanda, you're not gonna lose me," Rex promised, a promise he hoped was not in vain. He took her hand again and pressed it against his heart. "When all this is over, I want you to be my wife. I want us to get married and have that little house on the hill you want so bad."

Amanda's face lit up in a radiant smile. "Are you proposing marriage to me?"

"Yes, if you'll have me."

"On one condition."

Rex raised a brow. "What's this one condition?"

"You ask my brother for his blessing," Amanda finished. "It's good and proper, you know, and because Daddy's no longer here, Dave can take his place, can't he? Besides—"

"Amanda?"

Amanda looked at him with a flush on her face. "What?"

"I'll do it." Rex framed her face in his hands and kissed her before she could start to ramble again. He heard the back-screen door open but didn't care who saw them anymore; he was enjoying this kiss too much.

"I sure do hate to break up such a lovely moment," Al said, "but supper's on the table and it's gettin' cold."

Rex pulled away from Amanda and turned slowly to give Al a frown. "Al, you sure know how to pick 'em."

Al grinned. "Hey, pal, you can blame Peggy. I'm just the messenger."

Supper was pot roast, potatoes, and green beans with a side of Margaret's homemade rolls. It was a solemn affair because everyone was missing Ben and his absence was profoundly felt.

"Looks like a storm is coming," David remarked after hearing a distant rumble of thunder.

"Good," Margaret said. "We need the rain."

Rex warred with his thoughts all through supper, wondering when it would be the right time for him to fill Margaret and David in on his past—and the coming future. Certainly not now. Perhaps later, when supper was over and the coffee and cake were being served.

"That was a mighty fine meal, Peggy," Al praised at the end of supper. "Certainly the best I ever ate."

Margaret flushed with pleasure. "Thank you, Al. I made it especially for you." She gave his cheek an affectionate pat and disappeared into the kitchen to start the coffee. Al had only been here a few days, yet it seemed like he'd become a part of the family. Al was like that. He was charming and honorable, and he had a sense of humor for every occasion that endeared him to folks.

Amanda got up and started to clear the dishes. Rex helped her carry them into the kitchen, but was shooed away by Margaret, who insisted he go to the parlor and relax. Rex followed her order and found Al and David already there, discussing politics and other matters.

Rex sat down on the loveseat and felt nervous all of the sudden. But he wasn't a coward, and if this was the opportune moment to reveal his past, he wouldn't shy from that duty. He was ready to free his shoulders from the burden.

Amanda and Margaret entered, the latter carrying a tray of coffee things. She set it on the coffee table and took a seat beside her husband.

"Are you all right?" Amanda asked, settling down next to Rex. "You look like a deer that's been caught in the headlights."

Rex tried to smile, but failed. "Is your brother very forgiving?" he asked.

"I should say so. He's forgiven me on countless occasions."

"For what?"

"Never you mind. Are you going to tell him?" Amanda asked softly. "About Alcatraz and your brother?"

Rex nodded. Amanda took his hand and squeezed it encouragingly, something that greatly buoyed him into going through with what he was about to do. He stood up and cleared his throat.

"David, Margaret, I have something important I'd like to get off my chest," he said.

Margaret smiled. "By all means, dear. We're listening."

Rex sucked in a breath, then exhaled. "I haven't been very open or honest with you," he started. "From the moment you took me under your wing, I've lied to you."

David frowned. "What's this about?" he said warily.

"My past, and my future. My name isn't Moretti—it's Armati." And Rex dove in, starting from the beginning with his heritage and Tradition, to his betrayal to his Family, and his time spent in Alcatraz before his escape. He told them about his brother and how badly Stefano wanted to see him dead. The weight from his shoulders was gone by the time he finished. Even if the truth cost him his job, he felt all the better for getting it off his chest.

Rex stopped and a long, uncomfortable silence blanketed the room. He sat back down and Amanda took his hand, giving it a reassuring squeeze.

David looked appropriately stunned, as did Margaret. Rex wouldn't blame them if they no longer trusted him or considered him worthy of anything but their scorn. He deserved it for not telling them the truth about himself sooner.

David finally cleared his throat. He didn't look angry to Rex, just calm and thoughtful.

"I can understand why you didn't tell us the truth in the beginning," he said. "And although I'm a little angry, I've seen what kind of man you are, and I've judged you to be honorable as well as hardworking."

"So you're not going to fire him?" Amanda asked hopefully.

"Of course not."

Al spoke up. "Now that we're gettin' things off our chests, I'd like to clear the air on somethin'." He paused. "I ain't Rex's brother."

Margaret laughed, surprising everyone. "That I figured out for myself."

Rex and Al looked at her in simultaneous surprise.

"You did?"

"Yes. You see, it's quite obvious. Anyone could see past it if they really looked." Margaret smiled. "You two are nothing alike. You don't look alike, you don't talk alike. It's a simple observation. David and Amanda may have a considerable age gap between them, but they share many similarities."

"Oh," Al said. "That makes sense. But wait 'til you see Rex's other half. You won't be questionin' that relation, I assure you."

David's smile faded and he became serious. "Rex, about your brother. You mentioned he's out to kill you."

Rex inclined his head in a nod. "He is. That's why I thought you had a right to know about my past. Stefano is anything if not predictable, and if I know him, once he finds out where I am, he'll be comin' for me."

"What's one man against twelve?"

"Stefano won't come alone. He'll bring his men. I won't risk anyone's lives, you hear? This is between my brother and I."

Al stood up and jabbed a finger at Rex. "Stop tryin' to be the honorable man you are, Rex," he growled. "I'm gonna be beside you no matter what you say. You ain't my boss."

Rex put up his hands in defeat. "Fine. But if I give you an order, you follow it. Understood? I won't let you give up your life for the sake of mine."

"Count me in," David said.

"No," Rex said firmly.

David's counter was just as firm. "*Yes.* I'm your boss, remember? And this is my ranch. If I want to stand by you, then by golly I will."

Amanda made a sound of exasperation in the back of her throat. "All you men think about is taking up your guns and shooting at one another," she said indignantly. "How do you think this makes us women feel?"

"There's no other way to resolve this, sweetheart," Rex told her. "You have to believe me when I say I wish it could be different. I wish there didn't have to be bloodshed."

"When will this brother of yours be coming?" David asked mildly, like they were discussing the weather.

"When he's good and ready."

A loud, crackling boom of thunder shook the room. Al had never experienced a Wyoming summer storm and mistook it for something else.

"He's here!" Al cried, throwing himself to the floor.

Rex reacted to this exclamation by ducking down, thinking they were being shot at. All the while David, Amanda, and Margaret looked at the pair of them like they were some kind of crazy.

"Old habit," Rex said sheepishly, when he'd realized his error. It was only thunder, not gunfire.

"Sheesh," Al said, shaking his head. "We need to get a grip on ourselves, pal. We're a mess!"

Rex was normally a cautious man, and he knew it wasn't a good idea to expose himself while his brother was in town, but there was something he needed to do. He borrowed the truck from David and drove to town to run his important errand.

Last night had been an eventful one. Not only had he proposed marriage, but he'd gotten to tell the truth to David. He'd also taken the man aside and asked for Amanda's hand.

"On one condition," David had said.

Rex had tried to keep a straight face. Apparently, Amanda and David shared the same mindset. "What's that?"

"That you make my sister a happy woman. Got it?"

Rex could promise this and much more, but first he wanted to make it official. He wanted Amanda to wear his ring. He didn't have much, but he'd been saving half of his pay each month, and he knew just the ring he wanted to purchase. He'd seen it in the antique store window on the day he'd first taken Amanda to town all those months ago. Then he hadn't thought much of it, but now he knew it was just the ring he wanted.

Rex drove cautiously into town, keeping an eye out for the familiar face of Stefano. This wasn't the time or place for a confrontation. But he didn't see his brother anywhere, and that gave him a small measure of relief.

He pulled into the parking space in front of the antique store and went inside. There were no customers, only an elderly lady sitting behind the counter reading an old book with a worn-out cover.

Rex approached the counter and cleared his threat. "Ma'am?"

The woman looked up and gave him a warm smile. "Good day, dear," she greeted. "How may I help you?"

"There's something I'd like to purchase."

"Oh? Anything in particular?"

Rex couldn't help but smile. "As a matter of fact, yes. There's a ring you have displayed in the window. May I see it?"

"I believe I know the one." The old woman got stiffly to her feet and went to the front of the store. She carefully took the ring from the display and presented it to Rex. "Is this the one, dear?"

The diamond mounted on a silver band was lovely and it was just what Rex was looking for. Amanda didn't like frilly things, but he knew she'd like the simplicity of this ring.

"I'll take it," Rex said. He got out his wallet and paid the woman for the ring, then left the store with a smile tugging at his lips and the ring in his pocket.

The smile faded when he saw his brother strolling up the walkway with Beverly on his arm. Rex ducked quickly into the truck to avoid being seen, his heart hammering against his chest.

"Shit," he cursed under his breath. He watched the pair a moment, wondering what Stefano would do were he to catch sight of Rex. Rex didn't think he'd be foolish enough to confront him in a public place, but it was better to be safe than sorry.

Stefano was too enamored with Beverly to pay attention to his surroundings. Rex decided to take this chance and go before his brother could spot him. He started up the truck, put it in gear, and started off in the direction of the ranch.

All the way home, Rex had this nagging feeling in the pit of his stomach. Seeing his brother had made him on edge. He had the urge to turn the truck around mid-way and go back to face his brother, to finally put all this to an end. But he didn't. He tried to push Stefano from his mind and picture Amanda's reaction when he presented to her the ring. He knew she'd be pleased, and that mattered more to him than having dark thoughts towards his brother.

Rex wanted to give the ring to Amanda when they were alone. That evening, he took her to their favorite spot by the lake, a secluded place back in the trees where no one would bother them.

They walked hand-in-hand down to the dock. A cool breeze was blowing, bringing respite from summer's warmth. Rex stopped on the edge and looked down, studying the ripples in the water. He was suddenly nervous. Last night he'd proposed, but that had felt different. Today he was giving her a ring, and this moment was more defining than any other. He wanted to get his words right.

Rex turned to Amanda and stood there a moment, taking her in. The late-afternoon sun that shone on her turned her hair gold. Her beauty could never compare to another, he knew, inside and out. She was as pure as water.

"Amanda?"

Amanda turned to him, a soft smile touching her lips. "Yes, Rex?"

"I ... I got you something." Rex cleared his throat. He really wasn't good with words like Al was.

"You did?"

"Yeah." Rex reached inside his pocket and extracted the ring. "I asked for your brother's blessing, he said yes. This ring ... it's a token of my love."

Amanda's eyes teared up. She gave him her hand and Rex slid the ring on her finger. It was a perfect fit, much to his relief.

"I'll wear this always," Amanda vowed.

Rex drew her into his arms and hugged her. "Even on those days I get on your last nerves?" he teased.

Amanda drew away and gave his arm a playful nudge. "That depends on how frazzled my nerves are." She turned away from him and started to undo the buttons on her blouse. "We might as well not waste this lovely evening. I'm going swimming."

Rex watched her take all her clothes off, mesmerized. She took a running leap and gracefully cannon-balled into the lake. When she surfaced, she waved at him to join her.

Rex shed his clothes and joined her in the water. The icy shock of it no longer took him aback. He swam over to Amanda and encumbered her in his arms, going in for a kiss. Amanda wrapped her legs around his waist, clinging to him in a lover's embrace that ignited warmth in him.

"Rex, this is the first time I've seen you at ease all day," she said when they had drawn away. "What's troubling you?"

Rex rested his forehead against her chest and sighed. "I saw my brother in town today. It took every ounce of me not to confront him, just so I wouldn't have to put you and everyone else at the ranch in danger."

Amanda stroked his wet hair. "Rex, my brother and the hands will gladly stand by you. You are one of them now."

"What I want to know is how someone who is identical to me in so many ways turned out to be the opposite. My brother is a murderous bastard."

"I'm sure glad you're not like him," Amanda murmured.

Rex was glad, too. He'd die before he stooped to Stefano's level. The man had no values or honor, and he sure as hell didn't have an ounce of compassion in his body.

"We best be gettin' home," Rex suggested.

"Supper isn't for another hour," Amanda pointed out. "What's the rush?"

"I feel suddenly exposed out here, that's what."

"No one knows about this place except me and you and my brother. No one would know where to look."

Rex saw reason in this and decided he needed to calm himself before his nerves got the better of him. He looked around, but saw only peace and serenity in the clusters of trees and the gentle lapping of the water against the shore. In the distance, he heard an owl hoot mournfully.

"See? It's no one but us and nature," Amanda murmured close to his ear. Her lips touched his temple and he closed his eyes, enjoying the closeness of their bodies and the sweet scent of her perfume.

Amanda shivered from the chill of the air against her skin. They climbed back on the dock and Rex wrapped her up in his shirt to get her warm. His heart sang in response to the smile she gave him.

"Do you think anyone will miss us?" Rex asked, touching her cheek with the palm of his hand.

Amanda tilted her face into his touch. "No," she said. "Not for an hour at least."

Rex swept her up in his arms and kissed her again, losing himself in her beauty and thinking himself to be the luckiest man in the world to have a woman who loved him for who he was and stood by him no matter what.

Chapter Eleven

Joe was a regular patron at Annabelle's Diner. He enjoyed the burgers and the milkshakes and chatting with old friends that wandered in every now and then. He especially enjoyed flirting with Annabelle, the lovely widow who owned the place.

Today was no different. He went in during the lunch hour and took a seat at his favorite table near the back. As always, he scanned the many photographs that adorned the walls, depicting all walks of life and the history of Crowley. Annabelle came over to take his order, and as always, he complimented her on the new way she had styled her hair (she was always wearing new styles). And, as always, Annabelle blushed like a schoolgirl and bustled off to give his order to the cook.

Joe recognized all the faces. There was Mrs. Payton the gossip. And there were newlyweds Andrew and Nina, gazing lovingly at each other. Mr. Woolworth was occupying his usual seat, but today, he had a lady friend with him. And here was Miss Dottie and her best friend Miss Lily having milkshakes at the bar.

And here came…

Rex?

No. It couldn't be.

Joe had to do a double take. Either Rex had decided to spend all his earnings on a fancy new suit or he had a twin brother. Joe squinted. The guy certainly looked like Rex, but there were features of Rex's he lacked such as the long, jagged scar underneath the right eye. Joe noticed details like that.

When Annabelle bustled over with his meal, he asked who the feller was.

"Oh, that's Stefano Armati," she answered pleasantly. "He's new in town. I declare, doesn't he look an awful lot like Rex Moretti?"

"He sure does."

"Can I get you anything else, honey?"

"No, thank you. That'll be all, Annabelle."

She bustled off.

Joe ate in troubled silence. As soon as he was finished and had paid for his lunch, he headed out to the Chandler ranch. He just had to know if he was sane or just plain crazy. He got out of his automobile and wandered up to the house. He pulled open the screen door and stepped inside.

Margaret was seated at the table sorting through recipe cards. She looked up when the screen door shut with a gentle *clack*.

"I declare, Uncle Joe," she said, brows knitting together. "You look as though you've seen a ghost!"

"Somethin' like that," he agreed, taking off his hat and screwing it in his hands. "Is, er, Mr. Moretti around?"

"Which one?"

Joe thought his heart had plumb stopped for two beats. So there were *two* of them—he wasn't crazy after all. But now he was confused, for the man he saw in town was an Armati. If that were so, then who was the other Moretti?

"Rex is out with the boys searching for a calf that got loose," Margaret provided when he didn't specify which Moretti he wanted to speak to. "Al, Rex's friend from New York, is taking Billy for a ride in that fancy car of his."

"Is that so?"

"Al is a nice fellow. You'll like him."

Three Italians in Crowley. How about that.

Joe put his hat back on, said good-bye, and departed the house. He had a mind to stick around and wait for this Al fellow to return, but he also had duties to attend to and didn't have time to lallygag.

So he headed back to town.

* * *

Stefano sat on Beverly's front porch smoking a cigarette. He had decided to use her secluded, spacious house as a sort of headquarters, one where he and his men could lie low and plan without the sheriff becoming suspicious. Until his men arrived, Stefano bided his time by having a little fun with Bev. He stayed away from town as much as possible, intending on keeping a low profile until he made his move.

Life was like a game, he mused, exhaling smoke from his mouth and nostrils. You had your pawns, then there was you, making all the moves. The goal was to take down all your enemies and by doing so you scored points, which would determine your place in life. One could be first, or one could be last.

Stefano was always in second place. Rex always managed to hold first place. Soon, that would all change; Stefano would be first, and Rex would be knocked off the scoreboard—permanently.

Beverly knew his plan, knew who he was, and accepted it. She was a good little girl, submissive and meek. Although she wasn't the brightest, she learned quickly and efficiently. Stefano would keep her around just until she lost her value and became nothing more than a nuisance. She was a pleasant distraction, but that was all she'd ever be.

The front door opened and Beverly slipped out, wearing nothing but a slip, a cigarette clamped between her teeth. She wasn't much of a lady, Stefano observed. In fact, she was a far cry from the wealthy, sophisticated broads of New York. Stefano didn't much like tramps, but he tolerated Beverly on account of her beauty and her ability to make him laugh, which was no easy feat.

"If you want to make Rex suffer," Beverly said, sitting herself down beside him, "then I suggest you hurt the woman he loves."

Stefano put his cigarette out in the ashtray in order to give Bev his full attention. "And who is the dame you speak of?" he asked.

"Her name is Amanda. Amanda Chandler. I don't much like her."

"The woman my brother left you for?" Stefano guessed, and Beverly snorted.

"The very one. You'd be doing me a favor, Stef."

Stefano nodded thoughtfully. Hurting a woman was against his nature, unless that woman greatly annoyed him and deserved to be put in her place with a good beating. Stefano had no intention of hurting Amanda that way. There were other ways that did not involve physical violence, and one of them happened to be kidnapping, an innocent little business where the only people hurt were the victim's loved ones. Stefano could easily abduct Amanda, take her somewhere secluded and secure, and keep her there against her will.

But would he stoop to that level?

He thought about it. Chances were, the sheriff would get involved if a kidnapping was orchestrated in his very town. Then a search party would be dispatched. Fingers would go pointing. Rex would step forward and rat on Stefano.

The more Stefano thought about the plan, the more it began to appear stupid. He would be a fool for attempting such a thing.

"If you don't want to do the dirty work, ask Walker to do it for you," Beverly suggested as if she knew what he was thinking.

"Walker? Who's Walker?" Stefano asked, becoming curious.

"Amanda's old beau. He hurt her real bad. He used to work for the Chandlers but now he's doing odd jobs wherever he can find them."

Sounded promising. Stefano asked where he could find this Walker fellow, and Beverly supplied him with an address. Armed with this new information, Stefano headed to Saw Mill Road. He pulled into a rutted dirt driveway, sauntered up to a tiny, rundown house that had seen better days, and knocked on the door.

A grizzled, mean looking man answered the door wearing overalls, a strong, foul smell coming off him. Stefano took one step back, swept his gaze over the young man in disgust, and decided he looked like the kidnapping type.

Walker became wild-eyed with hate. "What do you want, Moretti?" he spat vehemently.

"The name is Stefano Armati, friend," Stefano corrected, slightly annoyed. "And you must be Walker."

"You sure do look like Moretti, feller."

"Rex is an Armati, just like me. Now, can I interest you in a little business?"

Walker became cautiously curious. "What kinda business, mister?" he asked.

"You look in dire need of some money. Perhaps I might entice you with this." He reached into an inner pocket of his sports coat and fished out a roll of bills.

Walker's eyes widened in disbelief.

"That sure is a lot of money, mister," he declared, a glow in his eyes. "I'm enticed all right. You must want me to do somethin' crazy, is that it?"

Stefano nodded. "You got it, my friend."

"What, then? I'm all ears."

"There's a thousand dollars here. Abduct Amanda and bring her here tomorrow evening. Make sure folks know you committed the crime. Once you've handed her over, one of my men will be waiting with a car. He'll take you wherever you'd like to go, even Canada."

"Will I get my money, too?"

"And much more, if you do your job properly."

Walker's eyes took on a greedy gleam. He accepted the offer, no more questions asked.

Stefano departed Saw Mill Road.

In the morning, five of his men arrived, including his second, Nicola. The rest would arrive later, perhaps at the end of the week.

Stefano gave the getaway job to Tomme.

* * *

Amanda took Billy into town for ice cream at Hudson Bros. Ice Cream Parlor on Main Street. The owner, the eldest Hudson, Marlon, was a nice old man who liked children. He welcomed all, knew everyone who came into the parlor, and remembered his customers' favorite flavors of ice cream.

As they stepped into the hot, almost humid air and headed for the truck, Billy's ice cream began to melt rapidly and he frantically went around the cone licking tiny rivers of chocolate threatening to soil his clean white shirt.

Amanda smiled warmly at the boy and rested one hand on his shoulder as they walked. Rex's ring glinted in the afternoon light, inspiring a thrill of excitement within her. She could scarcely wait to become Mrs. Rex Armati.

Her thoughts preoccupied with the future, she nearly missed seeing Walker watching her from across the street. He caught her looking and buried himself in a newspaper. The look on his face, still fresh in Amanda's mind, caused a pang of unease to kill her good mood.

She grabbed Billy's hand and hurried him to the truck. Unaware of her anxiety, Billy continued to lick happily at his cone, a content smile on his face. Children, so innocent and naive. They wouldn't know danger if it looked them in the eye. Amanda wished she was a child at that very moment, too, unaware that a man had given her what Al called the "scheming eye." The scheming eye, he explained, was when a fella or a dame was scheming of ways to kill you.

"You drive this truck real good now," Billy complimented as Amanda pulled out of Main Street onto the road that led home. He was finishing the last of his cone. "Rex is a good teacher."

"That he is," Amanda agreed, casting a look in the rear-view mirror. No sign of Walker. Perhaps she had just imagined it all. Perhaps Walker was still sore about the outcome of their relationship and was merely tossing her a nasty look of spite to quell his anger.

Yes. That was it. Nothing more, nothing less.

Amanda relaxed.

She listened to Billy chatter away about the new carving he was doing for David and Margaret's child for when he or she eventually came into the world. It was a little calf, he described, with big ears. He was going to paint in black and white.

Now, he chattered about Al's fancy automobile and how he wanted one just like it when he grew up. He also wanted to travel to New York City and see how the "Family business" was run for himself. Amanda thought Al was putting ideas where they oughtn't belong: in an adventurous child's head.

Billy finally fell silent. He rolled down his window and stuck his head out like a dog. Amanda contemplated telling him how unsafe that was, but she was too focused on driving, and being a new driver and all, she didn't want to lose that focus.

"Miss Amanda?" Billy suddenly asked.

"Yes?"

"Who's that man with the gun?"

"What?"

Billy pointed. "He looks mighty angry."

Amanda shot a quick glance over her shoulder and felt her heart plummet to her belly when she saw Walker pursuing them furiously and aiming a pistol out his window. With a screech of tires on pavement, he swerved to the left, then the right. His aim was hindered by his reckless driving, giving Amanda the advantage she needed to shift gears and floor the gas pedal. The truck shot forward and Billy slammed into the glove box.

"Shit!" he cursed.

Amanda didn't have the heart to correct him. She drove like the devil was after them and Billy hung on for dear life.

"Lord, we're gonna die!" he cried.

The pistol went off.

Billy screamed when one of the tires blew and Amanda lost control of the truck. It swerved into the grass and came to a complete stop when it struck a tree. Dazed and disoriented, Amanda clutched at the door handle and managed to get the door open. She crawled out of the totaled truck and nearly stumbled when she stood on shaky legs.

"Billy?" she called, turning to see if he was all right.

"I'm just swell all things considerin'," he remarked, scrambling out after her. He pointed, eyes widening. "Oh, look! That crazy man with the gun!"

Amanda whirled around. She shoved Billy behind her as Walker advanced upon them like a rabid animal.

"You're comin' with me, woman. You too, you little black bastard," he growled, pointing the pistol at them. "Move!"

Amanda took Billy's hand and propelled him forward. She rested her free hand on the small of his back, giving him a little nudge whenever he hesitated. Fear tightened her throat and made it impossible to breathe. She was too scared to cry. She had to be brave for Billy. He needed her right now, needed her protection.

With a badly trembling hand, she opened the passenger door of Walker's truck and climbed in. Billy scrambled in beside her and nestled close to her, seeking solace and safety. Amanda wrapped an arm around his shoulders and held him tight.

Walker got in and started the truck.

"Not one word, you hear?" he growled, waving the pistol in Amanda's face.

He pulled onto the road and drove at a slow, steady pace all the way to Saw Mill Road, where he pulled into a dirt driveway and stopped at a sad-looking house. He had parked the truck beside an expensive looking automobile against which a tall, intimidating man leaned smoking a cigarette.

Walker got out, ran around to the passenger's side, and opened the door. He grabbed Billy by the scruff of his neck and yanked him out. Next, he grabbed Amanda none-too-gently by the wrist, intending to exercise force, but she went willingly. Billy clung to her skirts as Walker escorted them to the porch.

"I got her!" he called to someone inside. "I made good. See?"

The front door creaked open and a well-dressed man emerged, a spitting image of Rex. Amanda gasped. Billy gawked.

"Stefano," she blurted, and Stefano smirked.

"Right you are, doll. And you must be Amanda."

"She is," Walker supplied, nodding vigorously.

"No one asked you, Hollister."

Stefano sized Amanda up in appreciation. He smiled in satisfaction, but frowned when he lay eyes on Billy. There was no hostility in the eyes so much like Rex's, until he looked at Walker.

"Hollister, I gave you specific orders. 'Abduct Amanda and bring her here,' I said. Simple enough, yes?" he asked, lighting a cigarette.

"Y-yes," Walker answered nervously. Sweat perspired on his forehead. "But the boy—"

"I don't wish to hear your petty excuses, son, I would merely like to know how you fared. Were you seen kidnapping the little lady and this boy?"

"No, sir." It was said confidently and with pride. "I successfully carried out a kidnappin' without being caught."

Stefano nodded calmly. He tossed his cigarette to the grass at Walker's feet.

"Do you remember my instructions or are you deaf?" he asked softly.

Walker looked confused. "Sir?"

"I said, 'Make sure folks know you committed the crime.' What part of that did you not understand?"

"But—"

Stefano held up a hand and Walker fell silent.

"No buts. You made a mistake. I understand and I forgive you. But lessons, they must be learned. Orders must be followed. Would you like to know what happens to folks who are ignorant and don't follow orders?"

"No, sir. I don't."

Stefano smiled coolly. As quick as an experienced gunslinger in a western picture, he drew the pistol from the holster strapped to his shoulder and fired a single shot.

The bullet struck Walker in the forehead.

Amanda screamed.

The man she'd seen earlier leaning up against the automobile appeared beside her and took hold of her arm. His hands were rough and calloused.

"Tomme, dispose of this filth," Stefano barked, and put the pistol away.

Tomme released Amanda and grabbed Walker by the wrists. As he dragged the body off, Stefano came off the porch to stand before Amanda, the cool smile still at his lips.

"Rex sure does know how to pick them," he murmured appreciatively, cupping her chin between his thumb and forefinger.

Amanda jerked her head away. "You bastard!" she cried softly. "You killed Walker. How could you do such a vile thing?"

"It's in my nature, honey."

Amanda couldn't understand how twin brothers could look so alike yet have vastly opposite personalities. She was mortally horrified that a man who looked so much like Rex—walked and talked like him, too—had killed a man without a second thought for making one little mistake. This was why the world thought the Mafia—or *Family,* as Rex called it—consisted of nothing but vile criminals who broke every law and went out of their way to commit unmerciful killings. Because of men like Stefano, Tradition was nothing but a farce. Family was nothing but an army of ruthless Sicilian men believing the world was their own personal empire.

Disgusted with the man that was Rex's twin brother, Amanda refused to look at him. She pressed Billy to her and cocooned him in her arms. If Stefano moved to touch him, she would make sure it was her he hurt and not Billy.

"Let's go," Stefano said, grabbing her arm and thrusting her to the back of the house where another expensive automobile sat, waiting. He opened the back passenger door for her and she and Billy got in without having to be asked twice.

"Stay close to me, you hear?" Amanda told Billy, and he nodded shakily.

"Yes'm," he said.

* * *

Rex sat at the kitchen table sipping a cup of coffee and reading a book. Al was in the living room napping on the sofa. Rex hadn't heard from Amanda all afternoon. Tonight, he had plans of throwing rocks at her window until she opened it so he could ask her to go down to the lake with him for a late-night swim.

Al muttered something about a pretty dame under his breath. When someone began to frantically hammer at the door, he sat up, reached for the pistol he had laid on the coffee table, and leapt to his feet.

Rex got up to answer the door. Realizing there was no danger, Al put the pistol away and raked splayed fingers through his already mussed-up hair, making it stand on end.

Ellen Sue stood on the doorstep, wringing her hands. Her eyes were bloodshot as if she'd been crying profusely. Rex felt his heart skip a beat. He began to come up with several explanations as to why Ellen Sue was so upset.

"Is it Billy?" he wanted to know.

"And Amanda." She began to cry anew. "Oh, Rex! Deputy Rowling found the truck on the side of Dappled Pony Road—crashed into a tree!"

Now, Rex's heart seemed to stop. His mind immediately went to a dark place and conjured images of Amanda lying bloodied and battered in grass sprinkled with shiny fragments of glass and mangled automobile parts.

Ellen Sue fell into his arms and began to sob. "They been kidnapped," she moaned, clinging to him. "There were signs ... Deputy says there was another automobile."

Rex felt overwhelming relief take hold of him. So Amanda wasn't dead. He closed his eyes and hugged Ellen Sue tightly for a brief moment before releasing her and holding her at arm's length.

"Tell me everything, Ellen Sue," he requested calmly.

"Sheriff Chandler is down at the house. He wants to see you, honey," was all she said.

So Rex and Al followed Ellen Sue down to the house and they went inside. Arthur, Solomon, David, and Margaret were seated at the table while Sheriff Chandler stood at the head. He turned when the screen door opened, and eyed Rex as if he were the perpetrator of some grand plot.

"Do you happen to have a twin brother, son?" he asked.

"I do," Rex admitted, and it suddenly hit him: Stefano had kidnapped Amanda and Billy.

"Your future brother-in-law has told me everything. I hear you're the son of a crime boss. And your name is Armati."

Rex winced. Not because David had confessed everything to the sheriff, but because he hated when those derogatory terms were used to refer to his Tradition. Damn the reporters who coined them.

"Yes, sir," he said with a nod. "This is true."

"And I ain't his brother," Al piped up. "I belong to another Family."

Sheriff Chandler narrowed his eyes in Al's direction, then in Rex's. He gripped the back of the chair he was standing behind until his knuckles whitened, and his eyes shown with hostility. But not towards Rex and Al, Rex soon found out.

"My deputies and I believe your brother has abducted my niece, Armati," he explained.

"How did you come to that conclusion?" Rex asked smartly. "Anyone could have done it."

"I know everyone in this town, Armati. Ain't no one would stoop so low as to kidnap a favorite, beloved teacher. A stranger newly arrived, now I wouldn't put it past 'em."

"If I knew where Stefano was, believe me when I say I'd go and confront him. Amanda is my fiancée. I love her. If Stefano lays one hand on her, I'll kill him."

"I wouldn't try to stop you, Armati," the Sheriff admitted without hesitation. "If you help us bring your brother in, I won't cast your reputation as a criminal in this here society of the US of A a second glance. If you kill him, my offer still stands. I just want my niece back. And Billy, too. He's a good kid."

"I want them back, too, Sheriff."

"Then it's settled. Tell us everythin' about Stefano."

"Everything?"

"Yep. Everything."

* * *

Stefano shoved Amanda up the front steps of Beverly's home. The negro child clung to her skirts and didn't say a word for which Stefano was grateful. He knew he couldn't hide them here forever, but for now, it would have to do.

He opened the door and they scrambled inside. Two of his men materialized with ropes and bound Amanda's and the child's hands together behind their backs, then forced them into chairs.

"Where's Beverly?" he barked at Enzo.

"Town, I reckon," Enzo replied, shrugging his shoulders in an I-don't-give-a-damn attitude.

"She don't talk to us," Pietro told Stefano.

"Yeah," Louis agreed from where he stood at the kitchen sink sipping a cup of coffee and peering out the window into the meticulous, well-manicured backyard. "She looks at us like were nothin' but mongrels that get underfoot and cause trouble."

Stefano gritted his teeth. Beverly ought to show respect towards his men. He would have to teach her a lesson, a lesson she wouldn't soon forget. A lesson in respect.

Amanda glared at him. He gazed at her for a moment, contemplating where to put her and the child for the time being. Perhaps he could put them in the basement.

Deciding that was the best option, he made his hostages get up. He herded them down the basement stairs, collected two dusty old chairs that sat forgotten behind the furnace, and sat them down. The little lady still glared at him, a spiteful look he wouldn't tolerate from any woman. She was an exception, he decided. Smiling, he flattened a palm against one of her smooth cheeks.

"Don't go anywhere, doll," he said playfully, and returned to the first floor.

"Shall I search for a better place to stash 'em, boss?" Nicola asked hopefully. "I got nothin' else to do but listen to your woman blabber on all day about frivolous matters that don't concern me, and quite frankly I'm gettin' sore."

Stefano made a sweeping gesture towards the front door. "Go."

Nicola eagerly headed for the door. Pietro hesitated and when Stefano nodded at him, he followed after Nicola. Stefano didn't blame them for wanting to escape the house. Beverly did indeed blabber about matters concerning no one but herself. Sometimes, it took every ounce of sheer willpower not to put a bullet in her mouth.

Downstairs in the basement, Amanda was scheming ways to free Billy and herself. She looked around for sharp objects, but found none—at least within sight and reach. She tried to slide her wrists free from the ropes, but that was a lost cause.

"Are we gonna die?" Billy asked, strangely at ease.

Amanda gave up trying to be free of the ropes to look at him. In spite of their situation, Billy appeared calm. His eyes, however, clearly spoke of the fear he was trying to keep hidden. He wanted to be brave, and Amanda felt a surge of tenderness for the boy for trying.

"Stefano won't kill us," Amanda assured Billy. Or would he?

Amanda quickly rid her mind of the dour thought, refusing to entertain the idea that Stefano was cold and ruthless. But he had killed Walker, had he not? What was to stop him from killing her and Billy?

Billy heaved a soft little sigh of misery.

"Suppose we do manage to escape, and that mean man shoots us in the back while we're a-runnin'?" he fretted, and gave an involuntary shiver.

"I don't think Stefano's a coward," Amanda once more tried to assure him.

"I wouldn't put it past him, Miss Amanda. He done shoot Mister Walker without a lick o' remorse. Suppose he don't care?"

"I don't know, Billy. I really don't."

Billy shrugged. "Suppose—oh, never mind."

Night was falling.

Amanda wondered if Stefano was going to make them sleep upright in these hard, uncomfortable chairs all night. She supposed she could manage it, but she dreaded the stiff neck that would surely ail her come morning.

The basement door opened. Someone was coming down the stairs. Amanda couldn't see a thing in this dark, damp basement. Stefano was a bad host for allowing his guests to live in such disgraceful conditions.

Speak of the devil.

"Who's hungry?"

Stefano appeared carrying two plates piled high with mashed potatoes, green beans, and meat loaf. Well, he was certainly generous when it came to providing meals for his guests, Amanda would give him that.

"How on earth are we going to eat tied up like this?" she muttered spitefully.

"I will untie you for the time being," Stefano answered pleasantly, setting their plates aside so he could do just that. "Now don't you contemplate running away, doll."

"I wouldn't dream of it, you're such a marvelous host," Amanda retorted sarcastically.

Stefano clicked his tongue in disapproval. "Now there's no need for that, sweetheart. Eat your supper. I might allow you to remain untied so long as you don't attempt to escape."

"How generous of you."

Stefano only smiled and gave them their supper. He vanished back upstairs, and once the door had slammed shut behind him, Billy dug in to his meal with enthusiasm. Amanda merely picked at hers. She wasn't that hungry.

"I wonder who made these taters," Billy wondered appreciatively.

"Ms. Lind," Amanda offered, rolling a green bean around on her plate with the fork Stefano had kindly provided.

Billy looked amazed. "She lives *here*?"

"Yes. As it just so happens."

Amanda set her plate aside and got up. She wandered around, poking around here and there, looking for sharp objects that might come in handy as a weapon. There were windows big enough to crawl through but too high up to reach. There were plenty of things to stand on, Amanda mused, but she felt it was too early to attempt an escape. Perhaps when Stefano was at ease, when he was sure his prisoners wouldn't try to escape and a false sense of security had replaced the alertness he must surely feel now, maybe then Amanda wouldn't hesitate to use those windows as a means of escaping.

Until then, her and Billy would have to bide their time.

* * *

"What's it going to take to rescue my sister?" David demanded Rex.

"Time," Rex answered simply. He hurried to explain when a vein in David's forehead throbbed suggesting he was on the verge of exploding in a rage. "If I know Stefano, he won't kill them. He's either using Amanda to lure me in, or he abducted her to hurt me. My guess is the latter, because we don't know where in hell my brother is hiding."

They were all seated in the living room, discussing Stefano, of course. It was agony, not knowing where the bastard was or where he had taken Amanda. Sheriff Chandler wanted to send a posse of his deputies out on a search party, but Rex told him no. When the sheriff asked why, Rex carefully explained to him that to go up against men of the old Tradition (or new, since Stefano seemed to have made up his own rules) was a death sentence. These men following Stefano were dangerous. They were sharpshooters and excellent at hiding in plain sight. They were killers.

More than anything, Rex wanted to find Stefano so he could kill him, but right now, that was out of the question. A good dose of patience was required at this very moment. And a plan. They had to come up with a plan.

In the meantime, they would regroup. The sheriff would return to town to rally his deputies. Rex, Al, Solomon, and Arthur would return to Bachelors' Row and put their heads together to formulate a plan. Perhaps they could recruit the other hands to their cause.

They would need all the help they could get.

Chapter Twelve

It was dawn, and sleep had eluded him entirely. Rex knew he wouldn't rest properly until Amanda and Billy were safe. Not knowing when that would be, he despaired, because every moment they spent under his brother was another moment he could change his mind and decide to end their lives.

Restless and anxious, Rex left his cabin and went to the barn. Prince looked out from his stall window and nickered a greeting when he saw Rex. The stallion reminded him of Amanda. She had raised this horse with a firm but gentle hand and it showed, in both the stallion's personality and demeanor.

Rex rested his elbows on the stall door and heaved a sigh. There was nothing more he wanted to do than head out this minute to find Stefano and end this. It had gone on long enough. But he knew he couldn't, or else Amanda and Billy might get caught in the cross-fire.

Suddenly, he wished he'd never come to Crowley, Wyoming. If he'd stayed put in Alcatraz, none of this would be happening. These folks would still be living their normal lives. Amanda would be safe, and Billy would be where he belonged, with Ellen Sue and Solomon.

But Rex realized the selfish part of him wouldn't trade the last few months for all the wealth in the world. Not only had he found a new home, he'd discovered another part of himself that he liked, and he'd fallen in love with the most wonderful woman. Nothing could take that away from him, even his brother.

Rex fisted his hands. He was angry, and there was nothing he could do to rid himself of what was building up inside him. He wanted to hit something hard, preferably his brother, whom all his wrath was currently turned towards. He wanted to make his brother suffer.

Prince seemed to sense this anger because he snorted uneasily and took a step back. Rex felt bad then, and sought to reassure the stallion. He gave him a gentle pat on the neck.

"I wasn't expectin' to find you up so early."

Rex glanced up. Solomon was standing in the doorway, regarding him with eyes that missed nothing, not even the emotions Rex tried so hard to suppress.

"I couldn't sleep," Rex said.

Solomon shrugged. "Neither could I. Keep thinkin' about Billy and worryin' myself sick over him."

"I'm sorry."

Solomon shook his head. "Don't go be sorry for me on the account of your brother. I don't blame you."

"I wouldn't hold it against you if you did."

"Son, life don't work like that. If I held resentment in my heart for everything that went wrong in my life, for every man who did me wrong, I wouldn't be a happy man, would I? No, I'd be sad and I wouldn't know how to be hopeful that everything's gonna be all right."

Rex pondered his words, and decided he'd try to be more like Solomon, although looking on the bright side had never been one of his strongest virtues. He'd seen so much darkness in his life that he no longer knew what being hopeful felt like.

"What do I do?" Rex asked, seeking Solomon's wisdom. "I'm not a good man, Solomon. I've done things in my life I'm not proud of. I've gone down paths I may never be able to return from."

Solomon put his hand on Rex's shoulder. "I can't tell you what to do, Rex," he said. "But what I can tell you is this: When all else fails, a little prayin' is what I do. I always manage to find an answer to my problems that way."

He gave Rex's shoulder a firm pat, then turned and left the barn. Rex stood in the same place for the longest time after that. He warred with himself, wanting to take Solomon's advice, but believing himself to be too far deep in his sinful ways to merit any sort of guidance or forgiveness.

But Rex had nothing to lose, and so after completing he chores, he borrowed David's truck and drove to the church down the road. It felt awkward walking through the doors of the little white church. He half expected lightning to come down from the sky and strike him dead.

It didn't. Inside, the church was as quiet as a tomb. Remembering his Catholic upbringing, he crossed himself. Rex took off his hat and walked up the aisle towards the alter. He gazed up solemnly at the crucifixion of Christ.

"I'm not a prayin' man," he muttered. "Far from it. But there's no one else I can turn to, and I've got an awful big request to make."

Rex screwed his hat in his hands and cleared his throat. "Amanda and Billy, they are the kindest souls I know. I ask that You keep them safe from harm. I know my brother, and if the nerve strikes him, he'll pull the trigger just to satisfy that need of his for blood-shed.

"I know I don't deserve much, but Amanda and Billy do. I'd trade my life if it meant they got to live and be spared from my brother's hand. If it comes down to a fight to the death, I might have to break that Commandment of Yours, but I don't do it lightly."

Rex heaved a sigh, feeling suddenly lighter. It was a nice feeling. "I'd hope this could be resolved peacefully, but I know it can't. I only hope a lot of good people won't die in the outcome."

He turned and walked back up the aisle, putting his hat on once he'd gotten outside. The sky above threatened a coming storm. It was a ways off, but Rex could smell rain in the air. He hoped wherever Stefano was keeping Amanda and Billy was a place that was warm and dry; and that, somewhere inside him, he still had some honor left in him, the very honor that kept him from harming women and children.

Rex got back in the truck and drove the half-hour back to the ranch. When he got there, an unsettling sight met him. A strange automobile was parked near the house. He had a feeling this visitor was tied to his brother, and that meant Stefano had a message for him; he was anxious to find out what.

Rex haphazardly parked the truck and hurried to the back door. When he went in, he found a dark-haired stranger sitting at the kitchen table with Al and David. Margaret was pouring him a cup of coffee, a pinched expression of wariness etched on her pretty face.

"Ah, there you are," the stranger drawled when he saw Rex. "We've been waitin' for you, Armati."

It took every bit of strength Rex had not to go at the man's throat and demand answers.

"Rex, this is Enzo," Al introduced. "Stefano sent him."

"I gathered as much," Rex said with forced calm. "What do you want, Enzo?"

Enzo clucked his tongue. "Is that any way to treat a guest?"

"The ones I don't like, yes." Rex took a step closer. "What news does my brother send? Out with it, man."

"It ain't news, but an invitation," Enzo said, losing his smile and becoming aloof. "Four o'clock, on Miller's Ford Road, where the bridge is. Come unarmed if you know what's good for you."

Rex scowled. "How like Stefano to make the odds in his favor," he retorted. "Tell my brother we'll be there—unarmed, but not unprepared."

Enzo rose from his chair and plopped his fedora on his head of thick black hair. He tipped it at Margaret. "Thank you for your fine hospitality, ma'am." He brushed past Rex and exited through the back door.

Al waited until he heard the automobile roar off before speaking. "Do you think it's a trap?" he asked Rex.

Rex shook his head. "No. Stefano's mind doesn't work that way."

"I don't like it," David said. "But if we can get answers, I say it's all we've got."

"You're stayin' here," Rex told him firmly. "Your responsibilities are *here*. I'm takin' Al and Solomon with me, and that's final."

"Are you sure that's wise?" Al said. "It's Solomon's son they've got. I don't know him well, but I know a man is unpredictable when he knows his kid's in danger."

"Solomon will do fine. It's me I'm worried about." Rex grimaced. "That's why I need you and Solomon along, to make sure I don't do anything rash."

David sighed and scrubbed his hands over his face. "I don't like any of this," he confessed. "It scares the hell out of me, knowing Amanda and Billy are in the middle of all this."

"My brother isn't goin' to hurt them," Rex assured him. "He wants to raise hell, that's what. The only people who are goin' to get hurt here are those who go up against him—armed. That'll provoke him faster than anything."

"You know him better than the rest of us. What do you think he's planning?"

Rex was uncertain about that. "I'm not sure, but it can't be good, whatever it is."

When four o'clock neared, Rex, Al, and Solomon piled into the truck and made the half-hour journey to Miller's Ford Road to rendezvous with Stefano. Tensions were high, especially because they were going unarmed. Solomon had balked at this but had respected the terms and had decided he had to do what was best for his son.

Al was unusually quiet. Rex had known him all his life and had never seen his friend like this. Al was worried. It showed in his rigid shoulders and clenched jaw. They both knew Stefano, whose actions were often predictable, but not today. Today there were no certainties as to what he had planned.

"I've never seen this brother of yours," Solomon said, out of the blue. "What's he look like?"

"Me," Rex said.

"They're identical twins," Al offered. "But don't take their likeness to mean they're both cut from the same cloth, because they ain't."

"How will I know which one to shoot if they ever get mixed up?" Solomon asked dryly.

"Easy. Rex has an ugly scar on his face. Stefano doesn't."

Rex scowled. "Thanks a lot, pal."

Rex caught Al's grin out of the corner of his eye. "It's the truth. You know I don't like to soften the truth, don't you?"

Rex didn't answer. They'd arrived on Miller's Ford Road. Up ahead was the bridge, which sat over Shady Pine River, and on the other side was a blockade of three vehicles. Rex felt outnumbered already. He tensed, wondering why he hadn't listened to his instincts and brought along the shotgun hanging above the back door of David and Margaret's house.

"Ain't that something," Al drawled. "A welcomin' party."

Rex was suddenly ill at ease. "I don't like this," he admitted. "Be ready for all possibilities, okay? I don't need one of you gettin' shot on my account."

"Hey, we tagged along because we wanted to, friend," Solomon said. "We're in this thing together."

"Ready?" When the other two nodded, Rex got out, prepared to duck if bullets started flying. Al and Solomon stood on either side of him. They walked a few feet from the truck and waited.

Stefano was the first to emerge from one of the vehicles. He paused to light a cigarette, then flourished a hand. The rest of his men got out and surrounded him; Rex counted seven in all. He was fine until he saw Amanda and Billy forced from one of the vehicles by two of his brother's men. He got angry when he saw the terrified look on Amanda's face, and almost couldn't control himself from acting impulsively.

"Damn you to hell, Stefano," he growled.

Solomon stiffened when he saw his son, and Al put a hand on both his and Rex's shoulders to steady them both.

"I'm fine," Solomon hissed under his breath.

"That's no way to greet your brother," Stefano drawled. "Mama would be mighty disappointed in you, Rex."

Rex laughed without humor. "Do you really want to go there, Stefano?"

"Not especially, but I *do* want to have a little chat with you. I hope you've come unarmed, because I'd hate for this to get ugly."

Rex shot a glance at Amanda and tried to reassure her with a small smile. His heart ached for her, but there was nothing he could do for her at the moment. His brother would have her killed if he tried anything.

Rex turned a steely gaze to Stefano. "What do you want?" he called icily.

Stefano didn't answer for several long moments as if contemplating his answer. Finally, he spoke.

"I want you dead, Alexander. But I'm willing to do it in a fair fight, so that you can die honorably. The time isn't now. But in three days, I will be ready, and I will want us to meet again. You may choose the time and place."

Rex pretended to think about it. He'd already guessed at what Stefano wanted, and he had an answer ready.

"Callahan's Meadow at noon, you and I. But I want Amanda and Billy returned safely to the Chandler ranch. If you hurt them, the deal is off."

Stefano smiled a slow smile. "That will be arranged on my terms. The woman and the boy will be returned safely, but until then, I keep them for insurance."

Rex clenched his fist. "Fine," he ground out through gritted teeth.

"Excellent. I look forward to our meeting, Alexander. Until then I hope you enjoy the remainder of your days."

Rex was afraid to look at Amanda again. He knew she'd be in tears, and seeing her cry would hurt him more than thinking about what might happen in three days. He looked away, filled with anger and resentment towards his brother.

"There's nothing more we can do," he told Al and Solomon. "Let's go."

Solomon hesitated, gazing longingly at his son. He forced himself to turn away and get back in the truck.

They drove away in silence, no one saying a word for the longest time. Rex knew he wouldn't be able to speak without betraying just how upset he was. Seeing Amanda and Billy like that, he could only image what they were going through.

"Are you really gonna let him kill you like that?" Solomon asked finally.

Rex swallowed to clear his throat. "You heard him. The fight's gonna be a fair one," he said listlessly.

"None of this is what I call fair," Al said angrily. He banged his first against the dashboard. "Damnit, Rex, be sensible. We need to come up with a plan that ensures the only ones gettin' what they deserve here is your brother and his men."

"I agree with Al," said Solomon.

Rex couldn't help but smile. Stefano might have had an army of men at his beck and call, but he sure didn't have friends. Rex was glad to have Al and Solomon to back him up.

"Have you got a plan?" he asked.

Al grinned. "Don't I always?"

* * *

Amanda knew they couldn't stay here any longer. It wasn't that Stefano was treating them poorly, it was his intentions towards Rex that fueled her desire to escape. If there was any way she could get to him, to convince him that there had to be another way, she would do it. The thought of seeing Rex lying in Callahan's Meadow, dead, was one that was too unbearable to contemplate.

Amanda had been working to loosen her bonds for the past two hours with little progress. Her wrists were raw with burns but she ignored the pain. There was much more at stake here than thinking about her own predicament. If she kept at it, she was certain she could get free within the hour.

Billy sat beside her in uncharacteristic silence. He hadn't said a word since their return from the rendezvous with Rex. Amanda feared all this was too much for him, but there was nothing she could say or do to soothe him, because she didn't want to lie. There was nothing worse to her than giving a child a false sense of security.

Amanda finally felt that the ropes were loose enough for her to get her hands free. Feeling triumphant, she wiggled and twisted until one hand was out, then the other.

"Whoah, Miss Amanda, you gonna get in trouble," Billy cried, looking worried.

Amanda rubbed her sore wrist. "Not if I can help it," she murmured. She stood on shaky legs and went around behind him to work on his ropes. Once he was free too, she started working on how they were going to escape.

Amanda looked around, hoping to be struck with inspiration. Her gaze froze on the window. It was a little high up, but it seemed as if it were the only option they had.

"Billy, if I give you a boost, do you think you can push open that window?" she asked, and Billy shrugged.

"Sure thing."

Amanda cupped her hands and crouched on her knee. Billy looked up at the window, frowning thoughtfully, then put one foot in her hands. She lifted him up to the window with only a little struggle; he wasn't at all heavy for his age.

Billy didn't have to push hard. The window was unlocked. He crawled through and turned, reaching down a hand to Amanda. She didn't think he had the physical strength to help her but was pleasantly surprised. It took a little time and effort, but when she was finally out from the confinement of the basement, she wasted no more of it. Time was precious now. It was starting to get dark, and it would be harder for them to navigate, but it would certainly help them stay hidden.

"Come on," Amanda whispered, taking Billy by the hand. She swept her gaze over the surrounding area, looking for Stefano's men; the coast was clear. Her and Billy took off for the safety of the woods.

Amanda was exhilarated and fueled by adrenaline. Running through the trees, she thought she could go on infinitely and never stop. She didn't want to stop; not until they were safe and far away from this place.

We are going to make it, she thought.

Amanda saw the break in the trees up ahead. She thought her heart was going to burst, but she kept going, thinking if they could just make it to the main road…

Stefano was waiting for them at the edge of the woods, leaning up against his automobile, arms folded across his chest. Amanda almost screamed when she saw him. She came to a halt, stunned and suddenly feeling numb with defeat. Beside her, she heard Billy curse.

Stefano pushed away from the automobile and sauntered over to them. He didn't look angry at them, only amused.

"You didn't think you could escape without someone noticing, did you?" he drawled. "You were clever, I'll give you that. I almost let you get away because of that alone."

Amanda felt her shoulders sag. She was afraid if she opened her mouth, she'd say something foul to him, and she didn't want Billy picking up another dirty word.

"Come now," Stefano said, almost tenderly. "I have a little surprise for you and the child. Would you like that?"

"I'd like nothing more than to belt you one," Amanda returned spitefully.

Stefano chuckled. "This I don't doubt, but we must remain civil to one another. I'd hate for things to get ugly."

He opened the back door of the automobile and flourished a hand. Amanda gave Billy a gentle push when he dug his feet in. Billy finally relented, but not before shooting Stefano his best glare.

Amanda paused before getting in and turned to face Stefano, who's arms were resting on the door, a patient if not bored expression on his face. He didn't look like Rex to her anymore. She had learned to spot the differences, and now that she had, she realized Stefano lacked a lot of what Rex had. One of those things, she decided, was a heart.

"Why do you have to do this to Billy?" she demanded. "He's just a boy. Let him go back to his parents."

Before Amanda could pull away, Stefano cupped her chin in his hand and skimmed his thumb over her jaw.

"Because I'm a considerate man, I will think about your proposal," he said, almost tenderly. "It's you I must keep. I believe Rex would give his life for you in a heartbeat, and I can see why. You are not only beautiful, but I see a heart made of gold."

Amanda tried to jerk away, but Stefano kept his hold on her. "Let go of me," she hissed.

Stefano's eyes flickered to her lips, and for a moment, Amanda thought he was going to kiss her. He didn't.

"Get in," he ordered brusquely. "My patience is wearing thin."

Amanda got in beside Billy, who scooted over to her and nestled into her side. Amanda hugged him tight. He clung to her as if his life depended on it, his head coming to rest on her shoulder.

Stefano got in and started up the automobile. Amanda assumed they were going back to Beverly's, but was dismayed when he drove right past the driveway without stopping.

"Where are we going?" she called warily.

"That's my surprise," Stefano answered. "I'm taking you and the child to your new home."

"New home?"

"Don't press for details, doll. Let's just say you'll be safer there than here. Understood?"

Amanda understood perfectly. He was making sure no one would be able to find them, and this was not at all a comforting thought. She swallowed down the lump that had formed in her throat.

It was too dark now to see clearly outside the windows. Amanda tried to guess where they were going, but she didn't recognize the road Stefano took them on. It wound and curved through a dark forest; there was no moon tonight.

Stefano slowed and made a right turn onto a dirt road. It went on for three miles before they emerged into a clearing. Warm light shone from the cabin nestled there, a homey sight, but one that failed to invoke warmth within Amanda. She couldn't suppress the feeling of despair that threatened to overcome her.

"Out," Stefano ordered, yanking open the door. "And no funny business."

Amanda and Billy got out and walked meekly towards the cabin. Two of Stefano's men were seated in chairs on the front porch playing cards by candlelight. One of them looked up and gave his boss a nod.

"I wouldn't bother trying to escape now," Stefano told Amanda after they went inside. "It's miles of forest in any direction. You'd just go and get yourselves good and lost."

Amanda didn't respond. Billy leaned up against her, trying hard to keep his eyes open. Stefano noticed.

"Go put the kid to bed in that back bedroom over there. Then you and me are going to have a nice, civil conversation." Stefano nodded curtly in the direction of the bedroom.

Amanda guided Billy inside a sparsely furnished bedroom and got him settled in the queen-sized bed. She stalled, dreading the inventible of having to face Stefano. Being civil to him was like trying to befriend a rattlesnake. Knowing what his intentions were made it worse, and she wanted nothing to do with him.

"Do you want me to tell you a story?" Amanda asked Billy, but he shook his head.

"I'm awful sleepy, Miss Amanda," he mumbled. "Maybe another time."

Amanda tucked in the covers around him and dropped a kiss on his forehead. Once he was settled, she reluctantly left the room. Stefano was waiting for her in the kitchen. He'd made coffee and was pouring them both a cup. The man was considerate, all right, but she didn't trust him. For all she knew he could have bad intentions towards her.

"Just so you know, there is nothing I wish to discuss with you," Amanda said icily, accepting the cup he handed her. "Unless you'd like to discuss your redemption and making peace with your brother. Killing him is not the answer."

Stefano gazed intently at her a moment. "When I make up my mind, I don't make it a habit of changing it," he said. "If it's of any consolation to you, Rex won't die dishonorably. There will be a fair fight."

Amanda wanted to scream at him. "I hope you rot in hell, Stefano Armati," she hissed, meaning it. She had never wished anyone ill will before, but she didn't much care what happened to Stefano; he was a vile man in her eyes.

Stefano set his cup down and came to stand in front of her. There was nowhere Amanda could go. She backed up, but was trapped between him and a wall.

"You don't know Rex as I do," Stefano said softly. "He isn't the man you believe him to be. I've heard him tell lies. I've seen him take another man's life. Why you've put such faith in my brother, I'll never understand, but it's misplaced."

Amanda fought back tears, but they came anyway, stinging her eyes. "I've seen in Rex what others haven't," she whispered. "I know what kind of man he is, and nothing that comes out of your mouth will change the way I feel."

Stefano brought his hand up to her face and tenderly wiped the tears away from her cheeks. Amanda looked away, not wanting to meet his gaze. She hated how he looked at her with those eyes so much like Rex's. She hated, too, that he was gentle, just like Rex; this made it hard to fully despise him.

"Stop touching me," Amanda bit out. "I don't like it."

Stefano dropped his hand to his side and leaned in closer. "Count yourself lucky I'm an honorable man," he murmured, his hot breath on her skin. Then he walked out the door, leaving Amanda standing there in the kitchen, fighting back the impulse to hurl her cup at him.

Chapter Thirteen

Stefano drummed impatient fingers on the kitchen table of his new hideout. Beverly was supposed to meet him here, bringing with her necessities like groceries and perhaps a home cooked meal. She was two hours late.

Where could she be, Stefano wondered, getting to his feet. He wasn't the sort to get impatient, but Beverly provoked him, and a woman who provoked her man was a woman not worth keeping. Still, she was useful, and Stefano had a rule about not harming a hair on a woman's head. Or a child's, for that matter. Men? Well, he'd shoot up a town of them without so much as a tinge of regret.

Stefano went outside. The air smelled good, unlike the air in New York City which smelled unnatural and adulterated. One could get a lungful of exhaust and cigarette smoke and be smelling it for days. Here, one could take in nature; not just a lungful, but an eyeful, too. It smelled wonderful, looked wonderful, and made one feel a sense of peace and belonging.

"Enzo," Stefano barked, "where the hell is Ms. Lind?"

Enzo, who had just pulled down the dirt driveway and was climbing out of his automobile, went white as a sheet. "Sir?"

"You were just in town, yes?"

"Yes."

"Did you see that vixen of mine while you were there?"

"As a matter of fact—"

"Was she doing what I asked of her?"

"No. Last I saw, she was headed into the radio station. That's on Ivy Bell Street."

"Thank you, Enzo."

Stefano got into his automobile. He was trying not to blow a gasket, but Lord, he was spitting mad and close to exploding. Almost all of his men were here and accounted for, which meant more mouths to feed. He had given

Beverly a simple job to go to the market and buy groceries. Apparently, she had deviated from her mission and was off at some radio station doing God knows what.

CCR was the only radio station in Crowley. It played nothing but country music. No Frank Sinatra or Bing Crosby to be found there. Disgusting. The disk jockey, by the name of Ralph White, sounded like a child who'd swallowed a marble. Stefano wondered if Beverly had stopped by to request a song. If she had, she was sure taking her sweet time. Perhaps she had stopped to chat with the marble kid. Stefano shrugged. He wasn't worried, because what woman in her right mind would fall for a guy like that?

He arrived at the station and walked in. The secretary, a woman in her mid-thirties, looked up from filing her nails.

"Can I help you, sir?" she asked, sounding bored and uninterested.

"Yes, ma'am. You certainly can. Where might I find Mr. White? is he in?"

"Do you have an appointment?"

"What is this? A doctor's office or a radio station?"

"Mr. White is a very busy man, Mr.–?"

"Armati."

The receptionist indicated to row of chairs with a lazy flick of her hand. "Have a seat, Mr. Armati. I'm sure Mr. White will be out shortly."

Stefano was indeed about to blow a gasket. This was an outrage! He could clearly see Mr. White wasn't busy, because the sign that read ON AIR above the door of the broadcasting room was unlit.

"Sir, you seem to have misheard me," the receptionist said as Stefano moved to open the door. "What are you doing? I'm going to call the police!"

Stefano was inclined to ignore her until she reached for the telephone. Calmly as could be, he produced his trusty pistol and whacked her across the temple. As she slumped in her seat, he caught and righted her.

"Idiots! My Lord, they're everywhere," he grumbled, gripping the rounded door handle and twisting it. He shoved open the door, and stopped dead in the entrance when his eyes sought out and froze on a sight that finally blew that gasket.

Beverly, seated on White's lap, fingers tangled in his hair, lips fused to his, gasped when Stefano made his entrance and quickly unfurled herself from the disc jockey.

Stefano saw nothing but red.

He drew his pistol, and without a second thought, he shot White, and then Beverly, both in the head. His anger subsided, he looked around, an idea coming to mind.

The town, he thought triumphantly, was his.

* * *

Rex headed into the police headquarters alone. He wanted to discuss something private with Sheriff Chandler, something he didn't want the others– even Al–to know.

Deputy Clarence led him into the sheriff's office and Sheriff Chandler indicated to a seat. Rex sat down.

"What can I do for you? You're obviously here on the account of your brother."

"I am," Rex conceded, nodding. "Stefano wants to meet me tomorrow afternoon at Callahan's Meadow. Alone. But I'm not going to be alone. You and some of your deputies are going to be there."

Sheriff Chandler, curiosity piqued, leaned forward. "What's the plan, Rex?"

"Stefano believes I'm coming alone. Let's keep it that way. You and your deputies will be close by, in ear shot. I'll pry Amanda and Billy's location from him. Once my brother reveals it, one of your deputies will call it in to headquarters and dispatch the rest of you deputies to rescue Amanda and Billy. Meanwhile, Stefano and I will be havin' a stand-off."

"Like in those old Western pictures?" Sheriff Chandler interrupted, sounding like an excited child.

"Well, if you want to see it that way, yes."

Sheriff Chandler started to grin, but quickly caught himself and cleared his throat.

"I don't want to die, and I don't want Stefano to die," Rex continued. "This is where you come in. On my signal, you and your deputies will surround Stefano. He'll have no choice but to surrender with all those guns on him."

"Sounds like a good plan. I like it."

"I thought you would, Sheriff."

The door opened and Deputy Smith stuck his head in. "Sir? You're gonna wanna hear this," he said.

"What is it, Deputy?"

"The radio, sir. Come and see for yourself."

Rex and Sheriff Chandler followed Deputy Smith from the office to the latter's desk around which seven deputies were crowded. Deputy Ian turned up the radio and Stefano's voice rang out loud and clear:

"Citizens of Crowley, you may not know me, but I am Stefano Salvatore Armati, brother of Alexander Alessio Armati. This is quite a lovely town you have got here. *Magnifico*! I believe I may stay awhile. Starting now, I am appointing myself mayor. My men will set you straight if you step out of line. My men, they number fifty. Very good sharp shooters."

"Who does this guy think he is?" hissed Deputy Smith.

"Hush!" Sheriff Chandler snapped.

"Alexander, if you are listening, I am calling off our meeting," Stefano continued, sounding pleased with himself. Rex knotted his hands. "*Arrivederci*, my brother."

"The nerve of him!" Sheriff Chandler cried when the broadcast ended. "Turn that damned thing off, Smith."

"We still have time to get him," Deputy Craig pointed out. "The radio station is two blocks from here."

"You're right, Deputy. Rex? You're riding with me."

Rex followed the sheriff and the deputies from the station. His blood was boiling, his thoughts a scrambled mess of words he couldn't decipher, blinded as he was by hate. Stefano had always wanted power. He'd wanted New York City, but the remaining Families hadn't allowed him to take it. Crowley was an easy target. The folks here had no idea what a Sicilian man of honor was capable of. They wouldn't see Stefano coming before it was too late. Before his men had caused chaos.

The sirens of the three police automobiles racing up the street was enough to wake the dead. Rex hung on tight as Sheriff Chandler swerved violently around the corner onto Ivy Bell Street. He slammed on the breaks and before the automobile had come to a complete stop, Rex was hopping out and running blindly into the station. The groaning secretary was collecting herself up off the floor and rubbing her head. Rex helped her to sit down in a chair, then proceeded to break down the door that led into the broadcasting room. Stefano was nowhere to be found, but the two bodies lying on the floor was a sure sign he'd been there.

Rex knelt down. His anger was rekindled when he realized one of the bodies was a woman. Stefano had never killed a woman before. Why now?

"Jesus Christ," Sheriff Chandler said from the doorway. "Poor Ralph. He was a good kid. Who's the gal, do you know?"

Rex found the woman's purse and rummaged around in it for an identification of some sort. He found a driver's license. The identity was revealed.

"Beverly," he said, feeling sick. He handed the license to the sheriff.

"Ms. Lind. I saw her with your brother at the diner."

Rex turned away and left the scene of the crime. Stefano had gone too far this time, between killing Beverly and announcing to the whole town he was taking it over. Stefano, Mama had once told Rex, had come out of her womb yellow and blue. He had barely survived. Perhaps that could explain why he was a little crazy. Always wanting more, even when he had enough. Always wanting to play God.

Rex had to do something about his brother, but he was at a loss. No ideas came to mind. He walked all the way back to the truck, got in, and went home. Chances were, folks at the Chandler ranch hadn't heard the broadcast. Rex needed to tell them, especially Al, who would know what to do. Al always knew what to do.

"Crazy fool," Al muttered when Rex had told his story to the folks at the Chandler ranch. "I'd call him something stronger but we're in mixed company."

"Oh, by all means," Margaret urged.

"I ain't no stranger to cussin'," Ellen Sue said. "He's got me so mad I'd call him the foulest name in the book."

"Call him what you want, but he's becoming a real problem," Rex told them grimly.

They were all gathered on and around the Chandler's front porch. Solomon and the hands, sweaty from working, seemed to have plenty on their mind. One of the many thoughts going through their heads, Rex reckoned, had something to do with wanting to murder Stefano. He had it, too, but he didn't want it to come to that. He would pull the trigger if need be, yes, but guilt and remorse would plague him the rest of his days. Rex still loved Stefano despite his ever-many flaws. They had a bond not even the closest of siblings shared. They were twins, cut from the same cloth.

"I say we ought to rally the town," Al suggested, and Arthur asked him to explain. "I saw this movie once with Devon Emond and Vivian Leigh. They rallied a town to help them take down Emond's character's ruthless cousin whose situation sounds an awful lot like Stefano's."

"This is reality, Al," David pointed out. "I don't think folks would risk their lives to defend our town."

"We'll see. When Stefano raises hell, the town'll get real desperate."

He had a point. Rex rubbed the beginnings of a beard he hadn't bothered to shave since Amanda and Billy had been abducted. He had no idea *how* exactly Stefano was going to go about taking over Crowley. If he did indeed have fifty men as he claimed, then the job would be as simple as setting those men loose and ordering them to knock some sense into whoever didn't comply with Stefano's rules. Or kill them. It depended on how far Stefano was willing to go.

* * *

The sweet smell of victory.

Stefano lounged on the front porch of his new headquarters, watching his men load their automobiles with ammunition, spare weapons, and containers of gasoline. He was proud to say he had an army. About fifty-seven men had come from New York to aid him in his cause, including the cousin of Emanuele Bonelli, the Father of the Bonelli Family. About twenty others were expected to arrive by tomorrow afternoon.

Stefano was sending all but three men out to take over the town. He had sent his Consigliere, Tomme, to stand in his place and give orders as orders needed given. It felt good to be the ruler of something, even if that something was just a small town in the middle of nowhere. Crowley paled in comparison to New York City, but at least it was civilized.

Stefano had wanted New York, but the city and state wasn't his for the taking. He would have to fight the remaining four families in order to secure his reign over "Pompeii" as Emanuele Bonelli's youngest son, Raffael, called it. That wasn't a risk worth taking, given the size of those vicious little Families.

The Moretti Family, especially, was not a Family to cross. Nor was the D'Amore Family or the Bonelli Family. The Alicino Family, on the other hand, was weak and susceptible to switching sides on a whim. It depended on who was winning.

Stefano lit a cigarette, his twentieth today. Mama had warned him his habit of smoking three packs of cigarettes a day would eventually kill him. As always, he respected her wisdom, but he was a grown man and taking risks was part of being one. In any case, Mama was sometimes wrong.

"All right, boys," Tomme announced, getting into the driver's seat of his automobile, "let's move!"

Stefano went inside to check on his prisoners. The child was sleeping, but Amanda was wide awake, peering forlornly out the window. Satisfied that they weren't doing anything suspicious, he left the room and went to the kitchen to fix himself a cup of coffee. Soon, he would join his men in town, and declare himself mayor. If he had to kill the current mayor to secure the job, then so be it. If the town attempted to call in higher authority, so be it. He'd kill every last one of them, starting with the meddlesome sheriff and his army of dim-witted deputies.

* * *

They were all over town, these damned bastards. Joe wouldn't stand for it, but there wasn't much he could do in terms of fighting them off and driving them out of town. Rex had warned him not to pick a fight with any of them. They were well-trained and could hit a bullseye from twenty yards away, or was it thirty? Joe didn't know, and he didn't care. That description alone told him he and his deputies would do well to leave these Italians—or Sicilians, what difference did it make?—alone. There was nothing he could do.

Walking along Main Street, he shook his head sadly. He couldn't call in the state police. One of those hooligans had taken out the telephone lines, thus cutting Crowley off from the outside world.

So, what was a man to do when his world was being upset by gangsters from New York?

Unfortunately, Joe didn't have an answer to that. Only God did, but his faith in the Lord was dwindling. Crowley didn't deserve such a fate. There were good people here—good, God-fearing people. They didn't deserve to die at the hands of Catholic bastards thinking they were above everything and everyone, including the law.

The streets were nigh-on empty. Folks were scared to go about their lives. Joe took one good look around, then returned to headquarters. His deputies were loitering about, miserable and angry. They wanted to do something about these no-good Italians, too, but they realized the danger they would be putting the town and themselves in if they even attempted to do their jobs. They hadn't been trained for something like this, they were merely small-town deputies whose duty was to keep the peace and put folks in line when they dared put a toe out of it, not start a street war with a bunch of armed sharpshooters.

"We should have run Rex Armati out of town when we had the chance," Deputy Grant grumbled.

The remark struck a chord in Joe. "Rex is my future kin, Deputy, and I'd thank you not to talk ill about him. His brother is the trouble here. Rex didn't mean for this to happen."

Deputy Grant muttered an apology.

"You men, get ahold of yourselves," Joe ordered sternly. "We ought to stand tall and firm, not hole up in here and moan about our failures. Do your jobs, but don't provoke those fools. We, unfortunately, don't know what they're capable of. What I do know is that they've each got one hell-of-a trigger finger. Now I ain't one to cower, but I sure as hell don't want to go up against 'em."

"Neither do I," Deputy Smith agreed. "I got a wife, and a baby on the way."

"We'll bide our time, gents. And then we will strike," Joe decided. But those words were only said to give his men hope. Joe had no intention of going up against Armati and his men. He wanted to survive, but most importantly, he wanted others to survive. No sense in causing any unnecessary deaths.

Going to his office, he sat at his desk, peered out the window, and scowled when he caught sight of those barbaric men patrolling the streets like soldiers protecting a fort. Getting up, he grabbed and pulled the cord to the blinds so that they fell and cloaked the room in complete darkness. He didn't want to see those ugly mugs anymore—they made him want to storm from these very headquarters, guns a-blazing, and shoot the lot of them to hell.

Maybe he would, but not in this life.

A week, perhaps more, had passed. Folks were getting scared; they refused to come out of their houses, refused to come into town. Some wanted to leave town, but Armati's men had road blocks on every road that led out of Crowley.

"Someone needs to send that fool to an asylum," Annabelle told Joe when he went in for coffee on Saturday morning. "He's crazy. It's time we stand up to him, Joe."

The diner was near empty. The only patrons were two of Armati's soldiers sipping coffee in a corner booth. Annabelle cast them a glare fit to raise the hair on a rabid raccoon's head.

"They're disturbing the peace," she pointed out as she refilled his coffee cup. "They ought to leave, and you ought to be the one to make them."

Joe shuttered as he pictured himself doing just that. "I'd be dead before I issued them an order to surrender or die," he said, quickly banishing the image from his mind. "I haven't had time to court you good and proper."

"I'll tell you what. You be brave for me and rid Crowley of these filth and I'll marry you."

He didn't know if she was being serious or if she was joking to lighten his mood. "Tempting. Real tempting, Annabelle."

"You think long and hard about my offer, Joe."

Joe lifted his mug to her. "Will do, honey."

* * *

Stefano was away in town. It was evening, and the three men whose jobs were to keep Amanda and Billy from escaping were on the front porch engaged in a game of poker. By the sounds of it, they were also drunk.

Amanda tested the window she'd been sitting at since their arrival and was delighted to find it wasn't locked. She lifted it all the way, and a cool evening breeze escaped inside.

"We escapin'?" Billy asked as Amanda peeked her head out.

"Yes, we are. Now stay close to me."

Amanda climbed out, then waited for Billy to do the same. Grabbing his hand, she tugged him towards the woods, her heart racing. They kept to the trees until they came to the main road. Even then, Amanda kept them close to the woods, and if she saw even the suggestion of headlights, they darted into the shadows the trees provided.

"What if we get eaten by mountain lions?" Billy fretted, voice high-pitched.

"Hush now, Billy," Amanda scolded. Mountain lions, she considered, were the least of their problems at this very moment. Stefano was much worse than a mountain lion. He was a rattlesnake, poised to strike at any moment. If he was the least bit provoked, that pistol of his, always at hand, would be the provoker's undoing. A bullet to the head solved all of Stefano's problems.

Amanda didn't know how long they'd walked, and she didn't care. When Crowley Baptist Church and the parsonage where Reverend Etlam and his family lived came into view, she wanted to cry. The reverend, his wife, and son would help them, she was sure of it. They wouldn't turn away lost sheep in need, would they?

Amanda and Billy hurried towards the parsonage. Amanda hammered on the door with one trembling fist.

Mrs. Etlam answered. When she saw them, she gasped and ushered them in. "Daniel!" she called, and her husband came running. "Look! It's Amanda and Billy. My goodness, they're safe!"

"Bring them into the parlor, Sylvia."

Amanda and Billy collapsed on the sofa, exhausted and ready to pass out. Reverend Etlam got his shotgun off the mantle above the fireplace and loaded it. Next, he ordered Mrs. Etlam to lock all the doors.

"I won't allow him to hurt you anymore, my children," he vowed, and Amanda was touched.

"He won't know where we've gone," she said, and hoped she was right.

"In any case, this gun is not leaving my side. Timothy? Where are you boy?"

A gangly kid of fifteen came running when his father called. "Yeah, Dad?"

"Get your gun. Saddle your horse and ride out to the Chandler's. David will want to know Amanda is safe. We could also use a few extra guns."

"Yes, sir."

Mrs. Etlam, of course, had something to say about this. "I protest! Timmy, you are not to go out there! Do you hear me?"

"With all due respect, Mama, you don't wear the pants in this family, Dad does."

"Why, I never!"

"I'll be fine, Mama. I promise."

Mrs. Etlam waved him off. She sniffed and brought out a white handkerchief to dab at her eyes. Composing herself, she brought Amanda and

Billy up to the spare bedroom, then showed Amanda to the bathroom so Amanda could bathe.

"I'll fetch you a change of clothes, darling. You too, young man."

Amanda smiled gratefully. "Thank you, Mrs. Etlam."

"Don't mention it."

Amanda was glad to finally be free of Stefano. That night, she and Billy rested easily, and in the morning, they were refreshed. Timothy hadn't returned yet, which didn't settle well with Mrs. Etlam. She fretted all through breakfast and only managed to get one bite of toast down. Billy, on the other hand, wolfed down a dozen pancakes, three slices of crisp bacon, a serving of eggs, and two pieces of buttered toast. His appetite was impressive, and Reverend Etlam stared at him in amazement.

"I wonder, who will attend church today?" he said, stirring sugar into his coffee. "Or will I be preaching to an invisible congregation?"

"If I was allowed in your church, sir, I'd attend," Billy declared around a mouthful of his third serving of toast.

"Son, everyone's welcome, saint or sinner, white or black, Catholic or Methodist."

"I didn't know that."

"Well, now you do."

After breakfast, Reverend Etlam went outside to survey the surrounding area. When he found only peace and scarcely a soul save for two doves sitting side-by-side in a tree, he herded Mrs. Etlam, Amanda, and Billy to church.

"You got a nice church here, sir," Billy complimented, and Reverend Etlam smiled down at him.

"Why thank you, son."

They hurried into the church and Reverend Etlam quickly shut the door. He looked around at the empty pews, and for a moment, his lips compressed together as if he was deeply disappointed in his absent congregation.

Amanda seated herself in a pew and Billy sat beside her. Reverend Etlam, shotgun in hand, went to his pulpit and stood gazing at the worn leather Bible he'd set on the surface.

"This is mighty awkward," he remarked with sincerity, looking to Amanda, then his wife. "I feel like a fool."

"We'll wait a few more minutes, Daniel," Mrs. Etlam suggested. "Folks might come, you wait and see."

Reverend Etlam shrugged, doubtful.

At that moment, someone burst through the doors, and Amanda jumped, thinking it was Stefano, but when she turned around, she sighed in relief to discover it was only Timothy.

"I brought 'em, Dad," the boy announced, looking pleased with himself. "Mr. Armati, Mr. Moretti, Mr. Chandler, Mr. Mason, *and* Mr. Elwood."

Rex. Amanda got to her feet.

"Did you kill anyone, son?" Reverend Etlam asked eagerly.

Mrs. Etlam went white with shock. "Daniel!"

"Nope," their son said with a tinge of regret in his voice. "I wasn't even detected."

"Amanda!" Rex called.

Amanda's heart fluttered. Her throat burned with raw emotion as her eyes found Rex running up the aisle towards her. She ran, too, and flung her arms around his neck as they met in the middle.

"Rex!" she sobbed, clinging to him.

"I'm here, baby. I'm right here," he soothed, holding her close. "He won't hurt you anymore, I promise."

"But he didn't hurt me. Not physically, anyway."

"Pa!" Billy cried, and laughed as his father swung him up in his arms. "I sure did miss you, Pa. Mama, too."

"We missed you too, son," Solomon said, choking up.

Next, Amanda embraced David, then Solomon. Even Arthur, who flushed crimson.

She returned to Rex and vowed never to leave his side again.

Chapter Fourteen

It wasn't pretty when Stefano found out his two prisoners were gone. The thing about Stefano, when he became enraged, he didn't yell or scream or raise his voice an octave or three. He spoke in a deadly soft voice that could send fear through even the toughest of men.

Several of Stefano's men, including Enzo, stood outside the cabin in tense silence. They were waiting to see the outcome. The three sentries who'd been on duty the night of the woman and child's escape were either going to pay for their lack of competence or be pardoned. Enzo was betting on the former.

A blood-curdling scream rent the air, then another. Enzo felt chills go up his spine. It seemed Stefano wasn't in the mood to be merciful today. Or any day, for that matter, but tensions were high and everyone knew how bad he wanted to see his brother dead. The obsession was going to eat him alive if he didn't do the deed soon.

The front door banged open and Stefano emerged from the cabin, his hands covered in blood. It was splattered on his face, too. Enzo whipped out his handkerchief from his pocket and silently handed it to his boss.

"At least I know I can count on you," Stefano growled, snatching up the handkerchief. He used it to mop the blood from his face, then hands. "Enzo, take two men and dispose of the bodies before they start to stink."

"Yes sir," Enzo said obediently. As much as he hated the duty of cleaning up Stefano's messes, he wasn't about to get on the man's bad side today. Not ever, come to it.

Stefano stalked away and got into his automobile. He roared out a moment later, probably headed back to town to make sure no one got out of line.

Enzo beckoned to Matteo and Antonio. "You heard the boss," he said. "Let's go clean up his mess."

Matteo made a face, but didn't dare complain. Both he and Antonio followed Enzo into the cabin, where they found the bodies of the three sentries lying in heaps, their throats slit. It was a gruesome sight.

"Poor bastards," Antonio muttered under his breath.

Enzo found himself getting nervous. He felt a cold sweat break out on his face, and wondered for the longest moment what would spare him from having the same fate as these three men lying dead on the floor. Sure he was loyal as they came, and he'd always been there at Stefano's every beck and call, but there had been too much death and gore as of late for his peace of mind. He had a wife and a couple of kids to look after. If Stefano suddenly snapped, and Enzo happened to be in his line of fire...

"Enzo," Antonio said, gripping Enzo's shoulder and shaking. "Let's get to work, pal."

Enzo swallowed down the vile and nodded. He crouched down to hoist one of the bodies to his shoulder. The poor bastard wouldn't get a proper burial, and that didn't sit well with him. He wondered if the man had family who'd be missing him.

This wasn't what the Tradition was supposed to be like. Stefano had more or less made his own code to satisfy his whim, and innocent folks were paying for it. Enzo was beginning to wonder if he was on the wrong side. Thoughts like that would get him killed, he knew, but he cared more for his honor than what the consequences might be.

* * *

Rex sat in one of the pews with Amanda and Al. The church was full now, full of scared men, women, and children seeking a safe haven. Stefano's men were everywhere. They had asserted their dominance, and now, they were unstoppable.

"Your brother is a very sick man," Annabelle remarked from the pew behind.

Rex turned around to acknowledge her with a nod. "I know that, ma'am." He had known since the day Stefano had tried to shoot his brains out when they were kids.

"What are we going to do? Folks are gettin' real scared."

Rex got to his feet. Amanda and Al gave him questioning looks, but they didn't speak. Folks watched him as he walked down the aisle to the pulpit and stood at it. He rested his hands on the smooth surface of the wood and cleared his throat.

"People of Crowley." He spoke loud enough for those in the back to hear. "Some of you may be angry. Actually, all of you may be angry. You probably want to hold me responsible for our predicament, and I don't blame you." He heaved a sigh. "My brother ... he needs to be stopped. We can either work together or we can stay holed up in here until he decides to blow us all to hell.

"I don't expect you to trust me. It would help matters if you did, though. I've got a plan, but I need help. Who's with me?"

Amanda, Al, Solomon, Arthur, David, and the rest of the Chandler hands stood up. Annabelle hesitated, then joined them. A few others stood up as well, including Timothy Etlam.

Rex nodded approval. "Good. Those of you who are too afraid to go out into the streets, stay here," he instructed, leaving the pulpit and striding down the aisle towards Amanda and the others. "The rest of you follow me."

He led his small army outside. It was mid-morning and already, the sun at its zenith, the heat was somewhat overbearing. The air was dry.

An automobile pulled into the parking lot. By the looks of it, it belonged to one of Stefano's men. Immediately on guard, Rex prepared to pull the hammer back on the rifle David had lent him. Al stiffened.

"If he makes a threatenin' move, blow his brains out," he suggested, flourishing his pistol.

"Let's hope it don't come to that," Solomon said wearily.

The automobile came to a stop, and the driver's door opened. Rex recognized Enzo as he stepped out and looked cautiously around. He was unarmed, but who was to say he didn't have a pistol hidden in a shoulder holster beneath that tailored sport coat of his?

Rex watched Enzo carefully, curious yet cautious. Poor fellow looked nervous. He kept looking around as if he would be ambushed at any moment by a gang of hoodlums.

"Did the boss send you, Enzo?" Al asked tersely.

Enzo scuffed one Oxford-clad foot on the pavement. "No. I came on my own accord," he said nervously. Sweat beaded his forehead.

"What do you want?" Rex demanded gently, sensing Enzo's unease. The man obviously had a purpose, and it wasn't a purpose meant to benefit Stefano, that was for certain.

"I gotta family, see. Stefano, he's goin' crazy. I think there's some loose screws in his brain or somethin', I don't know. He's gone far enough, harassing these poor folks just to get revenge."

Rex nodded. "I agree."

"Call me a turncoat, but I'm switchin' sides."

Al looked surprised. He looked at Rex, mouth slightly agape.

Rex grinned. "Welcome to the misfits, friend," he said, slapping Enzo on the back.

"I can provide you with valuable information," Enzo declared enthusiastically, looking eagerly from Rex to Al. "I overheard Stefano makin' plans with Nicola. Soon, they're going to take hostages and if you don't show your mug, Stefano's going to execute them one by one."

"Goddamnit," Rex swore, raking his hands through his hair and mussing it up. "I don't know what to do, Enzo. If I turn myself in, he'll only keep his iron fist closed around this town. There's only one option left to us, and that's to evacuate the town."

"You mean sneak them over the town line into Canesburg?" Solomon asked, and Rex nodded.

"But first, we'll need a distraction."

Al's eyes fairly gleamed with excitement. "Oh, boy!" he exclaimed, sounding like a little kid in a toy shop. "You name what needs blowin' up and I'll do it."

"There's the old abandoned mill," Amanda suggested, taking Rex's hand and squeezing. "It's on Hummingbird Creek Road. It ought to go up in moments, and it's close to town so Stefano will see it."

"I know where we can find some dynamite," Enzo offered, eager to redeem himself in Rex's and Al's eyes.

"All right, here's the plan," Rex announced, and everyone gathered round him. "Al, you're gonna take Enzo and Timothy and get that dynamite, then, you're gonna go blow that old mill to the sky. While Stefano and his men run towards the source in frantic alarm, Amanda, David, Solomon, Annabelle, and myself will be in charge of evacuating folks." He gestured to Arthur and the hands now. "Arthur, take these men and go to the town line. Make sure you get rid of any obstacles, if you get my meaning."

"Oh, I got your meaning all right, Rex. You can count on us."

Rex nodded. He was counting on all of them, especially the team in charge of blowing up the mill. He knew Al and Solomon would pull through, but he wasn't so sure he could trust Enzo. For all he knew, Stefano had sent Enzo to act as a spy.

Rex pulled Al aside to tell him this. Al assured him he would keep a close eye on Enzo, then slapped his back and went to join his team, who were loading up in Enzo's automobile.

Al claimed shotgun, wanting to keep an eye on Enzo. His pistol was in reach should Enzo pull any stunts, but Al was hoping the Sicilian was on their side and not acting as a spy for Stefano.

Timothy looked nervous yet exhilarated. Al wasn't so sure he liked the idea of a teenaged boy coming along on a dangerous mission, but he trusted Rex's instincts; and besides, the kid had heart, Al would give him that.

"So where's this dynamite?" Timothy asked Enzo, and quickly added, "Sir."

"We've got some hidden at Ms. Lind's home. Should be easy to retrieve."

"No guards?"

"No guards, unless Stefano's changed his mind as of late."

Al didn't fancy getting killed tonight. He intended to live a long, healthy life, raise a brood of kids with a pretty wife, and die old when his time came. He was certain the only way this could be achieved was to leave his Family. If it came down to that, he would give that life up for good. But today ... Today, he was a man of honor, a man of Tradition. He intended to serve his Family and his allies until he saw fit to leave them.

They arrived at the late Ms. Lind's house. No guards to be seen. The three men filed out of the automobile and crept towards the dark, empty little house, and Enzo used a spare key to gain access.

"This place gives me the spooks," Timothy remarked in a whisper. "Suppose Ms. Lind comes to haunt us?"

"What are you, a boy or man? I suggested you choose," Enzo whispered back, but not unkindly.

"Hey, ease up on the kid, will you? This place gives me the spooks, too," Al confessed unashamedly.

Enzo gestured to a door leading down to the basement. "Dynamite is down here, fellas," he pointed out, opening the door. He grinned at Al. "You first, Al."

"Me?" Al shook his head and took a step back. "Oh, no. I ain't gonna go first."

"What's the matter? Afraid of the dark?"

"I don't trust you not to shove the kid and I down the steps and lock us up so you can go tell your boss you captured the infamous Al Moretti."

Enzo looked hurt, but he shrugged it off and made to descend. "Okay, I'll go."

For a moment, Al felt guilty, but he quickly brushed the feeling aside in favor of suspicion, which was still very much present in his gut. When he would allow trust to take the place of the mistrust he so strongly felt was entirely up to Enzo.

Al took to the stairs last and shut the door behind them. Enzo turned on the little lamp affixed to the ceiling and a gentle glow bathed the somewhat cramped basement. A couple of crates of dynamite were stacked in one corner, enough to blow an entire town to the sky. They would only need a few for this mission.

After they had retrieved what they'd come for, they loaded their stash in the trunk of Enzo's automobile and drove off in search of the abandoned mill.

Located seven miles down Hummingbird Creek Road, the mill had once been an imposing building, but no more. In some places, the building looked unsafe. Glass and bricks and all sorts of debris lay scattered all over the ground.

"Wanna know a secret?" Timothy said, shoving his hands in the pockets of his jeans. He didn't wait for them to say yes. "I shared my first kiss here."

"Is this really relevant right now?" Enzo asked, although his eyes shone in quiet amusement.

"No, sir, I reckon it's not, I just like to recall fond memories. Especially when I'm back at the place I haven't been in years."

"My first kiss wasn't so memorable," Al said, just to keep the conversation going. The lightheartedness and innocence of first kisses offered a distraction from the intensity of a dangerous mission.

"What happened, sir?" Timothy prompted with subdued eagerness.

"I was eleven. I didn't like her, but she liked me, and, well … She said she'd give me a candy bar if I kissed her. Bein' the gullible sort when it came to candy, I accepted her offer." Al paused as they picked their way across a graveyard of glass and twisted metal. "Turned out she didn't have a candy bar. I got swindled all for a lousy kiss."

"Gee, I'm sorry."

"What for?" Al chuckled, amused. "I was young. It happens to the best of us, kid."

Enzo pried open a squeaky, rotting door and the three of them went inside, lugging their boxes of dynamite. This place would go up for sure, what with the dilapidated state this building was in.

Enzo had a plan. He instructed them to set the boxes down, then rushed outside to fetch something from his automobile. He returned with a can of gasoline, and poured it over each box, then made a trail to the door through which they had entered. Al was wary about this plan, but he also didn't care how this mission played out as long as it was successful.

"I'll get the car running," Enzo told Al, "while you light the fuse."

Al pointed at himself. "Me?" He shook his head. "Let's allow Timothy to light it. Get a taste of his first explosion."

Timothy's eyes gleamed as Enzo gave him a match and instructed him to light it, drop it, and run. The kid practically ran to his assigned position as Al and Enzo got into the escape vehicle.

"You sure this is a good idea?" Enzo asked, watching Timothy through the windshield. "After all, he's only a kid."

"Let him live his life."

Timothy struck the match. He dropped it, turned, and ran, literally diving into the automobile through the door Al had left open for him. Enzo stepped on the gas pedal and they roared away in a cloud of dust. As they were turning onto Hummingbird Creek Road, the mill blew in a blaze of brilliant glory. Al shared a grin with Enzo.

Timothy whooped.

"Yeah!" he cried, pumping the air with his fist in victory. "That ought to cause a decent enough distraction."

"Here's hoping," Al said.

* * *

"Golly day!" Billy exclaimed from where he sat perched on the railing of the steps that led up to the church.

"And there's our distraction," Rex announced solemnly, watching the orange and gray blaze reach for the sky.

He had relayed his plan to the folks inside the church. Some were horrified by the explosion bit (particularly the mayor), but they were too eager to escape the impending chaos to demand why Rex would do such a thing as blow up an old, washed-up relic they considered an important part of the town's humble history.

Town was a few blocks away. Reverend Etlam and quite a few others had offered to help coax people from their houses and apartments. Rex was grateful for the extra help, as he realized the small group originally supposed to help him wouldn't be able to cover enough ground before Stefano came back.

Rex didn't consider the fact that Stefano might have only sent a few of his men to investigate. He carelessly started off for town in Al's automobile, going solely on instinct and personal knowledge. If he knew Stefano, that bastard brother of his had sent the whole gang to investigate the source of the explosion, and he himself would be at the lead. Stefano sure did love a good thrill. He always had.

"Rex, I'm scared," Amanda announced, sliding over to him and looping her arm through his. "What if one of us doesn't make it tonight?"

"Don't talk like that, sweetheart. Of course we're gonna make it. After this chaos is over, we're gonna get married and I'm gonna build you that little house on the hill."

Amanda teared up, getting all sentimental on him. He smiled at her tenderly and pressed a quick kiss to her temple.

"What are you going to do to your brother, Rex?" she asked hesitantly.

He shrugged. He hadn't decided yet, and told her so. He was weighing two options in his mind: option one was making a citizen's arrest and hauling his worthless brother to jail and leaving him in Sheriff Chandler's hands. Rex would be sure Stefano was tried in some big court in New York, found guilty, and taken to prison where he would spend the remainder of his days.

Option two was simply this: death. If it came down to it, Rex would kill Stefano and that would be the end of it.

Rex was veering towards the honorable side. Option one sounded more favorable.

He parked at the very edge of town, and reached for the door handle. Amanda lay a hand on his arm, and he paused to look at her, waiting for her to speak. She simply brought her lips to his and they shared a long, tender kiss, after which they both got out and joined the others.

The plan was to coax folks from their homes and urge them to go to the church. There was a large section of little white houses on Strawberry Lane, and another on Charlotte Street. There was also an apartment building on Main Street, but thankfully it was the only one.

After folks were assembled at the church, they would be led by David and Reverend Etlam to the town line. Rex predicted some would refuse to leave, and as he and Amanda, Solomon and a few others went down Charlotte Street knocking on doors and instructing people where to go, he realized the "some" was quickly amounting to a "multitude".

Rex couldn't worry about the ones who refused to leave. He just prayed they remained out of sight from Stefano, who appeared to be in the killing mood, which he was well known for back in New York. Rex recalled a time when Stefano had shot up an entire neighborhood because he had lost a round of Poker. The memory made him shudder.

About fifty-four people were coaxed from their homes and herded to the church like frantic sheep by David and Reverend Etlam. Rex felt better knowing he had done his best to protect these people, even if there were some too stubborn to listen to reason.

"What is the meaning of this?" Sheriff Chandler demanded as Rex and Amanda made their way down the sidewalk towards the edge of town where they had left the automobiles. "Why the hell are you drivin' folks out? They were safe where they were, Armati!"

"I don't see you protecting anyone," Rex retorted sharply. "Stefano plans to start shootin' the place up. The least I can do is warn folks before he does."

"You don't have to get excited," the sheriff grumbled, taking off his hat and slapping it against his thigh. "Where are those bastards, anyway?"

"Didn't you hear the explosion, Uncle?" Amanda asked.

"Explosion? What explosion?"

"Never mind what explosion," Rex snapped impatiently. Time was running out. "Sheriff, my brother will be back any minute now. I suggest you rally your men. I sense a battle coming."

Sheriff Chandler jammed his hat back on his head and jabbed a finger at Rex's chest. "Look here, you, I'm about this close"–he demonstrated just how close with two, bony index fingers–"to shootin' that damned brother of yours in the head. 'Cept that ain't possible because I can't get a clean shot and besides … I'd be killed before I even pulled the trigger, what with him havin' a big army."

At that moment, Enzo's automobile roared down the street. With a screech of tires on pavement, the vehicle came to an abrupt stop and Al popped out of the passenger side, as giddy as a kid who'd just pulled a prank on his friends.

"Did it work?" he asked, all smiles.

Rex made a sweeping motion with one hand to indicate the emptiness of the streets. "It sure did."

Sheriff Chandler crossed his arms over his chest in disapproval. "I don't even want to know," he grumbled, making to head back into the station.

"Sir—Sheriff—we could use your help," Rex pleaded, and the old man turned around, narrowing eyes so like Amanda's into slits.

"What do you think I was doing? Fleein' to safety like a yellow-bellied coward? No, I was just about to fetch my men."

"Thank you, sir."

He waved impatiently. "Don't mention it. It's my job to protect this town."

"Boy, is Stefano gonna be cross," Al said, and smiled so wide, Rex thought his friend's face might split. "I'd used a stronger word but we're in mixed company here."

"Hey, I know lots'a swear words," Timothy announced and dared anyone to contradict him by crossing his arms over his chest and jutting his chin out.

Rex patted the kid on the shoulder. "Go home, son," he ordered the boy. "I'm sure your mother is worried."

"But I want to stay and fight."

"Amanda's not gonna stay. Nor is Miss Annabelle. They'll take you back to the church."

"But—"

"No buts. I like your courage, but this is no place for a boy who's got a long life ahead of him."

Timothy heaved a crestfallen sigh. "Yes, sir," he mumbled, as Amanda took his arm and guided him in the direction of the vehicles. Rex called her back so he could toss her the keys to Al's automobile.

"Amanda..." He took her hand and gave it a gentle squeeze, not wanting to sound like he was saying good-bye. That was too permanent. "I love you."

Amanda smiled, understanding. "I love you too, Rex." She let go of his hand and walked away.

Rex smiled after her but as soon as she was gone, he allowed his lips to curve down in a frown. He had doubts, doubts that involved ultimate annihilation, deaths including his own, and a victory for Stefano. Sure, these doubts were a bit exaggerated but that didn't stop them from plaguing him and making him feel like a failure. Looking at Al, he realized his best friend was confident. No worries shown in those wise blue eyes, and an easy, relaxed smile lent to his carefree look. Rex wished he could be more like Al.

"Are you sure you want to do this?" Rex asked. "It could mean your life."

Al responded as Rex knew he would. "Pal, I'm with you 'til the end."

Rex started forward, resting his rifle on his shoulder. "Let's go."

Stefano was waiting for Rex in front of the court house, surrounded by his men. They were all armed, their trigger-fingers itchy. As Rex walked up the deserted street, Al by his side, Sheriff Chandler joined him with his deputies, followed by David's ranch hands and a couple of other armed men who had decided to join Rex in the fight to take back their town. They weren't an army, but they were determined, and that was all a man needed to win.

"That little distraction of yours was clever, Alexander," Stefano called out. "But it was blatantly obvious. I know what goes on in that head of yours, brother. Nothing you do surprises me."

Rex laughed without humor. "You'd be thrilled to know I think the same about you," he said coolly.

Stefano's gaze drifted away from Rex and he scoffed. "Do you really believe you can overrun me with that pathetic little army of yours?"

Behind him, Rex heard Sheriff Chandler mutter a dark expletive under his breath. He smiled. These men were angry, all right. If Stefano kept up with his goads, he'd soon find out just how capable a group of small-town men armed with rifles and shotguns were.

"I didn't come to fight. But if that's the way you want it, then that's the way it's gonna be."

An automobile roared up behind Rex and the men. Enzo got out, his face stoic. He grabbed a rifle and hoisted it on his shoulder.

"Ah, it's about time you showed up," Stefano growled. "Where the hell have you been, man?"

"Sortin' my thoughts," Enzo answered coldly. "I decided to place my allegiances in a man of honor, and that ain't you, Stefano."

Stefano's face became stony. "I expect more from my men." He reached swiftly into his coat and pulled out his pistol, and without missing a beat, fired. Enzo looked surprised, then dismayed. Blood bloomed on his chest.

"Jesus Christ," Al exclaimed.

Enzo toppled over, dead before he hit the ground. Rex saw his lifeless body, thought of the man's wife and children, who would now be widowed and fatherless, and he saw red.

"Rex," Solomon warned. He put a restraining hand on Rex's shoulder, which nearly trembled with his rage. "Keep a cool head. Think of Amanda."

"I am, goddamnit," Rex hissed under his breath. He took a deep breath and exhaled. That didn't calm him much, but nothing short of pummeling Stefano's face into the ground would satisfy the anger bubbling up inside him.

Stefano smiled, a slow smile that revealed his satisfaction over getting his brother riled up.

"It's a shame, really," he said without emotion. "Enzo was a good man. But I detest traitors."

Rex's grip on his riffle tightened until his knuckles turned white. "You know what I detest? Men without honor." He raised the riffle. "Now I don't want things to get ugly, but I won't hesitate to pull this trigger."

Stefano's smile faded. "You and I both know you don't have the guts to pull that trigger," he said in a low, mocking voice.

Rex's finger hovered over the trigger. In response, Stefano's men raised their own weapons, prepared to defend him, prepared to kill if Stefano gave the order. Rex swallowed. If he pulled the trigger now, every man standing at his side was going to die. He didn't want that.

"This is between you and I," he said. "Call your men off."

Stefano held up a hand and slowly, but with reluctance, his men lowered their guns.

Stefano stepped forward. "This is between me and you, yes, but I'm calling all the shots."

"I only ask one thing."

"What is it?"

"Leave these people alone." Rex spread his arms wide. "Leave them to live their lives and never return. Those are my conditions."

Stefano nodded. "Your conditions are accepted." He moved his coat aside to reveal the gun holstered at his side. "Now it's my turn. Let us finish what I came here to do. I am giving you a chance to die honorably, and that's in a fair fight."

Rex lowered his head. It wasn't in defeat, but acceptance of his fate. There was no possible way to end this without some form of destruction and death. He greatly cherished the last few months, as they'd been the happiest of his life. Perhaps now it was his time to go.

"I'm not goin' to kill you, Stefano." Rex threw down the gun. "Not today, not in a million years. You're my brother. If you're still set on killing me, I ain't stoppin' you."

"Alexander," Al hissed. "What are you doin', you crazy bastard?"

Rex turned his head to smile at him. "You've been a good friend to me, Al. Tell Amanda she's the best thing that's ever happened to me." He looked away from Al and nodded at Solomon. "Solomon, thank you."

Solomon looked confused. "For what?"

"For bein' my equal. I learned how to respect because of you. You taught me that we're all the same, and I owe you my gratitude."

Rex stepped forward to meet his brother. He expected to be afraid, but he felt nothing. Not even fear.

Stefano raised his gun, his hand trembling. "Just so you know, Rex, I don't want to kill you, either," he muttered in a voice that was hoarse. "But in the end, it has to be that way."

He pulled the trigger. As the shot rang out, Rex was thrust aside forcefully. He landed hard on the pavement. There was pain, but it wasn't from a bullet. Sitting up, feeling momentarily stunned, he looked and saw Solomon lying on the ground, his shirt red with blood.

"No, no, no!" Rex cried. He scrambled over to Solomon on his hands and knees and pressed his hands into the wound to try and stop the bleeding.

"Don't," Solomon sputtered, pushing Rex's hand away. "Just listen, boy."

Rex gripped the hand Solomon gave him, tying hard to fight the overwhelming pain that stabbed at his heart.

"You're wrong about yourself," Solomon went on weakly. "You're a good man, Rex. You go and make Miss Amanda a happy woman."

Rex nodded, his throat feeling tight. He was afraid to speak in fear of revealing his true emotions.

"Tell ... Ellen Sue ... and Billy ... I love them." Then Solomon became still, his eyes gazing lifelessly at the sky. Rex looked away. It took him several moments to recover his bearings, which had nearly been lost.

He realized, as he sat there by the side of the man who had once been his friend, that he'd been giving a second chance. But he didn't feel deserving of it.

"Rex?" Al put his hand on Rex's shoulder. "Talk to me, pal."

"I'm fine," Rex said hoarsely. He slowly got to his feet and turned to face Stefano.

Stefano was standing there, looking bemused. The change was unsettling. Rex cautiously went towards him so as not to alarm his brother or his men. No one moved.

"Stefano," Rex said, surprised that he had no hostile feelings for him. Solomon wouldn't have wanted that.

"He actually gave his life for you," Stefano muttered, more to himself than Rex.

Rex reached his brother and pried the gun from Stefano's hand. He tossed it aside. Stefano's men stared, unsure what to do without guidance from their boss.

"Sheriff, I could use some help," Rex called.

Sheriff Chandler jogged over and handed Rex a pair of cuffs. Stefano didn't try to fight when Rex put them on. Something had come over him, something that had subdued the rage that had been roaring inside him like an angered lion. Rex wasn't sure what to think about this.

Instead, he turned to address Stefano's men. "I suggest you men run on home now," he said. "Not unless you want to be arrested and charged for disrupting the peace."

Nicola hesitated, then nodded curtly to the rest of the men. They followed him off to where they'd left their automobiles, and were soon gone, disappearing around the bend.

It was all over. Rex couldn't quite take it all in at once, afraid if he did, he wouldn't be able to handle himself well. He was thinking about Solomon's sacrifice and still feeling undeserving of it. Ellen Sue and Billy came to mind, tormenting him.

He sat there on the top step of the courthouse, staring off into the distance, wondering why life had so much twists and turns. Everything was unexpected. He hadn't expected to live, but here he was.

You're a good man, Rex...

Solomon's words kept replaying in his mind. Rex closed his eyes, wondering if he judged himself too harshly. He wished he could see himself through the eyes of others. He tried to be a good man, but he'd made too much mistakes and bad decisions in his life to deserve that title.

But Solomon had believed in him. He'd proven that by giving his life so that Rex could live. Somehow, Rex would make sure the man's sacrifice wasn't in vain.

Someone touched Rex's shoulder. He opened his eyes and saw Amanda standing there, and his resolve all but broke.

"It's all over," he said.

"Yes," Amanda murmured.

Rex exhaled sharply. "He's gone. Solomon. He…" He squeezed his eyes shut, but he could no longer hold back. A traitorous tear escaped his lashes.

"Oh, Rex…" Amanda gathered him up in her arms and held him while he unashamedly cried into her neck. It felt good to unleash what he'd been holding in for far too long. Amanda stroked his hair, whispering words of comfort to him.

She was his rock. Rex would indeed make her a happy woman for the rest of their lives. His journey to find her had been one strewn with many obstacles, but it had been worth every step and every hardship. He thanked Solomon for giving him this second chance, and he thanked God for men like Solomon Elwood.

Epilogue

June, 1954

Rex wiped sweat and dirt from his brow as he headed up to the little white house he'd built with his own hands, aided by David and Arthur. It wasn't a grand house with lots of fancy things to go with it, but it had all the things a man could want, and Rex wouldn't trade it for anything in the world.

For the past four-and-a-half years, he'd raised up his own little ranch after buying a small two-hundred acre spread. He'd decided to raise horses instead of cattle, seeing as he liked them better, and his operation was now thriving. He was proud of what he'd accomplished and he had his wife to thank. Without her by his side he didn't think he could have done any of this and succeeded; after all, he used to be a city slicker with no knowledge at all on the art of ranching.

Rex climbed the porch steps and slipped out of his boots. He heard giggling and couldn't help the smile that tugged at his lips. That sound never ceased to fill him with joy. He walked inside the kitchen and found Amanda there instructing their four-year-old daughter, Rose, how to make bread. There was a dusting of flour on her dress and on her cherubic cheeks. She was the picture of innocence, with dark curly hair and magnificent blue eyes. She was Rex's angel.

"Daddy!" Rose cried, jumping off the chair she'd been standing on and running to him with open arms. Rex swung her up and gave her a hug.

"How's my little gal?" he asked.

"Good. Daddy, you smell," Rose said, and Rex couldn't help but laugh.

"So do you, but all sweet, like roses and sunshine."

Rex put his daughter down and went to kiss his wife. He rested his hand on her abdomen, round with their second child. He was hoping for another daughter, but Amanda wanted a son. She was convinced that, soon, they'd have a little Rex running around the house.

"Rose is right," Amanda said, laughing. "You do smell, Rex."

"I promise to wash up real good before dinner," Rex assured her.

"We're having your favorite, Daddy," Rose informed him. "Pot roast and potatoes."

"Sounds mighty good."

"And I'm helping Mama make bread."

Amanda smiled. "You're doing a fine job, too, honey. Oh, Rex, before I forget, Ellen Sue and Billy are coming over for supper, and there's a letter that came for you on the hall table. It's from Al."

Rex nodded and went out to the hall to get the letter. He and Al had been corresponding back-and-forth after promising they'd stay in touch. Al wasn't a man who said a lot in his letters, but he kept Rex up-to-date of the happenings in the city.

Rex opened the letter carefully with his pocket knife and took out a neatly-folded piece of paper.

Dear Rex,

You wouldn't believe the heat wave we've been having here in New York. Not that I mind, but it gets real annoying having to listen to other folks complain about it. I say if they've got a problem with the heat, they can haul their bums to the arctic where they'd freeze and I wouldn't have to listen to them anymore.

Anyhow, not much is going on here, but I sense a change. There's something big on the horizon but I don't know what. I hope it's nothing bad, if you get my meaning.

Speaking of changes, I'm thinking of finding me a girl and settling down. It's about time, I think. You always sound so damn happy in your letters, and when you send me photographs of Rosie, it makes me wonder if I'd be a good father or not.

Say hello to Rosie and Amanda for me.

Yours truly,
Al

Rex put the letter away, tucking it into the pocket of his pants. He hoped Al found himself a lovely, good-hearted woman to settle down with. Al was a good man, and he deserved the best.

He wondered what kind of big change his friend was talking about, but decided not to worry about it. Supper was almost ready and he still had to get cleaned up.

By the time Rex had showered and changed, Ellen Sue and Billy had arrived. Billy, who was almost twelve, was getting tall. He was still scrawny but he more than made up for it with the strength in his arms. He was a bright kid, and Rose adored him. Billy had told Amanda when she was carrying Rose that, if Amanda had a daughter, he was going to marry her someday. Rex didn't know how he felt about that. As a father, the thought of his daughter being sweet on anyone didn't sit well with him; he was very protective of her.

Rex gave Ellen Sue a kiss on the cheek. "How are you doing?" he asked. Since her husband's death, Ellen Sue had held up well, but it wasn't hard to miss the sadness ever-present in her eyes.

"I'm doing fine, Rex," Ellen Sue answered, giving his cheek an affectionate pat. "I take each day as it comes."

"That's good."

"I ought to be asking you that, you know. You're about to be the father of two young'uns. If it's a boy, like Miss Amanda says, God help you."

Rex couldn't decide whether or not she was joking with him, but didn't ask. He went to the screen door and looked out, his heart warming when he saw Billy pushing Rose on the swing that hung from the branch of a big old oak tree. The smiles on their faces were infectious. He watched them a moment, hoping their future was going to be one of promise. He knew they'd face hardships, but there was no such thing as an easy path, and as long as they knew they had a loving home to come to when the day was done, they'd be all right.

Rex felt peace fill him. He never thought he'd experience it, but now that he had, he knew he was complete. If only Al could find it, too. Rex would write him back tonight and wish him the best of luck in his endeavors, hoping that perhaps someday he'd be just as content as Rex was now.

* * *

Mrs. Armati—now Bonanno—looked like someone had spilled a bucket of sunshine over her, if that was possible. She looked ten years younger, too, and as she pecked Al on the cheek and thanked him for everything he'd done for her these past few years, Al decided the change was miraculous.

Today, Mrs. Bonanno was leaving for Wyoming with her new husband, Marcus, to see her grandchildren. After the visit, the new husband and wife were taking off for California to start a new life and Al couldn't be happier for them.

Now, Mrs. Bonanno pressed a key and an envelope in Al's hand, and smiled tenderly at him. "I've arranged everything with Mr. Steinfeldt," she explained upon his quizzical look. "This is the lease and the key to my apartment. I'd like you to take care of it for me. I know you have already got a home in Lorenville, but should you become tired of suburban life, the apartment is here and waiting. If you want it, of course."

Al was touched, but he had no use for an apartment. Still, he accepted Mrs. Bonanno's offer with a thank you and a smile. Who knows? It might come in handy someday.

"Mr. Bonanno is here, Mrs. Armati—I mean Bonanno," Gabriel announced as he came down the hall towards them. "Shall I inform him you're ready?"

"Yes, Gabriel, thank you."

"It's my pleasure."

Al picked up Mrs. Bonanno's suitcases and followed her outside where a tall, handsome Italian stood waiting, a wide, friendly smile on his lips. He was a nice guy, Al thought, loading the suitcases in the trunk of Mr. Bonanno's automobile. He didn't belong to a Family, but he was of good Italian stock, and was the friendliest guy Al had ever met. A widower of ten years, he and Mrs. Armati had met at the *Iris* and got to talking. Soon, they were courting, and a year after their courtship had begun, Marcus had popped the question. A small wedding to which Al and his family and a few other close friends and relatives had been invited was held at a small Catholic Church in New Rochelle, where Mr. Bonanno lived. Rex and Amanda couldn't make it, but Mrs. Armati had understood and didn't fault her son for missing her wedding.

"I'm going to miss you dreadfully," Gabriel confessed, a sad smile on his lips. "You were a pleasant tenant and a good friend."

Mrs. Bonanno kissed Gabriel's cheek. "And you a good landlord, Gabriel. Tell you sisters good-bye for me."

"I will. Have a safe trip."

"Thank you."

She turned to Al, now, and embraced him. They said good-bye, and she and her new husband drove away.

Al went home to Lorenville and his empty house on Maple Berry Street. As he was coming through his front door, the telephone in the kitchen started to ring and he dashed to get it.

"Hello?"

"Al, it's me. Luke."

"What's wrong? You sound morose."

"Peter gave me a message to pass on."

"Peter who?"

"Peter Di Stasi, of the Alicino Family."

Al picked up the base and brought it to the table, where he settled down in a chair and prepared himself for whatever his brother had to say. "What's the message?" he prompted.

"Peter wants you to meet him in front of that swanky nightclub a couple blocks from the *Iris* at seven tonight. He says he's got somethin' to tell you. Could be a trap."

"Yeah. The Alicinos never did like us Morettis very much."

Luke sighed, the sound coming out crackly on Al's end. "It may be important, too."

"Who knows? I'll go. I'll be vigilant, I promise."

"If you're assassinated, Ma will kill me. Good luck." Before he hung up, Al heard him mutter, "This is a fool's errand."

The line went dead.

Al returned the base to the counter and checked his wristwatch. He went to the living room, and from the big book shelf in the corner he grabbed the hollow book he kept there and opened it. Inside was his pistol, hidden for emergencies. He grabbed it and tucked it inside his inner jacket pocket. Now, he grabbed the keys to his automobile and hurried out.

Al arrived at the *Blue Sparrow*, the nightclub a few blocks from the *Iris*. He had a bad feeling in the pit of his belly, but he chose to ignore it. Peter was the nervous sort. He was also a fool and prone to acts of cowardice. If he intended to kill Al, he'd probably have someone hide in some building or an alleyway across the street with a sniper rifle. But an assassination attempt was unlikely because no matter how much the Morettis and the Alicinos hated each other, they would never do anything so stupid as to provoke a war by killing their enemy.

The *Blue Sparrow* appeared to be closed. Al stuffed his hands in his pockets and stared up at the sky, mesmerized. He smiled. It wasn't as pretty as the Wyoming sky, but it sure was something.

Al felt something cool and smooth in one of his pockets. He closed his fingers around it and retracted his hand. Uncurling his fingers, he frowned at the ring lying in his palm, glinting in the low lighting of the street lamps. It was the ring Mrs. Bonanno–then Armati–had given to him to give to Rex. The thing of it was, Al had never felt giving the ring to Rex was the right thing to do, not then when he had the chance, and not now because Rex seemed happy to remain in Wyoming on his little ranch with Amanda and their children. Giving this ring to Rex would signify many things, including a load of responsibilities which would be unceremoniously dumped on Rex's shoulders.

Perhaps when the time was right, Al would give Rex this ring. But until then, he would carry it with him as a reminder the Armati Family was Fatherless and sorely in need of a leader.

"Hey, you."

Al looked up, and his heart did a somersault as his eyes froze on the cop coming towards him.

"You Al Moretti?"

"I am," Al confirmed.

"Put your hands where we can see them. You're under arrest."

Aghast, Al did as he was told, and a second cop materialized to cuff him. He was promptly and unceremoniously forced into the back of a cramped police automobile and driven to the police station, where he was tossed into a holding cell. Confused, his head swirling with scenarios, he simply stood there, wondering if Peter had set him up. It was a possibility. That dirty rat!

Al muttered a curse under his breath. Even if he was allowed one call, he wouldn't call any one of his family members to come bail him out because he didn't want to endanger them like that. Besides, he had distanced himself from them in the last few years and he didn't feel right calling upon them for help.

There was always the Bradens, or the Steinfeldts, but he didn't feel right calling them up, either.

Al sat down. Still wondering what he was framed for, he put his head in hands and decided the only thing left to do was accept his fate. Perhaps by some stroke of luck he'd get out of here.

All he had to do was wait.

And that's exactly what he did.

CPSIA information can be obtained
at www.ICGtesting.com
Printed in the USA
BVHW060347261122
652770BV00004B/607